Days Without End

A Novel

Sebastian Barry

W F HOWES LTD

This large print edition published in 2017 by
W F Howes Ltd
Unit 5, St George's House, Rearsby Business Park,
Gaddesby Lane, Rearsby, Leicester LE7 4YH

1 3 5 7 9 10 8 6 4 2

First published in the United Kingdom in 2016
by Faber & Faber Limited

A CIP catalogue record for this book is available
from the British Library

ISBN 978 1 51007 385 2

Typeset by Palimpsest Book Production Limited,
Falkirk, Stirlingshire

Printforc   erlands

Days Without End

For my son Toby

I saw a wayworn trav'ler
In tattered garments clad

JOHN MATHIAS

CHAPTER 1

The method of laying out a corpse in Missouri sure took the proverbial cake. Like decking out our poor lost troopers for marriage rather than death. All their uniforms brushed down with lamp-oil into a state never seen when they were alive. Their faces clean shaved, as if the embalmer sure didn't like no whiskers showing. No one that knew him could have recognised Trooper Watchorn because those famous Dundrearies was gone. Anyway Death likes to make a stranger of your face. True enough their boxes weren't but cheap wood but that was not the point. You lift one of those boxes and the body makes a big sag in it. Wood cut so thin at the mill it was more a wafer than a plank. But dead boys don't mind things like that. The point was, we were glad to see them so well turned out, considering.

I am talking now about the finale of my first engagement in the business of war. 1851 it was most likely. Since the bloom was gone off me, I had volunteered aged seventeen in Missouri. If you had all your limbs they took you. If you were a one-eyed boy they might take you too even so. The only pay worse than the worst pay in America was army pay. And they fed you queer stuff till your shit just stank. But you were glad to get work because if you didn't work for the few dollars in America you hungered, I had learned that lesson. Well, I was sick of hungering.

Believe me when I say there is a certain type of man loves soldiering, no matter how mean the pay. First thing, you got a horse. He might be a spavined nag, he might be plagued by colic, he might show a goitre in his neck the size of a globe, but he was a horse. Second place, you got a uniform. It might have certain shortcomings in the stitching department, but it was a uniform. Blue as a bluebottle's hide.

Swear to God, army was a good life. I was seventeen or thereabouts beginning, I could not say for certain. I will not say the years going up to my army days was easy. But all that dancing put muscle on me, in a wiry sort of way. I'm not speaking against my customers, I'm speaking for them. If you pay a dollar for a dance you like a good few sweeps of the floor for that, God knows.

Yes, the army took me, I'm proud to say. Thank God John Cole was my first friend in America and so in the army too and the last friend for that matter. He was with me nearly all through this exceeding surprising Yankee sort of life which was good going in every way. No more than a boy like me but even at sixteen years old he looked like a man right enough. I first saw him when he was fourteen or so, very different. That's what the saloon owner said too. Time's up, fellas, you ain't kids no more, he says. Dark face, black eyes, Indian eyes they called them that time. Glittering. Older fellas in the platoon said Indians were just evil boys, blank-faced evil boys fit to kill you soon as look at you. Said Indians were to be cleared off the face of the earth, most like that would be the best policy. Soldiers like to talk high. That's how courage is made most like, said John Cole, being an understanding man.

John Cole and me we came to the volunteering point together of course. We was offering ourselves in a joint sale I guess and the same look of the arse out of his trousers that I had he had too. Like twins. Well when we finished up at the saloon we didn't leave in no dresses. We must have looked like beggar boys. He was born in New England where the strength died out of his father's earth. John Cole was only twelve when he lit out a-wandering. First moment I saw him I thought, there's a pal. That's what it was. Thought he was a dandy-looking sort of boy. Pinched though he was in the face by hunger. Met him under a hedge in goddamn Missouri. We was only under the hedge as a consequence the heavens were open in a downpour. Way out on those mudflats beyond old St Louis. Expect to see a sheltering duck sooner than a human. Heavens open. I scarper for cover and suddenly he's there. Might have never

3

seen him otherwise. Friend for a whole life. Strange and fateful encounter you could say. Lucky. But first thing he draws a little sharp knife he carried made of a broken spike. He was intending to stick it in me if I looked to go vicious against him. He was a very kept-back-looking thirteen years old I reckon. Anyhows under the hedge aforementioned when we got to talking he said his great-grandma was a Indian whose people were run out of the east long since. Over in Indian country now. He had never met them. Don't know why he told me that so soon only I was very friendly and maybe he thought he would lose that blast of friendship if I didn't know the bad things quickly. Well. I told him how best to look at that. Me, the child of poor Sligonians blighted likewise. No, us McNultys didn't got much to crow about.

Maybe out of respect for the vulnerable soul of John Cole I might skip ahead violently and avoid an account of our earlier years. Except he might also acknowledge that those years were important in their way and I cannot say either that they constituted in any way a time of shameful suffering in particular. Were they shameful? I don't see eye to eye with that. Let me call them our dancing days. Why the hell not. After all we was only children obliged to survive in a dangerous terrain. And survive we did and as you see I have lived to tell the tale. Having made our acquaintance under an anonymous hedge it seemed natural and easy to join together in the enterprise of continuing survival. That is John Cole in his minority and I placed our steps side by side on the rainy road and proceeded into the next town in that frontier district where there were hundreds of rough miners working and a half dozen tumultuous saloons set up in a muddy thoroughfare endeavouring to entertain them.

Not that we knew much of that. In these times John Cole was a slight boy as I have laboured to illustrate with his river-black eyes and his lean face as sharp as a hunting dog. I was my younger self. That is though I was maybe fifteen after my Irish and Canadian and American adventures I looked as young as him. But I had no idea what I looked like. Children may feel epic and large to theyselves and yet be only scraps to view.

Just sick of stumbling round. Two is better together, he said.

So then our idea was to find work slopping out or any of the jobs abhorrent to decent folk. We didn't know much about adult persons. We just didn't know hardly a thing. We were willing to do anything and even exulted in the fact. We were ready to go down into sewers and shovel the shit along. We might have been happy to commit obscure murders, if it didn't involve capture and punishment, we didn't know. We were two wood-shavings of humanity in a rough world. We were of the opinion our share of food was there if we sought it out. The bread of heaven John Cole called it because after the fall of his father he has much frequented those places where hymns and meagre food was put into him in equal measure.

Weren't many places like that in Daggsville. Weren't any. Daggsville was all uproar, mucky horses, banging doors, queer shouting. By this time in my biographical ventures I must confess I was wearing an old wheat-sack, tied at the waist. It sorta looked like clothing but not much. John Cole was better in an old queer black suit that musta been three hundred years old, judging by the gaps in it. Anyway he was having a breezy time of it about the crotch, far as I could see. You could nearly reach in and measure his manhood, so your eyes did their best to be kept looking away. I devised a good method to deal with such a thing and fixed fiercely on his face, which was no work in itself, it was a pleasing face. Next thing comes up in our view a spanking new building all fresh wood and even a last sparkle in the recently beaten nailheads. *Saloon* a sign said, no more nor less. And underneath, on a smaller sign hanging from a string, *Clean boys wanted.*

Look, see, says John Cole, who didn't have the great learning I had, but had a little none the less. Well, he says, by my mother's loving heart, we do fulfil half of that requirement.

Straight in, and there was a highly pleasant quotient of good dark wood, dark panelling floor to ceiling, a long bar as sleek and black as an oil-seep. Then we felt like bugs in a girl's bonnet. Alien. Pictures of those fine American scenes of

6

grandeur that are more comfortable to gaze on than to be in. Man there behind the bar, complete with chamois cloth, philosophically polishing a surface that needed no polishing. It was plain to see all was a new enterprise. There was a carpenter finishing up on the stairs going to the upward rooms, fitting the last section of a rail. The bartender had his eyes closed or he might have seen us sooner. Might even have given us the bum's rush. Then the eyes open and instead of the drawing back and cussing at us we expected this more discerning individual smiled, looked pleased to see us.

You looking for clean boys? says John Cole, a tincture pugilistic right enough, still prophesying menaces.

You are right welcome, the man says.

We are? said John Cole.

You are. You are just the thing, especially the smaller one there, he says. That was me he was meaning. Then, as if he feared John Cole might take offence and stamp out away – But you'll do too, he says. I'm giving fifty cents a night, fifty cents a night each, and all you can drink, if you drink easy, and you can bunk down in the stable behind us, yes indeed, cosy and comfortable and warm as cats. That's if you give satisfaction.

And what's the work? says John, suspicious.

Easiest work in the world, he says.

Such as?

Why, dancing, dancing is all it is. Just dancing.

7

We ain't no dancers far as I know, says John, flummoxed now, violently disappointed.

You don't need to be dancers as such in the accepted dictionary definition of the word, says the man. It's not high-kicking anyhow.

Alright, says John, lost now just from a sense aspect – but, we ain't got no clothes to be dancing in, that's for sure, he said, displaying his very particular condition.

Why, all's supplied, all's supplied, he says.

The carpenter had paused in his work and was sitting on the steps now, smiling big.

Come with me, gentlemen, says the bartender, likely the owner too, with his swank, and I will show you your clothing of work.

Then he strode over his spanking new floor in his noisy boots, and opened the door into his office. It had a sign on it said *Office* so we knew. Why, boys, after you, he said, holding the door. I got my manners. And I hope you got your manners, because even rough miners love manners, yes indeed.

So we troop in, all eyes. There's a rack of clothes like a gaggle of hanged women. Because it's women's clothes. Dresses. There was nothing else there, and we looked around thoroughly, we did.

Dancing starts eight sharp, he says. Pick something that fits. Fifty cents, each. And any tips you get is yours to keep.

But, mister, says John Cole, like he was talking to a pitiful insane person. We ain't no women. Can't you see. I is a boy and so is Thomas here.

No, you ain't women, I can see. I could verify that second you came in. You fine young boys. Sign says looking for boys. I would gladly sign up women but ain't no women in Daggsville but the storeman's wife and the stableman's little daughter. Otherwise it's all men here. But men without women can get to pining. It's a sort of sadness gets into their hearts. I aim to get it out and make a few bucks in the process, yes, sir, the great American way. They need only the illusion, only the illusion of the gentler sex. You're it, if you take this employment. It's just the dancing. No kissing, cuddling, feeling, or fumbling. Why, just the nicest, the most genteel dancing. You won't hardly credit how nice, how gentle a rough miner dances. Make you cry to see it. You sure is pretty enough in your way, if you don't mind me saying, especially the smaller one. But you'll do too, you'll do too, he says, seeing John Cole's newly acquired professional pride coming up again. Then he cocks an eyebrow, interrogatory like.

John Cole looks at me. I didn't care. Better than starving in a wheat-sack.

Alright, he says.

Gonna put a bath for you in the stable. Gonna give you soap. Gonna supply the underwears, *muy importante*. Brought with me from St Louis. You'll fill them fine, boys, I reckon you'll fill them fine, and after a few glasses no man I know will object. A new era in the history of Daggsville. When the lonesome men got girls to dance with. And all in a comely fashion, in a comely fashion.

9

And so we trooped out again, shrugging our shoulders, as if to say, it was a mad world, but a lucky one too, now and then. Fifty cents, each. How many times, in how many bowers before sleep in our army days, out on the prairie, in lonesome declivities, we liked to repeat that, John and me, over and over, and never failing in our laughter, Fifty cents – each.

That particular night in the lost history of the world Mr Titus Noone, for that was his name, helped us into our dresses with a sort of manly discretion. Give him his due, he seemed to know about buttons and ribbons and such. He had even had the foresight to sprinkle us with perfumes. This was the cleanest I had been in three years, maybe ever. I had not been noted in Ireland for my cleanliness truth be told, poor farmers don't see baths. When there is no food to eat the first thing that goes is even a flimsy grasp of hygiene.

The saloon filled quickly. Posters had been speedily put up around town, and the miners had answered the call. Me and John Cole sat on two chairs against a wall. Very girl-like, well behaved, sedate, and nice. We never even looked at the miners, we stared straight ahead. We hadn't ever seen too many sedate girls but a inspiration got into us. I had a yellow wig of hair and John had a red one. We musta looked like the flag of some country from the neck up, sitting there. Mr Noone had thoughtfully filled out our bodices with cotton.

Okay but our feet were bare, he said he had forgotten shoes in St Louis. They might be a later addition. He said to mind where the miners stepped, we said we would. Funny how as soon as we hove into those dresses everything changed. I never felt so contented in my life. All miseries and worries fled away. I was a new man now, a new girl. I was freed, like those slaves were freed in the coming war. I was ready for anything. I felt dainty, strong, and perfected. That's the truth. I don't know how it took John Cole, he never said. You had to love John Cole for what he chose never to say. He said plenty of the useful stuff. But he never speaked against that line of work, even when it went bad for us, no. We were the first girls in Daggsville and we weren't the worst.

Every citizen knows that miners are all sorts of souls. They come into a country, I seen it a thousand times, and strip away all the beauty, and then there is black filth in the rivers and the trees just seem to wither back like affronted maids. They like rough food, rough whisky, rough nights, and truth to tell, if you is a Indian girl, they will like you in all the wrong ways. Miners go into tent towns and do their worst. There were never such raping men as miners, some of them. Other miners are teachers, professors in more civilised lands, fallen priests and bankrupt storeowners, men whose women have abandoned them as useless fixtures. Every brand and gradation of soul, as the crop measurer might say, and will say.

But they all came into Noone's saloon and there was a change, a mighty change. Because we were pretty girls and we were the darlings of their souls. And anyhow, Mr Noone was standing at the bar with a shotgun handy in front of him, in plain sight. You wouldn't believe the latitude the law allows in America for a saloon owner to be killing miners, it's wide.

Maybe we were like memories of elsewhere. Maybe we were the girls of their youth, the girls they had first loved. Man, we was so clean and nice, I wished I could of met myself. Maybe for some, we were the first girls they loved. Every night for two years we danced with them, there was never a moment of unwelcome movements. That's a fact. It might be more exciting to say we had crotches pushed against us, and tongues pushed into our mouths, or calloused hands grabbing at our imaginary breasts, but no. They was the gentlemen of the frontier, in that saloon. They fell down pulverised by whisky in the small hours, they roared with songs, they shot at each other betimes over cards, they battered each other with fists of iron, but when it came to dancing they were that pleasing d'Artagnan in the old romances. Big pigs' bellies seemed to flatten out and speak of more elegant animals. Men shaved for us, washed for us, and put on their finery for us, such as it was. John was Joanna, myself was Thomasina. We danced and we danced. We whirled and we whirled. Matter of fact, end of all we were good

12

dancers. We could waltz, slow and fast, foxtrot and even against the Yankee politics of that district, the Charleston. We swirled about in our dresses and Mr Carmody the storeman's wife, Mrs Carmody of course by name, being a seamstress, let out our outfits as the months went by. Maybe it is a mistake to feed vagrants, but mostly we grew upward instead of out. Maybe we were changing, but we were still the girls we had been in our customers' eyes. They spoke well of us and men came in from miles around to view us and get their name on our little cardboard lists. 'Why, miss, will you do me the honour of a dance?' 'Why, yes, sir, I have ten minutes left at quarter of twelve, if you care to fill that vacancy.' 'I will be most obliged.' Two useless, dirt-risen boys never had such entertainment. We was asked our hands in marriage, we was offered carts and horses if we would consent to go into camp with such and such a fella, we was given gifts such as would not have embarrassed a desert Arab in Arabia, seeking his bride. But of course, we knew the story in our story. They knew it too, maybe, now I am considering it. They were free to offer themselves into the penitentiary of matrimony because they knew it was imaginary. It was all aspects of freedom, happiness, and joy.

For that filthy vile life of a miner is a bleak life and only one in ten thousand finds his gold, truth to tell. Course in Daggsville they was digging for lead so all the more true. Mostly that life is all muck and water. But in Mr Noone's saloon was two diamonds, Mr Noone said.

But nature will have his way and bit by bit the bloom wore off us, and we was more like boys than girls, and more like men than women. John Cole anyhow in particular saw big changes in them two years. He was beginning to give giraffes a run for their money, height-wise. Mr Noone couldn't find dresses to fit him, and Mrs Carmody couldn't stitch fast enough. It was the end of an era, God knowed. One of the happiest works I ever had. Then the day came when Mr Noone had to speak. And we was shaking hands then in the dawnlight, and tears even were shed, and we were going to be just memories of diamonds in Daggsville. Mr Noone says he will send us a letter every feast day of St Thomas and St John and give us all the news. And we was to do likewise. And we lit out with our bit of dollars saved for our hoped-for cavalry days. And the queer thing was, Daggsville was deserted that morning, and no one to cheer us away. We knew we was just fragments of legend and had never really existed in that town. There is no better feeling.

14

CHAPTER 2

All this to say, we joined up together. Well, our old business has gone bust just from what nature does naturally to the body. Soon after training we were being hiked out across the Oregon trail towards California. It was supposed to be weeks and weeks of riding and then turn left at some place I forget, otherwise you would find yourself in Oregon. It was supposed to be and it was. Lots of dilapidated Indians in Missouri as we rode through, they were even riding the rivers, moving about a great deal anyhows, some of them travelling to get their government annuities maybe, even as far as up Canada way. Sad, dirty-looking people. And plenty of New Englanders heading west, maybe a few Scandinavians, but mostly Americans, upping sticks and off they'd go. You kept away from the Mormons heading into Utah, you couldn't trust those mad boys. They had the devil's rep. If you fight them you got to kill them, our sergeant said, but I don't know if he ever did. Then you had the desert that wasn't really a desert. Lots of bones of pilgrims' cattle though, and now and then along the way, a piano thrown out from a wagon, or a cupboard, as the oxen weakened at their task. Drought was the worst thing there. It was a mighty queer thing to see a black piano in the half-true desert.

Hey, John Cole, what in the name of tarnation that piano doing there in the dust?

Must be looking for a saloon, he says.

Man, we were laughing. The sergeant gave us his black look, but the major ignored us, he was probably thinking about that desert. Where's the water going to come from in a few days, when the water-bottles are empty? We were hoping he had a map, something marked there, we hoped he had. People had been coming through there for a few years now, they said the trail was widening all the time, a mile-wide dirty mark on the prairie, every time army came through they noticed. Half of our company were crusty older men, we wondered they could still ride, some of them. It's hard on the bollocks, and the lower back, God damn it. But how else were they to live? You rode or you died. It was always a dangerous route. One of the young men like us, that was the aforementioned Watchorn, the last year had seen wagons spread out in their hundreds, and he saw a great herd of buffalo stampede right across them, hundreds of wagoners trampled and killed. That time we were passing, he reckoned the buffalo were keeping away, he didn't know why. They didn't like this class of humans maybe. Never seemed to mind the Indians much. White boys were noisy smelly

16

sonsabitches maybe, Watchorn opined. And all their whiny, caterwauling, snot-nosed kids going out to California, or up to Oregon. But all the same, said Trooper Watchorn, yep, I do wants a parcel of kids myself someday. He reckoned he would like fourteen, like his ma. He was a Catholic man, rare in America outside the Irish, but then, he was Irish, or his pa had been, in the long ago. So he said. Watchorn had a fine face, a beautiful face, he looked like a president on a coin, but he was awful damn small, maybe five foot and one measly inch, on a horse it made no odds, he just rode on a short stirrup, that worked well. He was an exceptionally agreeable man, yes, indeed.

We were out there, on the longer grass then, nearer the mountains, just passing along. We were going into someplace to get our close orders. The major knew already though, John Cole said, because he had heard him talking in the night. As for night, we slept on the ground just as we were, our uniforms stinking, the pickets guarding the horses, the horses muttering all through the small hours, talking to God as John Cole said. He couldn't make that lingo out. It was going to be a week of riding yet, us three hundred souls, and now our scouts came in, two Shawnee lads with their sign language as good as words, and told us they'd seen buffalo seven miles to the north-east, so we were going to choose a party tomorrow to go north and try and kill a few. If I was not the best shot of three hundred I was a liar. I don't know why, I never shot a gun till training. You got a beady eye, said the drill sergeant. I could soon shoot a hare dead, centre of the head, a hundred feet, no trouble. Better not starve before we go to do our work. We knew in our hearts our work was to be Indians. People in California wanted rid of them. Wanted them routed out. Troopers couldn't take the bounty legal-wise of course but someone high up had agreed to help. There was two dollars per scalp for a civilian, for God's sake. It was a funny way to earn your card-money. Volunteers were going out and shoot maybe sixty bucks and bring the bodies in.

The major said he liked Indians well enough, he couldn't see the harm in those Diggers, so called. They're not the same as the Indians on the plains, he said. Diggers didn't even have horses, he said, and this time of year you could find them all in one place praying. The major had a melancholy sort of look when he said this, like he had said too darn much, or maybe knew too much. I was looking at him. The sergeant, his name was Wellington, snorted through his dusty nostrils. Goddamn Injuns, we'll show 'em, he said, all to himself nearly, grinning, as if he were among pals, which he was not. No one could prize a man with a tongue like a bolus of knives. He hated the Irish, said the English were stupid, the Germans worse. Where the hell was he from? John Cole wanted to know. Little village, he said, you never heard of it. Did he say Detroit? We didn't know what that sergeant was saying half the time, because he kind of laughed

18

when he talked, except when he was giving orders, then all was clear enough. Forward! Advance! Slacken off! Dismount! It made our Irish, English and German ears sore.

So what happens next day was me and John Cole and Watchorn himself and also a nice sonofabitch called Pearl, we went up with the scouts to find that herd. We came into marshy ground first but the Shawnee boys knew the path through and we weaved along it content enough. Cook had put some of his cooked sparrows in our stomachs. We were after something bigger. Shawnees, seem to remember one of them was called Birdsong, as it happens, cool-minded, timber-skinned boys they were, giving themselves the old information in their own lingo, had done up their prayer bags the night before. Kinda lucky charms they liked to put together in an old bag made from the scrotum of a buffalo. They were lashed to their ponies' necks now, they rode without saddles. Long before we had news of it, they were going slower, they knew something was close, they brought us about a mile sideways so we could start to work in up the wind. There was a big low sickle-shaped hill before us, covered in a dark grass, and the country there was quiet and almost windless, except for a sound you were guessing might be the sound of the sea. There was no sea thereabouts, we knew. Then we breasted the hill, it was giving a horizon of maybe four miles, and I drew in my breath, amazed, because right down below us was a herd of maybe two or three thousand buffalo. They musta taken a vow of silence that morning. Shawnees now were putting their ponies into a polite trotting, and ourselves likewise, we were to go down as close to the buffalo as we could without stirring them. Maybe buffalo isn't the smartest chicken in the coop. We had the wind in our faces such as it was. We knew as soon as they felt us there was going to be fireworks. Sure enough, the nearest dozen must of felt us. They started to stumble forward all of a sudden, nearly falling down. We must have smelled like death to them. We hoped we did. Birdsong kicked forward and we kicked forward, John Cole was a beautiful rider, he streaked through the Indians and fled after the biggest cow he could spot. I had a line on a big cow too, must have been that we preferred the cow meat. Then the land dipped again, the near buffalo had set everything moving, it was ten thousand hooves then drumming the hard earth and the whole cavalcade pouring down into the declivity. Seemed to swallow them, every last one, then the ground rose in front of us, and there they were again, the flood of buffalo, like a big boil of black molasses in a skillet, surging up. Goddamn blackberries they were as black as. My cow had taken a wild run to the right, she was gearing herself to go through her comrades, I don't know if an angel hadn't given her a message I was on her tail. You gotta treat a buffalo like a killer, like a rattlesnake on legs, she wants to kill you before you kill her. She wants to lure you on too, and then she wants to suddenly run sideways at you, knock down your horse in full flight and then come back before Saturday and stamp you to death. You never want to fall to the ground on a buffalo hunt, if I can just instruct you in that. My cow won't act out of character, but I got to get myself in close, get a shot into her head as best I can, it's no easy task to keep your rifle raised and ready, when your horse was seeming to be an aficionado of every goddamn rabbit hole out there. He better keep his footing. Maybe we are moving at thirty, forty miles an hour now, maybe we are sheeting along like the wind, maybe the herd is making a noise like a great storm coming down from the mountains, but my heart was up and I couldn't care what happened unless I could get my bullet into her. Blooms in my head the picture of the troopers roasting her and cutting great steaks out of her. The blood running down the meat. Well, I am caterwauling now, and I see the other Shawnee now nameless in my memory, he is riding down a most splendid bull, he is sitting back on his pony Indian style, and he is shooting arrows into the bull, who is only a raging roaring mass of meat and hair. That sight vanishes in a vanishing second. My own task is at hand. Sure enough, she makes a brilliant-minded lunge sideways at me, just as I think I am steady to strike. But my horse isn't the first time out against buffalo, and he skips to the right, like a good dancer, and now we have drawn a bead on that cow, and I fire, and the lovely orange flame shoots the bullet forth, and the burning black steel is absorbed into her shoulder. That girl is all shoulder. We burn along the grasses together, the herd seems to take a violent turn left, as if to escape her approaching fate, I fire again, I fire again, then I see her right haunch sort of dip down, just a half a foot, well, glory be to God, that's the good sign, my heart swells, my pride explodes in my breast, down, down she goes, a blaze of dust and power, and she takes fifteen feet to reach a stop. Must have pierced her heart. That's a dead buffalo. Then I got to keep riding, riding away out right, or the herd might swing back and kill me. Then I am galloping, galloping, and hollering, and hallooing, gone berserk, and I guess nearly crying for joy. Was there ever such excitement as that. And now I am a quarter mile off, and my horse is just busted, but I think I smell his sense of victory too, and I wheel about, and take a watching stand on a short run of hill. And my horse is breaking his chest trying to breathe, and it is very glorious and crazy the feeling. And then the herd has passed on, how quickly it utterly vanishes across the horizon, but me and John Cole and Birdsong have killed six, and they are left behind like the dead after a battle, the long grasses all flattened like the fur on a mangy dog, and Birdsong laughing, I can see him, and John Cole being a devotee of silences sort of laughing without laughing, without even a smile, funny old dog that he is, and in the next while we know we will kneel to the task of skinning and we'll take the best meat off the bones, and lash it to our horses in huge wet slabs, and leave the enormous heads to moulder there, so noble in their aspect, so astonishing, so that God Himself might marvel at them. Our knives flashed through. Birdsong cut the best. He made a sign to tell me, laughing, this is women's work. Strong women if so, I signed, best as I knew. This was a big joke for Birdsong. He's roaring, Man, I guess he's thinking, these stupid whitemen. Maybe we are. The knives opened the flesh like they were painting paintings of a new country, sheer plains of dark land, with the red rivers bursting their banks everywhere, till we were sloshing in God knows what and the dry earth was suddenly turned to noisy mud. The Shawnees ate the lights raw. Their mouths were sinkholes of dark blood.

Only Trooper Pearl looked sad as a sad baby not to have killed. But he got the first cut around the fires that night, the raw meat spitting and blackening in the flames. The men hunched around, talking with the gaiety of souls about to eat plentifully, with the empty dark country about us, and the strange fabric of frost and frozen wind falling on our shoulders, and the great black sky of stars above us like a huge tray of gems and diamonds. The Shawnees singing in their own camp all night till at last Sergeant Wellington rose up from his blanket and was desirous to shoot them.

23

CHAPTER 3

In the army you meet a dozen men a month came from Ireland but you never hear them talk about it much. You know a Irishman because he has it writ all over him. He speaks some other way and he is not a great man for hair cutting generally and there's something about a Irish when he is drinking that just ain't like any other human being. Don't tell me a Irish is an example of civilised humanity. He may be an angel in the clothes of a devil or a devil in the clothes of an angel but either way you're talking to two when you talk to one Irishman. He can't help you enough and he can't double-cross you deep enough ever either. An Irish trooper is the bravest man in the field and the most cowardly. I don't know what it is. I seen killer Irishmen and gentle souls but they're both the same, they both have an awful fire burning inside them, like they were just the carapace of a furnace. That's what being a Irish does to you. If you cross a Irish for half a dollar he's going to burn your house in revenge. He will work at that till he drops dead from the desire to do you mischance. I was never no different neither.

I'll say quickly what happened to me and brought me to America but I don't feel much in the way of saying too much. Least said soonest mended is the old saw. It's damnable true.

My father was a butter exporter man in a small way sending butter in barrels out of Sligo port into England. All good things was sent there. Cows, beeves, pigs, sheep, goats, wheat, barley, English corn, beets, carrots, cabbages, and all the rest of the paraphernalia of existence. All that was left in Ireland was the potato for eating and when the potato was lost there was nothing left in old Ireland. She starved in her stocking feet. And she had no stockings. Rags. My father was a better sort of man and wore a high black hat but even that was knocked-about-looking because it had already lived a long eventful life in England. We sent food to England and she sent rags and battered hats. I don't know because I was only a child. In '47 the harvest was so bad even my father had nothing then. My sister died and my mother, on the stone floor of our house in Sligo town, in a street called the Lungey. The Lungey meant in Irish Luaighne, which was the kingdom my ances- tors was kings of, or so my father said. He was a very living man while he was alive. He loved to sing, he was a dancer, and he loved to make a bargain on the wharf with his captains.

Butter kept flowing in the time of hunger but how it happened that my father fell out of life I do not know but he lost that business and then as I say my sister and mother perished. They perished like stray cats, no one caring much. But the whole town was perishing. On the riverbank, where the port was, the ships were still coming into harbour and embarking, but not by my father's order no more. The old ships started to bring ruined people to Canada, people that were so hungry they might eat each other in the holds. I am not saying I saw that. But I was thirteen or so and I knew in my heart and soul I had to flee. I crept onto one of those ships in the darkness. I am telling this best I can. It's long ago, before America. I was among the destitute, the ruined and the starving for six weeks. Many went over-board, that's how it was.

The captain hisself he died of fever, when we reached Canada we were a ship without a steward. Into the fever sheds with us and that's where hundreds died. I'm just writing all this down. The point is, we were nothing. No one wanted us. Canada was a-feared of us. We were a plague. We were only rats of people. Hunger takes away what you are. Everything we were was just nothing then. Talk, music, Sligo, stories, future, past, it was all turned to something very like the shit of animals. When I met John Cole that's who I was, a human louse, even evil people shunned me and the good had no use for me. That's where I started. Gives an idea of the victory meeting John Cole was. First time I felt like a human person again. And that's enough of that, I say, I don't want to say no more. Silence.

I only say it because without saying I don't think anything can be properly understood. How we were able to see slaughter without flinching. Because we were nothing ourselves, to begin with. We knew what to do with nothing, we were at home there. I almost wasn't able to say, my father died too. I saw his body. Hunger is a sort of fire, a furnace. I loved my father when I was a human person formerly. Then he died and I was hungry and then the ship. Then nothing. Then America. Then John Cole. John Cole was my love, all my love.

Let me go back to my beginning time in the army. We reached Fort Kearney, it was just near one of the new mining settlements, in a northern part of California that was mostly wilderness. Wild knotted country, said to be full to the brim with gold. Indians owned it, Yurok people. Maybe it wasn't Kearney, I forget, Kearney is an Irish name. The mind is a wild liar and I don't trust much in it that I find there. To tell a story I have to trust it but I can issue a warning like a ticket master issuing a ticket for a western-bound train that will be obliged to go through wilderness, Indians, outlaws, and storms. There was a local militia made up of the townsmen and some of the miners scattered about on the claims. They just couldn't live with the thought of Indians and they went out in parties and scoured through the hills and tried to kill them. They could of captured the men and put them to work sluicing and digging if they had wished, that was California-style law. They could of took in the women and children for slaves and concubines but at this time they preferred just to shoot what they could find.

In Fort Kearney that night when we dusted off the bunks and had our grub, the townsmen came in and told us of the latest awful happenings from the Indians. There was a miner they said on the far edge of the settlement and the Yurok had stolen his mule. The way they told it it was the finest mule ever seen in the world. They stole his mule and tied him down in the dust and whipped his face a little. They told him he was digging in a graveyard and he must desist. These Yuroks were not big in stature but little men. The townsmen said the women were the ugliest women in creation. There was one New England man called Henryson said this and he was laughing about it. The major listened patiently enough but when Henryson said about the women he told him to shut up, we didn't know why. Henryson shut up obediently enough. He said he was glad to see the cavalry there. It was a boon to the town. Then we felt quite proud. Well pride is the fool's breakfast.

The sergeant was silent all through, he just sat on a two-legged brace stool and glowered at the ground like he couldn't wait to hear the end of this deposition and get out there and do what we came to do. What that was seemed to comprise of finishing what the militia had begun. Henryson said they wanted the country cleared and the major

28

said nothing then. He just nodded in his quiet way and his face looked sorta handsome and good, especially against the face of Henryson, which looked quite queer and black, like he had bitten off too many powder caps in his time. Then the townsmen gave the troopers a keg and we drank that into the small hours and played cards and there was those brief fights that you'd expect and men were ill as poisoned dogs.

Me and John Cole, staggering back to the hard bunks but knowing whisky would be our pillow, paused at the designated pissing spot by the boundary wall. There was a picket on the top of the wall, and all we saw was the hump of his dark back. He could have been sleeping for all the back said. The major was just finishing, pulling the strings of his flies tight again.

Goodnight, Major, sir, I said, to his own dark shoulders. He looked back at us. I saluted him as I was bound to do. In his whisky-sodden state his head weren't quite as moored as usual on his neck. He seemed to be in a sort of fury. He saluted chaotically and shook his head and then turned it upward to the stars.

Are you alright, Major, sir? I said.

It's a long way to come for a stolen mule, he said, ferociously, like an actor on the stage.

Then he was muttering, I heard the name Henryson, and something about letters to the colonel, and depredations, and murders of settlers, and damn lies. But this speech seemed to be directed at the wall. He was moving about awkwardly, trying to keep his feet on the sodden ground. Three hundred men make quite a bit of mud. And the stench was ferocious, it was a wonder the picket stood it.

It's a long way to come for a stolen mule, and a whupping, he said, with an emphasis on the last word, like it was something he might like to administer to Henryson.

We helped him back to his quarters and then steered our own way back to ours.

He's a good man, that major, said John Cole, with all the definiteness of the drunken man.

And then we quietly fucked and then we slept.

Next morning bright early despite the depredations to our bodies we saddled up. It was cold as dark dreams because now it was late in the year and the sun wasn't just as keen as it had been previously. There was a frost across all that ground and we could see great shrouds of frost hanging in the redwoods that grew thereabouts. Long low hills waved with grasses where the trees had failed or been felled, we didn't know. We were told we had about fourteen hours' riding ahead. The scouts seemed to know the way after the instructions of the militia the night before. We were told the militia had rode ahead in the darkness, which vexed the major hugely. He shook his head and cursed civilians. Well our muskets were primed and we had food in our bellies and we were inclined to think well of the enterprise. The sore backs of the long journey west seemed less to the fore of our minds. All that riding grinds down your backbone till I believe you gain for yourself a little store of bone dust in your buttocks. That's what it felt like. Every rut, every slip of your horse is a jolt of pain. But my horse that time was a sleek grey creature that you couldn't feel displeasure with. John Cole was mounted on a broken-hearted nightmare right enough. He had to pull the mouth off of her to get his way. The mare had snapped her martingale somewhere in the desert so she was free to saw her head up and down just as she liked. But he put up with it. The horse was black as a crow and John Cole liked that.

The breath of three hundred horses makes a curling twisting mist in the cold November air. Their warm bodies were steaming from their exertions. We were obliged to try and keep formation but the ancient redwoods didn't care about that. They were parting us and cutting us as if they were moving themselves. You could have tethered fifty horses to the girth of some of them. The curious birds of America were calling among the trees and from the far heights dropped the myriad speckles of frost. Now and then something cracked in the forest like musket-fire. There wasn't any sense the trees needed us there. They were about their own business certainly. We made a racket of harness, spurs, equipment, things knocking and shrugging from movement, and hooves skittering and clacking on the earth, but the troopers barely spoke a word and for the most part we rode in silence as if by prior agreement. But it was the trees that pressed the silence on us. The major issued his orders with his arms and hands, and these were replicated down the line. Something was going on ahead, we sensed it before we saw it. Suddenly a huge nervousness invaded us, and you could almost hear the bones in our bodies tightening, closing, and our hearts seemed captive in our chests and desirous to escape. Men coughed to clear the spit of fright from their throats. We could hear a great sound of burning up ahead, as if ten thousand starlings were massing there, and through the trees we saw violent yellow and red flames, and a great pulse of black and white smoke everywhere. We came out of the trees at last. The fire was burning at the bottom of a wide meadow. There were four or five big lodges made of logs of redwood, and only one of these was burning, creating the storm of flames and smoke all on its own. The major spread us out across the meadow, as if he might be intending to charge against this conflagration. Then we were told to trot down slowly, our muskets at the ready. The townsmen were everywhere it seemed, running along the length of the Indian encampment, shouting at each other, and soon I saw the figure of Henryson, holding a big firebrand aloft. They were as busy as lawyers whatever was the work. Soon we were close and Henryson came back to talk to the major, but I couldn't hear what he was saying. Then we were broken into sections and we were told there were Indians down in the copses to the right. We spurred on our horses and what with the steep decline felt like we were fleeing down the slope. Troopers Pearl and Watchorn were near me as normal, and then the thickness of the smaller trees obliged us to dismount, and a few dozen pushed on into the copse on foot. Then there was screaming and calling, and shrieking cries. We fixed bayonets to our muskets and now rushed forward, trying to avoid the springing undergrowth. Down from the burning lodge the smoke had plundered everywhere, into the copses, into every cranny, so that it was nigh impossible to see and our eyes smarted horribly. We saw the shapes of Indians and stabbed them with our bayonets. We worked back and forth through the milling bodies and tried to kill everything that moved in the murk. Two, three, four fell to my thrusts, and I was astonished not to be fired on, astonished at the speed and the horror of the task, and the exhilaration of it, my heart now not racing but burning in my breast like a huge coal. I stabbed and I stabbed. I saw John Cole stabbing, I heard him grunting and cursing. We wanted the enemy stilled and destroyed so that we could live ourselves. Every second I thought I would feel the famous tomahawk split my Irish skull, or the molten bullet pierce my chest. But nothing seemed to happen except our savage grunting and thrusting. We were a-feared to fire our muskets in case of murdering each other. Then all the work seemed done and all we heard then was the crying of survivors, the terrible groaning of the wounded. The smoke cleared and we saw at last something of our battlefield. Then my heart shrank in its nest of ribs. It was just women and children all around us. Not a brave among them. We had torn into the little hiding place of the squaws, where they had tried to take refuge from the burning and the killing. I was affrighted and strangely affronted, but mostly at myself, because I knew I had taken strange pleasure from the attack. It was as if I had drank six whiskies in a row. Watchorn and Pearl were dragging a woman from the ground and into the trees. I knew they were going to take their pleasure from her. I knew well. Babies that had spilled from their mothers' arms were now stabbed and killed with the rest. The troopers worked until I believe their arms could do no more. Watchorn and Pearl rutting and shouting, then ruthlessly killing again. Till in runs the major shouting the loudest of all, with true horror in his face, shouting his orders, wild to bring a stop to things. Then we were all of us standing there panting, our cold sweat pouring down exhausted faces, our eyes glittering, our legs trembling, just like you would see dogs do after they have been killing lambs.

Wearily, wearily, we walked back. The townsmen were standing twenty feet back from the flames. It was still a ferocious turmoil of smoke and fire and resins sparking and spitting like some old painting of hell. The troopers massed together, not talking much yet, watching the flames and watching the townsmen. We didn't know where we were. We didn't for those moments know our names. We were different then, we were other people. We were killers, like no other killers that had ever been. Then with a huge queer sighing, the roof of the lodge fell in. It collapsed in a great smoulder and shatter of sparks. The sparks rushed into the air above and tumbled there, joyous and black and red. An enormous stormcloud of sparks. Then the walls of the building tumbled, and fierce in the dark worst flames burned the bodies, brave upon brave piled six deep, you could see the ruined faces and smell the roasting flesh, the corpses twisted strangely in the heat, fell and rolled onto the scorched grasses, no longer held by the walls. More sparks flew up, it was a complete vision of world's end and death, in those moments I could think no more, my head bloodless, empty, racketing, astonished. Troopers wept, but they were not tears I knew. Others threw their hats into the air, as if it were a crazy celebration. Others held their heads as if they had just heard of the death of their own loved ones. There didn't seem to be anything alive, including ourselves. We were dislocated, we were not there, now we were ghosts.

CHAPTER 4

The townspeople were set to put on a huge feast to show their gratitude. One short street with a few new buildings each side was the town. Troopers Pearl and Watchorn had been quietly detained by the major and were now in the lock-up at the fort, giving out betimes through the meal hatch, I do not doubt. Major said he would deal with them in due course. The town otherwise was heaving with preparations and general to-do for the following day. They had a bear for to butcher and also deer meat, they said, and a rake of dogs. Seemingly the Indians had a whole pack of them and the townspeople had rounded them up like sheep, drove them back to town, with all the crazy yapping and barking.

The major meanwhile sent back a detail with spades he got off the iron-goods store and we dug two long pits out in the wilds beside the deserted encampment and then we started to drag the bodies to them, and tipped them in. Major was loath to let wolves have them, though the townsmen didn't seem to mind. Expressed a great deal of surprise at the major's thoroughness, but the major, while polite, and even-tenored in his voice, wasn't going just to think like everyone else. Major was of the opinion, and communicated it to us as we lined up reluctantly with our spades for the work, in that hateful and haunted place, that an Indian got a soul just like another man. I would like to tell you how I felt except it was all taking me back to Canada and the fever sheds that time and there's no use going back there in my mind. Pits that time too, and people put in, thousands, babies too. I seen all that as a child myself. It's a dark thing when the world sets no value on you or your kin, and then Death comes stalking in, in his bloody boots.

So we dug like frightened heroes. John Cole I noted was the best digger, it wasn't the first time he had turned the earth, you could tell. So I copied him. I had only ever pulled up potatoes with my hands as a little boy in Ireland, after my father shook the earth around them with his spade, that was just a little patch he had kept behind our house, it wasn't like he was a true farmer. The frost was still on the ground everywhere and the temperature had started to freeze the little river that wound past the camp, making it I suppose a good choice for a stopping place. The grasses were sere and indifferent really, scratching the horizon of the sky with their sharp stems. That sky was clear and high and the lightest blue. We were four hours digging out the trenches. The troopers were singing as they worked, dirty-worded songs we all knew. We were sweating like window-glass in the winter. The major drove us on in his strange way, sort of cold, indifferent, like the grasses. He was set to do something and he was doing it. In the town he had asked the padre to come out but the townsmen vetoed that. After the hours of digging we were sent then to fetch across the bodies and we brought the bodies of the women and the children to the pit and after that we went to the burnt-out lodge and fetched in among the debris and the black dirt and got whatever we could of the bones of the braves, heads and such. Threw them in. You might have had a worried look when you saw how gently some of the men threw. Others throwing like they was throwing nothing of particular importance. But the gentle ones throwing gently. John Cole for instance. As for talk there were only the usual repartee that means nothing but somehow saves the heart and the day. It became clear to me that many of the squaws and the children had got out of the copsewood, because you could see still the trampling effect of their rushing off on the underwood. I found myself hoping many of the bucks had got away too but maybe I was asking for trouble thinking that. It was such a beautiful spot and the work was so lousy. You couldn't help almost a more human thought. Nature asks you to go back a little and forget things. Gets under your hardened nature like a burrowing creature. When all the bodies were in, we covered over the pits with the soil we had left, like we were putting pastry tops on two enormous pies. It was wretched. Then we stood and took our hats off at the major's behest and he spoke his few words. God bless these people, he said, and though we was doing our work as we were bound and ordered, may God forgive us. Amen, we said.

It was dark and we had hours of riding before us and we were not disappointed to mount up and head back.

Next day we were risen early at the fort and we washed off all our dirt at the water butts and put on our finery for the feast. That was, our usual uniforms brushed down best we could, and Bailey the barberman cut as many of the hairs as he could and shaved as many of the faces as he could too. There was a big line of men in their vests, waiting. The hair was bagged up in a linen sack and burned because of the nits carousing there. Then we were nigh ready, and rode with what grace and style we could muster back into town. It is a fine thing to see three hundred men riding, and we all felt the fineness in it, I suppose we did. Some of us had drunk our livers clean in half, though we were young enough still. I weren't even eighteen. Lower backs ground away by the hard saddles. Pain everywhere on waking. But the little grandeur of the line of riders affected us too. We were about the people's business, we had done something for the people. Something like that. Puts a fire into your belly somehow. Sense of rightness.

Not justice exactly. Fulfilling the wishes of the majority, something along those lines, I don't know. That's how it was with us. I guess it's long ago now. Seems to sit right up in front of my eyes just now though.

Major let Watchorn and Pearl out for the festivities, he seemed to think that was the right thing to do. He said he would tend to them later. Where were they going to run? Wasn't nothing around us only nothing.

I would have to say it was lovely how the town composed itself to welcome us. They had set banners all along their little street and they lit lanterns they had made from old packing paper, the candles burning in them like souls. The padre made a huge prayer out in the open and the whole town went down on its knees, right there, and praised the Lord. This was the section of humanity favoured in that place, the Indians had no place no more there. Their tickets of passage were rescinded and the bailiffs of God had took back the papers for their souls. I did feel a seeping tincture of sadness for them. I did feel some strange toiling seeping sadness for them. Seven hours off buried in their pits, the redwoods towering, the silence pitted by birds and passing creatures. The solemn awfulness of it maybe. There weren't no padre praying in exultation for them. They were the boys with the losing hand. Then niceties all done, the town rose and cheered wildly, and then it was a maelstrom of meat eating and

40

keg broaching, and all the usual mayhem. We were dancing, we were clapping backs, we were telling old stories. Men were listening with their ears cocked, till they judged when they could let loose the laughter. Time was not something then we thought of as an item that possessed an ending, but something that would go on forever, all rested and stopped in that moment. Hard to say what I mean by that. You look back at all the endless years when you never had that thought. I am doing that now as I write these words in Tennessee. I am thinking of the days without end of my life. And it is not like that now. I am wondering what words we said so carelessly that night, what vigorous nonsense we spoke, what drunken shouts we shouted, what stupid joy there was in that, and how John Cole was only young then and as handsome as any person that has ever lived. Young, and there would never be a change for that. The heart rising, and the soul singing. Fully alive in life and content as the house-martins under the eaves of the house.

The army had in mind for us to brave out the winter in the fort and then come spring be seeing what else could be done for to pacify the country. Although I have given the impression that them Yuroks were small and ineffectual people nevertheless listening to the townspeople did put us in suspicion that the Indians were not always so tolerable. There were stories everywhere of rapes and robberies and sudden and vicious visits on

41

out-of-the-way premises. Unless you were a witness how could you say what was true. Anyhows in due course a herd of some hundreds of cattle arrived, driven up from southern California on an army requisition docket. That was for our sustenance. On the saint's day of St John I get a letter from Mr Noone just as he promised. All his news. There was good water under the thickening ice. All the stores would keep fresh in those low temperatures. There was a forest of wood to burn. We washed our shirts and trews and when we went out to get them off the bushes, they were as stiff as corpses in the cold. Some poor cows froze where they were standing like they had peered into the face of old Medusa. Men lost the wages of three years hence at cards. They bet their boots and then pled for the pity of the winner. The piss froze as it left our peckers and woe betide the man with an obstruction or hesitation to their shit, because soon they had a brown icicle on their arse. The whisky continued its work of eating our livers. It was as good a life as most of us had ever knowed. Watchorn and Pearl mingled with the rest, as if the major had forgotten their offence. The Missouri men sang their Missouri songs, rough Kansas men sang theirs, and those queer New England types sang no doubt the ancient songs of England, who could tell.

Then rain began to fall in an extravagant tantrum. High up in mountain country though we were, every little river became a huge muscled snake, and the water wanted to find out everything, the meaning of our sad roofs for instance, the meaning of our bunk beds beginning to take the character of little barks, the sure calculation that if it fell day and night no human man was going to get his uniform dry. We was wet to the ribs.

Crazy California weather, how come anyone ever come out here? said John Cole, with the voice of one who has not exactly chosen this destination.

We was lying out on the aforesaid bunks. Now the spring was supposed to be afoot was just as well as no one had dollars left to lose at cards, except the damn sergeant, who had won most of it. There were sharks in other segments of our unit too, Patterson and Wilks, both evil good card-players. Now they were likely struggling to keep their winnings dry. Those Yankee dollars were inclined to rust. The high snow melted and down that came too.

Next morning John Cole was shaking my arm to wake me. You need to do something other than lie there, he says. Sure enough the water was up over his bunk and just about to engulf mine. There was a smell of rats' urine if you ever smelt that. Now that I think of it, we saw dozens of the critters swimming for their lives. We sloshed out onto the parade ground so called. Men were coming out of the sheds trying to hitch their braces. Well we had no high ground to go to. How come we got a flood here, we were saying? The way some genius built this place. True enough, now that we had the rain and meltwater to show us, the camp was kinda built in a odd way. If you can imagine a great scallop shape there, and the hills behind, and what was formerly the helpful little stream going past the boundary wall. Now blotted out. The night pickets were standing on the wall looking very doubtful. Some brave bugler bugled reveille but damn it we were all reveilled by then. The major was actually swimming up the way. Now the three hundred were looking to get up on the roofs, seemed the only way, and dozens of others shimmied up into the shade trees, if they were dizzy from heights they didn't show it, up they went like monkeys in uniform. Myself and John Cole pushed over through the lead-heavy water and clumb a tree likewise.

We weren't even all up there when something queer was stirring in the distance. No one had ever seen the like. It looked like someone had put the ocean on top of the forest, just thrun it down there, and now the ocean was doing the inevitable in the scientific way and was hammering and surging down towards us. We felt like three hundred very small and foolish creatures when we saw that, standing as we were on a bunch of low roofs. Major almost screams out his orders, and then the sergeants were echoing him, and then the men were trying to respond. But what had the major said? What had the sergeants called out? Where to go? We were already the citizens of a shallow sea. That coming wave looked like twenty feet of death.

The flood came so quickly you couldn't have laid a bet on it. You couldn't a got the book open quick enough to mark the wager. Then the wild vicious thing reached our camp and spread itself over it carrying half of the forest with it. Trees and branches and bushes and bears and deer and God knows, birds and alligators, though I never saw alligators up there to be truthful. Wolves and mountain cats and snakes. Everything was gone then with the flood, that was able to be unmoored and move. Those fellas on the roofs had the shittiest cards in the deal, it was like nature's hand just swept them off the table. I could feel our shade tree bending with the force and it was twelve feet round at the base. Man, it bent. Then unbent. Now we were nearly arrows being fired. Hold on there, John Cole! Hold on, Thomas! So we held, we gripped, we fastened ourselves, the great old tree whanged in the boiling waters, I doubt I will ever hear such a sound again, it was well nigh musical.

Dozens of troopers musta drowned. Maybe Watchorn and Pearl might have wished to be among them, but they survived. Me and John Cole. Thank God, John Cole. The major, and two hundred others. It was the men in the trees was mostly saved. Those roofs too low. We found bodies for the next weeks, lower down, as the flood waters fell. The townspeople came down and helped us with the burying. They hadn't been so crazy as to build their town in a flood path anyhow. Guess we knew then what had scalloped out that ground. Goddamn engineers.

Then a queer fever went through the camp. Maybe it was yellow fever, something like that, something that liked a lot of wetness. Our cattle were gone of course and all our dry goods were wet goods. The townspeople gave us what they could but the major said we had to go back to Missouri even though the grass would only be coming small on the prairie.

This little tour is done, he said, drily. The major's wit. It was the driest thing in the camp.

Now winter was tightening her noose on the world everywhere and we were headed back for Missouri. To say we were a bedraggled troop is not quite saying enough. Maybe we were being punished for our shabby acts. There was no game below the mountains this time and soon our bellies were gnawed by hunger. It was weeks of a journey and now we were a-feared of what hunger might do. A hunger knower like myself was a-feared more than most. I seen the cold deeds of hunger. The world got a lot of people in it, and when it comes to slaughter and famine, whether we're to live or die, it don't care much either way. The world got so many it don't need to. We could have starved out there on the badlands, on that desert that wasn't a desert, on that journey that wasn't a journey so much as a fleeing eastward. Thousands die everywhere always. The world don't care much, it just don't mind much. That's what I notice about it. There is that great wailing and distress and then the pacifying waters close over everything, old Father Time washes his hands. On he plods to the next place. It suits us well to know these things, that you may exert yourself to survive. Just surviving is the victory. Now that I can no longer exert myself in that way, I think back to that lonesome troop of soldiers, trying to make it back. Desolate, and decimated though we were, there was something good there. Something that couldn't be extinguished by flood and hunger. That human will. You got to give homage to it. I seen it many times. It ain't so rare. But it is the best of us.

Now we were praying like priests or virgin girls that we would meet some wagons plying west. Except, by the time they passed us, they might be lean on victuals also of course. But we just gotta see other human faces. Mile upon mile of the sere little bushes of America and the scraggy up-and-down terrain. In the far distance to the south sometimes we thought we could see piled-up square hills, we knew we mustn't go down there. That was Apache and Comanche country certainly. Boys would eat you for their supper quick as see you. The major knew the lean Apache boys, he had fought with them for fifteen years, he said. Just about the worst devils you will ever hear about or see, he said. He said they was going down regular into Mexico, chewing up farmers. Kill everyone they could find, take the cattle, horses, women and oftentimes children back to their countries. Be gone a month, riding like ghosts through the spectral lands. You could chase after them with men and guns but you would never find them. Never even see them. You'd wake in the morning and there wouldn't be a horse tethered no more, fifty of them vanished in the night, and the pickets dead as stones where they had been sitting. He said they took you prisoner you would regret it. Take you back to their villages for sport, the women with their little sharp knives cutting you with a thousand cuts, the slowest death in the book. Bleed out on the warm prairie dust. Or bury you to the neck, let the ants eat your face, the dogs gnaw your ears and nose, if the women hadn't cut them off already. Thing was, a warrior was never to cry out. Show how brave you were by not crying out, that's what they thought was a decent exit. But white men, troopers, they'd be roaring just to see the women coming with the knives. Anyhow, you died either way. Thing was, if a warrior was missing something important, if the head was parted from the trunk for instance, there was an opinion among them that you wouldn't be able to reach the happy hunting grounds then. So they were careful not to take too much. Just little bits. The ear and eye, say, or trim off the bollocks. So you could still reach heaven. But the trouble was, Mexican bandits, and rough riding white men of any description, evil outlaws, murderous rustlers, all those wild class of beings that were ubiquitous in that time, they thought they better cut up an Indian when they killed him. Took off the hair firstly, hair was a big thing for an Indian. Scalping. Long silky black hair down to the waist and the skin on top of the head with it. Chop off the head with a machete. Chop off the arms. That didn't show no respect and no thought either for the warrior's aftertime. That sort of thing inflamed the Apache, the Comanche, then he was out on a revenge spree. He was going to take your fingers off one by one. He was going to take your toes, and then your balls, and then your pecker. Slowly, slowly. You better not get in his way then.

White men doesn't understand Indians and vice versa, said the major, shaking his head in his even-toned way. That's what brings the trouble, he says.

Well, now we were fearing the Indians just as much as the hunger, though the hunger was winning too.

CHAPTER 5

Imagine our horror and distress then when we saw those Oglala boys sitting on their horses on the horizon. Two hundred, three, just sitting there. Our own horses were skeletons. They were getting water but little else. Horses need regular fodder, grass and such. My poor horse was showing his bones like they was metal levers sticking out. Watchorn had been a small plumpish man but he weren't no more. You coulda used John Cole for a pencil if you coulda threaded some lead through him. We were a day out on the prairie and the horses only had the first bright green slivers of grass to graze on. Half an inch. It was too early in the year. We were yearning to see wagons, our crazy wish was to see a herd of them buffalo, we started to dream of buffalo, thousands upon thousands, stampeding through our dreams, and then we'd wake in the moonlight and see only that, piss yellow and thin in the chill darkness. Temperature dropping down the glass till it was hard to breathe it was so cold. The little streams smelling of iron. At night the troopers slept close together in their blankets, we looked like a mess of prairie dogs, sleeping close for life. Snoring through frosty nostrils. The horses stamping, stamping and steaming out frosted tendrils and flowers of breath in the darkness. Now in these different districts, the sun came up that bit earlier, more eagerly, more like the baker putting fire into his bread-oven, in the small hours, so the women in the town would have bread bright early. Lord, that sun rose regular and sere, he didn't care who saw him, naked and round and white. Then the rains came walking over the land, exciting the new grasses, thundering down, hammering like fearsome little bullets, making the shards and dusts of the earth dance a violent jig. Making the grass seeds drunk with ambition. Then the sun pouring in after the rain, and the wide endless prairie steaming, a vast and endless vista of white steam rising, and the flocks of birds wheeling and turning, a million birds to one cloud, we'd a needed a blunderbuss to harvest them, small black fleet wondrous birds. We were riding on and all the while, ten fifteen miles, the Oglala moving with us, watching. Might have been wondering why we didn't stop for eats. Didn't have no eats to eat. It was Trooper Pearl knew they were Sioux. Said he recognised them. Don't know how he did, seeing as they were so far off. The flood had took our Shawnee scouts who'd a known. With our diminished numbers we were two hundred now, maybe a little less. The major hadn't done a roll call for days. Sergeant Wellington was the only one indifferent, it would seem. If he knew

51

one song out of the mountains of Virginia he knew a hundred. If he knew one song about a poor dying mother lonesome and her children far away he knew a thousand. And the cruel creeping raw vicious scraping voice he had. Mile after mile. And the goddamned Oglala Sioux or whoever it was out there keeping pace with every painful step. I was beginning to think it would be a welcome release if they just charged up now and did for us. It would stop that miserable caterwauling anyhow.

Mid morning then of this drear day Sergeant perks up suddenly, his singing dying away. He points out on the plain a horseman detaching from the distant group. Had a high pole with a pennant on it, waving in the fluttering breeze. The major stopped our whole troop and got us to clump together. He was giving a sight of ten lines of men with twenty riders each ready with muskets to the approaching Indian. The Indian didn't seem to think much of this, he came on, we could see him clearer now. Then he stops half way, just sits there, his horse stirring about a little like they do. Champing, backing off a step, being settled again by his rider. He was just beyond musket range. Sergeant was anxious to try a shot but the major stayed his hand. Then the major spurs his horse and goes forward out of position, heads off across the scutty grasses. The sergeant bites his lip, because he doesn't like this, but can't air an objection. Major thinks Indians gentlemen like hisself, he hisses.

So we're paused there and of course the flies find us quickly and if we have nothing to gorge on, they do. Ears and faces and backs of hands get a going over. Damn little black devils. But we almost don't heed them, you can see all the men sitting forward on their saddles, as if they could hear the parlay about to take place, but no chance of that. Off there now we see the major reach the rider and now he is stopped and now we can see the mouth of the Indian moving, and the head nodding, and the hands going in sign language. The air is so tense even the flies seem to stop biting. The prairie is as quiet as a library. Just the tremendous grasses folding, unfolding, showing their dark underbellies, hiding them, showing. The little shucking sound of that. But most of the business was sky. Huge endless sky all the way to heaven most likely. The major and the Indian talked for about twenty minutes, then the major suddenly wheels around, comes trotting back. The Indian watches him for a few moments, sergeant begins to draw a bead on him then, but there's no emergency, the Indian pulls the head of his pony round, and goes back placidly to his friends. The major comes on daintily enough, that's one fine horse he has, one of those pricy mounts, skinnied up now though.

What's the news? says the sergeant.

He wanted to know what we're doing out here, says the major. Looks like we're north of where we thought. These ain't treaty Indians.

53

Goddamn mongrel sonsabitches what they are, the sergeant says, and spits.

Well, he said they have meat and he would give it to us, says the major.

The sergeant didn't seem to have an answer to that. The men were amazed, relieved. Could it be true? Sure enough we saw the Indians leaving the meat. Then we went over to get it, by which time they had cleared off completely. Just vanished away like they do. The fire-makers and the cooks got going and then we had roasted buffalo. We were pulling it a bit raw from the fire but no matter.

It was such a wild crazy pleasure simply to eat. To champ on actual sustenance. It was like the first time we ever ate. Mother's milk. Everything we were that had started to seep away because of the hunger was returning. Men were talking again and then the laughter was returning. The sergeant was affecting to be angry and perplexed. Said the meat was likely poisoned. But it weren't poisoned. Sergeant said no one ever likely understood Indians. They'd had their damn chance to kill us and they hadn't took it. Goddamn stupid Injuns, coyotes had more sense. The major must of decided to say nothing. He was quiet. The two hundred sets of teeth chewing away. Swallowing the big blackened lumps, bellies growling.

Well, I gotta say, said Trooper Pearl. I be thinking well of Indians now.

The sergeant looking at him with a wolf's eyes.

I gotta say, thinking well of them, Pearl says again.

The sergeant gets up in a big huff for himself and goes off a piece and sits by himself on a grassy mound.

It got to be accounted a happy day.

We were four or five days from the frontier, we reckoned, just a bit of a ride now to Missouri and what we called home, when a storm came in over us. It was one of those bleak ice storms, everything it touched freezing, including the bits of our bodies showing. I never rode in anything so cold. We had nowhere to shelter and so were obliged to push on. After the first day the storm decided to go worse. It made the world into a perpetual night but when the real night came the temperature maybe was down to forty minus, we didn't know exactly. Our blood said bottom of the scale. It's a queer wild feeling, that freezing. We laid neckerchiefs across our mouths and chins but after a while little good it did. Our gloves froze and soon our fingers were fixed fast around the reins like our hands had deceased and gone to their reward. Couldn't feel them which was maybe just as well. The wind was all icy blades and might have shaved the beards and whiskers of the men but that they had already froze to metal. We all went white, frosted from our crowns to our toes, and the black, the grey, and brown horses were all turned white now. The blankets of chill white rheum over everything was not warming. Picture us, two hundred men riding into that wind. The grasses themselves crackling under the hooves. Above in the black sky torn and rent by invisible violence just now and then fleetingly the burning white orb of the moon went flying. We feared to open our mouths for one second or the moisture would freeze them ajar. The storm had a lot of prairie to cross and all the days of the world to do it. It must have been as wide as two countries. It passed over us and through us. But for the Indian victuals we would of died in the second day. It was just enough belly fuel to carry us out the other side. Then we saw other trouble. Big sunlight followed the storm, and our clothes seemed half-melted, like unravelling felt. Many of the men were in atrocious pain just as soon as the ice melted off them. Trooper Watchorn's face was as red as radishes and when he pulled off his boots we could see his feet were no good either. Next day his nose was black as soot. It was like he was wearing something on it, burning dark and sore. He couldn't put his boots back on for any money and he wasn't the only one in travail. There were dozens in a bad way. Soon we come to the river that marked the frontier in that part and we push the column forward into the shallow waters. The river was two miles wide and about a foot deep all the way. The horses threw up the water and soon we were drenched. That didn't do Trooper Watchorn much good, howling now. There was pain in him like no man could bear. There was others as bad but Watchorn had headed further in his brain somehow and when we reached the far bank the major was required to pull him from the horse and get him trussed up somehow, because he wasn't no human creature now exactly, Watchorn. We were spooked as hell. That howling man, and pain so painful we seemed to feel it too somehow. Then they trussed him up because he was banging his face with his hands and he had to suffer the indignity of being lashed belly down to his mount. Then in a strange mercy he sank into a stupor, and in that condition we reached our destination much bedraggled and harassed. In the fort hospital in the coming months men lost toes and fingers. Frostbite the doctor called it, frost carnage more like. Trooper Watchorn and two others didn't live past the summer. Gangrene got in and that's a dancing partner no trooper chooses. And then they were in the funeral parlour like I told, all decked out in spare uniforms, and additions made to their losses, Watchorn with a wax nose and shaved clean as a stone courtesy of that embalmer. But looking dandy enough. It sure took the proverbial cake.

I guess poor Trooper Pearl had the worse fate. The major hadn't forgotten after all. Court martial and even though the officers presiding had no real notion of what his offence might have been given that Trooper Pearl was a victor in an Indian engagement something about the major's high moral tone got into proceedings and then Pearl's goose was cooked. It was me and five other troopers were gave the job of dispatching him. He made a noble end of things. Looking a bit like Jehovah now because he had grown a long black beard in captivity all down his breast. We shot him through the beard to reach his heart. Joe Pearl went down. His father came in from Massachusetts where they was from and took the body home.

John Cole said he might have enough of Indian fighting just presently but we got to serve out our term agreed and we were content to do that because we got to be. We sure getting poorer and uglier in the army but better than be shot, he said.

CHAPTER 6

You can be tired all you like of something I guess but the Fates say you got to go back out and rub your nose in it. How come we left cosy Jefferson again to traipse back just next and nigh the way we had come with so much hardship might have been a question. That just the army way. Well we had got three months in barracks and that was a fine endowment. Wise old hands brought their bearskins. They weren't going to freeze again like the late Trooper Watchorn. Army had no good clothes to give us for the cold. Meant to give us wool jobs but we never seen them. First bloody Sergeant Wellington said we was cunts deserved to die of frostbite. Every man Jack got a printed sheet showing us the saving outfits which was supposed to arrive at barracks instanter. Never damn did. Can't wear a picture, says John Cole, my beau.

But now was the season for all those hopeful hearts going out to pick up gold nuggets as they thought from the ground of forsaken places. This year more than was seen before. If you ever set eyes on three thousand lily-faced white boys and their families you'll know what I mean. Was like they was going to a picnic but the meadow was six weeks off and death guaranteed for many. We was told in St Louis to take a northern route because every blade of grass was eaten between Missouri and Fort Laramie. Them thousand thousand horses, cattle, oxen, and mules. Lots of new boys in the 6th, lots of forlorn Irish, usual big dark boys. Joking, all that teasing Irish do, but somewhere behind it the dark wolves staring, the hunger wolves under the hunger moons. We were to augment the military presence in Fort Laramie because there was to be a great gathering of Indians out there on the plains. The major and the colonel is going to ask them to stop killing the goddamn emigrants.

The colonel sends out messengers to every tribe he knows of ever set foot on the whiteman's trail. Thousands come, driven in by want and hunger. The whole thing is set up a few miles north of the fort in a place called Horse Creek. The colonel puts the army on the lower bank of the river. Up go our rows of tents. The summer sun leans down on everything and bakes the canvas and if you can sleep at night you must be deceased. Nice easygoing river there and not much bother to cross it, and the colonel he ranges the government men and the quick-chance traders over a ways and across the water itself he requests the tribes to be establishing their wigwams. Now there was maybe three four thousand pointed dwellings bedecked in painted skins and banners. The famed Shoshone, the lofty Sioux boys both Teton and Oglala, the Arapaho, the Assiniboine come down from Canada, blazed out in the midday heat in all their finery. Major knows the Oglala because it's the same crowd fed us in our time of trial. That same chief's here, Caught-His-Horse-First. And the noise that come up from the whole lot of them is a tremendous music in itself. A special awning is erected and the officers in their best bibs assemble there on chairs. At length the cloaked backs of the chiefs was seen ranged darkly in the shadows and the sun-red faces of the officers sort of bleakly looking out from under hatbrims, everyone starching they-selves up into a mighty fit of seriousness. Big speeches is made, while the mounted infantry and the cavalry respectfully stood off at a distance, and on the other bank the tribes seat themselves in a silence such as you might know just before a thunderstorm, when the land draws in its chest and holds a limitless breath, and across the valley drifts the voice of the colonel. Annuities and food supplies is offered in exchange for the emigrants to be let through. The interpreters do their work and agreement is reached. The colonel looks mighty pleased. We were all thinking that a new day was dawning on the plains, and we was happy to think it might be so. Them Indians is wore out from slaughter and so are we.

Starling Carlton, one of the fellas in our company, says there's so much hot air in the colonel it's a wonder he don't float off. But soldiers like to take the dim view. It cheers them up. I won't say what the sergeant said of all this, the only truly unhappy man.

Empurpled rapturous hills I guess and the long day brushstroke by brushstroke enfeebling into darkness and then the fires blooming on the pitch plains. In the beautiful blue night there was plenty of visiting and the braves was proud and ready to offer a lonesome soldier a squaw for the duration of his passion. John Cole and me sought out a hollow away from prying eyes. Then with the ease of men who have rid themselves of worry we strolled among the Indian tents and heard the sleeping babies breathing and spied out the wondrous kind called by the Indians *winkte* or by white men *berdache*, braves dressed in the finery of squaws. John Cole gazes on them but he don't like to let his eyes linger too long in case he gives offence. But he's like the plough-horse that got the whins. All woken in a way I don't see before. The *berdache* puts on men's garb when he goes to war, this I know. Then war over it's back to the bright dress. We move on and he's just shaking like a cold child. Two soldiers walking under the bright nails of the stars. John Cole's long face, long stride. The moonlight not able to flatter him because he was already beautiful.

Next morning was a final gift-giving to the Indians. A man called Titian Finch had arrived with a daguerreotype machine to make a record of these clement days. The tribes is photographed in great assemblies and the major has his picture done with Caught-His-Horse-First like they was old friends. A sunlight as white as a maiden's bosom floods the country. They have to move real close. A naked Indian and a braided major. They stand beside each other in casual earnestness, the Indian's right hand gripping the major's silver-threaded sleeve, as if to alert him to some danger, or guard him from it. Titian Finch bids them both hold still as stones, and for one eternal moment they are there, the very picture of human equanimity and gratitude.

Then these friendly acts were done and the Indians dispersed and we was returned to ordinary days. Nathan Noland, Starling Carlton, Lige Magan the sharpshooter, these was boys of the regiment that came close to us in that time, me and John Cole. Because it was now that John Cole started to show the illness that afflicted him. He was obliged to lie quiet for days because there weren't one cup of steam in him. Doc had no name for it. A rattlesnake could of trailed across his breast and he couldn't a done nothing about it. The boys abovementioned was the ones that shown regard for John Cole in his extremity. Handsome John Cole they called him. Got the cooks to make him broth and so forth. Bringing it in to him like he was a emperor. Not to say that Lige Magan and the rest weren't broken-backed moaning clap-ridden drunken loons betimes. Man they was. Lige Magan I liked best I can say. Elijah was his full name so I guess he was a wonder worker. Nice ox-faced boy of some forty-five years out of Tennessee. His people had hogs there till the bottom fell out of hogs. The bottom was always falling out of something in America far as I could see. So it was with the world, restless, kind of brutal. Always going on. Not waiting for no man. Then John Cole would wax good again and it was like nothing had ailed him. Then down again. Then up again. We was dizzy.

Now it was inching into autumn and those treaty Indians had to make way in their villages for that old murderer called Famine. That filthy dark-hearted scrawny creature that wants the ransom of lives. Because government food that was promised was late or never coming. The major was looking vexed and tormented. His honest heart had made promises, that how he saw it.

It was in the time of noisy weather that the first trouble came. We rode forth to meet it. Thunderstorms busted open the air and threw heaven-cast pails of light over that landscape that had no walls, no ends. God in his farmer's apron, scattering the great seeds of yellow brightness. The hinterlands beyond the mountains breathing a fiery white breath. Nathan Noland with his tender ears already ruined by years of musket-fire deaf for three days after. Riding in a bruised becalmed gap between that ravenous display and the coming clatter of the rain. Then rain flattening the grasses like bear grease flattens a squaw's hair. Sergeant Wellington was happy now because Sioux from some village westward had fallen on some strayed emigrants and ripped them from hopeful life. So the colonel had gave him fifty men and said to put a stop to that. Seems it was those Oglala friends of the major but that didn't stop the order.

First Lieutenant puts us into two companies and he takes twenty men and goes sharp westward by his compass and us and the sergeant set off scouring out a little river ravine where he reckons that village might lie. The watercourse runs for ten miles north-east looks like. The whole country has started to steam because the sunlight is roasting off the rain. The grasses start to sit up again almost naked to the eye. A giant rousing. Three thousand bears throwing off the winter looks like. The stream itself mad as goaded bulls tearing down between its drenched rocks. Meadowlarks larking everywhere looking pleased with themselves and the skeeters in wholesale flocks everywhere. We ain't feeling cheerful because rocks above you favours the enemy. That's in all history. We were expecting to see the sergeant's savages any moment popping up. But we went on all that day and further up the country where there were no streams only the baking silence of the plains. Then the sergeant disgruntled gives the order to retrace our steps and he is cursing that he let the new Pawnee scouts go with the lieutenant. These are very elegant boys in good uniforms better than what I had. But the lieutenant took them.

White men just no good for tracking cross country like this, he said, surprising us. Sounded like praise.

We camped up where our paths had furcated and we slept as best we could in our nightcaps of skeeters. We was happy men to climb out of blankets at earliest dawn. We washed our weary faces in the stream now calmed by the hours passed between. Rains in it must have passed on towards the Platte river and soon enough pour down into the Missouri. Strange to think of all that as we tried to shave our cheeks with blunted razors in the sparkling waters. Handsome John Cole whistling a waltz still residing in him out of New England.

Then we're just poking about the place there waiting for the lieutenant to come back. Sergeant tells us to dry the lurking rain off our sabres or they will rust for sure. Then we fodder the horses best we can. Ain't a trooper alive don't love his horses. Spavined brute is loved. Nothing much to do then. Lige shows his skill at cards again and cleans out Starling Carlton. But we're only playing for blades of grass, we ain't got no money till the end of the month, if it comes then. Pawnee scouts were nearly going off last month because their pay didn't come and then they seen we had nothing either so they calm down. Sometimes when you're far from the sweet bells of town nothing comes out to you. Feels like they forget you. The goddamned boys in blue.

So the sergeant tells us to mount up and then we ready the horses and then we ride out along the way the lieutenant went, following the hoofprints best we could after the big rubber of the rain. Rain likes to keep things discreet, not show the way. But we go like that, Sergeant cursing all the while. Sergeant has a big hard stomach these days, says it's his liver. Way he drinks whisky it might be. Youth has gone out of him anyhow and he looks like a old man. Like we got ten faces to wear in our lives and we wear them one by one.

Two miles on we got the shackles of the heat lying on us again, so hot the country begins to shimmer like the desert. We had the sun half behind us to the south which was some mercy. Wasn't a man among hadn't had his nose skinned off a hundred times. Bear grease is good for that but it stinks like an arsehole and anyhow we ain't seen bears for a long time.

Jeez Christ, says Starling Carlton, if this ain't hot.

So then it got hotter. You can feel your back begin to cook. Pinch of salt and a few sprigs of rosemary and you got a dinner. God Almighty, the heat. My horse don't like it much and is beginning to stumble along. Sergeant is riding a nice mule he got in St Louis because he says mules is best and he ain't wrong. We're just going along while the sun hammers on us without anyone able to stop it. You could arrest sunlight for attempted murder out on the plains. God damn it. Then Starling Carlton just falls off his horse. If he knew when he was born and had a paper it wouldn't show too many years. Falls clean off his saddle and strikes the powdery earth. So the sergeant and another trooper push him back up and give him water from the bottle and he looks all startled and ashamed like a girl farting in chapel. But we're too hot to mock him. On we go. Then off in the distance Sergeant thinks he sees something. Truth to tell Sergeant is as good as a scout for seeing things but we don't like to tell him that. So now we dismount and are leading our mounts and we are keeping best we can to a low line of scrub and other rubbishy rocks that happily snakes off towards whatever the sergeant seen. Feet swole in the boots and now every inch sweating including feels like the very eyeballs.

Quarter mile off the sergeant stops and makes a reckoning. He can't see nothing moving he says but he sees plenty wigwams there and we can see them too, black shapes pointing up to the stupendous white acres of the sky. He don't like what he sees. Then he barks a quick order and we're into the saddles again and we don't feel no heat now. Sergeant puts us into a double line and then by God he gives the order to charge. Out there in the silent prairie with only the perpetual wind for music and he tells us to charge. Ain't there an old story about a windmill? But we spur the flanks till we draw little scratches of beaded blood. Horses wake up out of their stupor and catch the atmosphere. Sergeant shouts draw sabres so he does and now we show our thirty swords to the sunlight and the sunlight ravishes every inch of them. Sergeant never has given that order in all our time because you might as well light a fire as draw a sabre in the brightness as far as signals go. But something has the wind up him. Suddenly an old sense of life we haven't remembered floods back into us. The air of manhood fills our skins. Some can't help hollering and the sergeant screams at us to keep the line. We wonder what he is thinking. Soon we are at the fringes of the tent town, we tear through in a second, like riders in an old storybook, sweeping in. Suddenly we reach the centre. Suddenly we rein in mighty fast. Horses are flighty, excited, snorting, they're spinning round so it's hard to keep a bead on what's to be seen. What's to be seen is our twenty other troopers all dead looks like. They're all dead lying about in the centre of the camp, clumped up, looks like shot really sudden, so that most of the heads are pointing nigh in the same direction. Lieutenant's head in addition cut from his body. Hats gone, belts, guns, sabres, shoes, and scalps. Nathan Noland with his copper-coloured beard and eyes open to the sun. Tall wiry man from Nova Scotia, R.I.P. Halo of black blood. There's only two Indians there, dead as dollars. We're surprised the Indians didn't take their dead with them. Must be a story there. Otherwise the camp is clean empty. You see the pole marks where the Indians left. Had to go so quick they didn't pack the wigwams. Kettles still, here and there, with fires under them still. Sergeant dismounts and lets his mule walk off. Walk to Jericho for all he cared. He takes off his campaign cap and scratches his bald pate with his right hand. Tears in his eyes. God have mercy.

CHAPTER 7

We're scuffing about the camp trying to figure out what happened and looking for clues. We don't know if the Indians are nearby or coming back. Then a trooper's found in a wigwam where he must of crawled in. It's like a miracle and for a moment an exultation floods my breast. He has a bullet in the cheek but he's still breathing. Caleb Booth's alive, shouts the man who finds him. We all crowd to the tent door. We fetch him a swallow of water and then the sergeant holds up his head and tries to get him to drink but most of the water runs out through his cheek. We found them early this morning, says Caleb Booth. He's young like me and John Cole, so he doesn't understand dying. Probably thinks he'll come through all right. Wants to tell us the history. Says the Pawnee scouts took off for some reason and then the lieutenant rode them right in and asked the chief was he involved in killing those emigrants. Chief said he was because they was moving over ground that was forbid in the treaty and why was that and had he not by God every right to kill them? Caleb Booth said the lieutenant just lost his temper then at the easy mentioning of the Lord and just shot the man standing next nigh the chief. Then the chief calls out and there is a dozen other braves in the tents unbeknownst and they rush out and start shooting and there's only time to shoot another Indian and then all the troopers are shot. And Caleb lay in the grass face down and keeps quiet. Then the Indians go off in a big hurry and Caleb creeps into the wigwam as the sun starts to rise higher in the sky since he don't wish to be fried. He knew we would come, he says, he just knew. Darned glad to see us. So then the sergeant pokes around the wound a bit to see where the bullet went and looks like it went right through and out somewhere. Flying like a gemstone over the plains. Sergeant nods his head like someone asked him something.

Digging holes for nineteen men in earth never ploughed is taxing work. But the bodies are already swelling and we ain't got a cart to carry them home. We gather up all the wigwams and all the bits and pieces and pile them up and then we fire the lot. Lige Magan says he hopes the Injuns can see the smoke and hurry back to save their dirty rags. He says the best thing to do is bury the men and then light out after the killers. Kill every one of them for a change, he says. I'm thinking but not saying that we don't have the supplies for that and what about Caleb Booth. They could be a day away and what's more cavalry can never find Indians like that, they're wilier than wolves. And

Lige knows all that as well as me but he goes busting on about doing it. Tells us what he thinks we can do when we find them. Seems to have a lot of plans. More than likely the sergeant can hear him but the sergeant is standing alone now beyond the wigwams. The grass is so baked by the sun that it looks blue, it shines like blue blades beside the sergeant's old boots. He has his back turned to us and he doesn't say anything in response to Lige. Lige shakes his head and goes on digging. Starling Carlton has gone puce-red in the face and is panting like an old dog, but he keeps the shovel moving. Bangs his foot down on it and keeps it moving. They say Starling Carlton killed men in his time outside the law but no one knows for sure. Some say he was a child-catcher, taking Indian children for slaves in California. He sure would give you a clatter if you looked sideways at him. You gotta treat him with due caution. He don't mind losing at cards and has a jolly aspect to him sometimes but you don't want to find out the thing that irritates him because it might be the last thing you find out. There's no one on earth would say he's a polite man. How he carries his big weight out here on a job like this is anyone's guess and he don't seem to eat much more than the next man and he sweats like a cut cactus all the time. It's washing down his face now and he rubs it away with his filthy hands. He digs nearly as good as John Cole, has a little steady knack to his spadework, which is agreeable to watch even as we mourn. We don't know rightly what to do with the dead Indians so we just leave them. Sergeant comes over suddenly and cuts off their noses because he don't want them to reach the happy hunting grounds, he says. He throws the noses out onto the prairie like he thinks the dead might rise to try and put them back. He fetches the papers and them little travelling Bibles and the like off of our boys. Wives and mothers to send them to. On we go, then we respectfully drop the men into their holes and then we cover them up with a bedding of earth and every man in due course has a mound of the same earth over him like eider-downs in a fancy hotel. The sergeant rouses himself and says a few words appropriate to the moment and then he bids us mount up and Lige puts Caleb Booth up behind him because it's Lige who has the strongest gelding and then we ride off. No one looks back.

Caught-His-Horse-First and his band is pinned up in barracks as the number one criminal. Sergeant pins the notice up himself. Colonel signs the order. Doesn't take the terror and the sorrow out of it but puts revenge in beside it as a brother. Like cutting beer with whisky. The Pawnee scouts come in eventually but when they can't give a good account for hightailing it the colonel reckons it's as good as desertion and they're shot. The major don't like it and says scouts ain't soldiers proper, you can't shoot them. Apart from that old and useful phrase *nahwah* which means howdy, no one speaks Pawnee and sign language don't cover this. Indians look very puzzled, surprised and offended to be shot but they go to the wall with noble mien I must allow. You can't have nothing good in war without you punishing the guilty, the sergeant says with a savage air and no one says nothing against that. John Cole whispers to me that most times that sergeant he just wrong but just now and then he's right and he's right this time. I guess I'm thinking this is true. We get drunk then and the sergeant is clutching his belly all evening and then everything is blotted out till you awake in the bright early morning needing a piss and then it all floods back into your brain what happened and it makes your heart yelp like a dog.

Least Caleb Booth was coming good in the infirmary and that might be a tribute to his innocent belief in the darn permanence of life.

But I was remembering in particular Nathan Noland my friend and John Cole's. And I remembered John Cole putting a sprig into the hole with Nathan of some goddamn weed he called Wolf's-bane but I said it was a goddamn Lupine, don't he know his flowers? He said he knowed them a heck better than me being a farmboy but we was out in foreign country now and names were not the same here. Wolf's-bane was used in New England for poisoning captured wolves, said John Cole. You crushed it up and fed it with meat. I said you can crush that up and try kill a wolf with it but the wolf will bite you because it's just a Lupine. Then he was laughing. We was sorrowful in the extreme for Nathan Noland and the flower looked good along his bloodied face, Lupine or Wolf's-bane or whatever was its name. It was a small stack of purple smoke it looked like lying there and the drear pull of the skin on Nathan's face was somehow eased a little by it. John Cole had closed his eyes and we was sorry to see his end.

As drear winter returns again we hunker down in the fort and hope our bodies can rise in spring like the bears. Soldiers coming out of winter have those swimming rheumy eyes of drinkers. Their skins is pale from poor eats. Awful endless yards of dry meats from the long cold pantries and maybe for a while potatoes from New York and Maine come out in huge wagons and even some oranges coming back the other way from California. But mostly filthy dreck of things like things dogs won't eat except in extremities. But Indians too go to ground and God knows how they stretch their goods from fall to spring because an Indian he never plans for nothing. If he got a pile of something he eats it, if he got a barrel of whisky he drinks it. He drinks it till he falls down drunker than a pollen-drunk bumblebee. We're hoping Caught-His-Horse-First is feeling the same murdering hunger we do. Only the sergeant keeps his swole belly, like a girl six month gone, and of course Starling Carlton never sheds an ounce. The fort is scattered with other Indians, they sit out on the roofs like emperors, and the women work for favours with the troopers. Troopers have red peckers and God knows what the squaws. Troopers that can't afford even squaws lie with troopers so that's more devilment to their equipment. Doesn't do to dwell your mind on it. Major instituted an Indian school for the many children racing about and the offspring of the troopers that have took Indian wives. Most of the three-card tricksters, hucksters, coffin makers, snakebite serum sellers, miracle medicine men, volunteer militiamen, do-anything merchants, and all the candidates for the worst examples of humanity, and so on and so on, hove off east just as soon as the lead dropped in the glass. The major himself went east just nearly alone with a company of ten men because news is he is to be married there to a Boston beauty, so Lige Magan has ascertained, but how we don't know, unless he reads it in one of those ancient newspapers that crawl out to us with the pilgrims. The buglers and our drummer boys played him out onto the trail and we gave him a friendly cheer for luck. Plenty pilgrims also in the fort putting a lean on the rations, and how many have resolved to return east I don't know, but nearly every soul here was gone out to California or Oregon and found nothing there they liked, and back they wended eastward, reaching only here before the winter. Guess the Promised Land is draped in hues of grey in the upshot. It's a hard task to make

77

something out of nothing as even God might attest. Me, sharpshooter Lige Magan, Caleb Booth back from the dead, Starling Carlton, Handsome John Cole, we were keeping a little understanding going that we was a special outfit of friends, for the purposes of cards not least. Starling, heaving with his accustomed fat, in the dead of winter when we might have ate rats heartily enough, we suspected of cheating against himself. Either that or he was losing his famous touch. But our small economy was moving about between ourselves anyhow, our few cents and tokens passing from pocket to pocket and back again, and I remember that winter as one of uproarious laughter. We was on best terms because we had seen slaughter together. Caleb was almost a holy man among the soldiers. He could of taken a collection in his hat every Sunday. A man that comes through murder and horror is a special man, men look at him as he passes and they say such and such about him – there goes Caleb Booth, the lucky man. A lucky man is a man you want fighting near you and he gives the needful sense that the world is a thing of mysteries and wonders. That it's bigger than you, bigger than all the shit and blood you seen. That God might be in it somehow looking out for you. Troopers maybe are rough souls and the regular padre don't get much joy out of us. But that don't say we don't have things we cherish. Stories that tell another story just the whole while they are being told. Things you can't ever quite put your finger on. Every man alive has asked why he is here on the earth and what was the likely purpose of that. To watch Caleb Booth come back from the door of death with his mortal wound, well, somewhere in there all mixed up with not knowing was knowing something. I ain't saying we knowed what we knowed, I ain't saying Starling Carlton or Lige Magan jumped up and said he knowed something, or anyone else. I ain't saying that.

No, sir.

Late spring's bringing the first of the wagon trains and also the major with his new bride. She ain't riding side-saddle. Kitted out in proper ladies' britches. In the gates she comes like a message from a far far country, where things is different and people eat off nice plates. Country opens like an enormous parcel and the plains is sparkling with ten thousand flowers and you can feel that first tincture of healing warmth in the days. And across this great carpet of colours has come the major and his bride. God Almighty. He carries her indoors as custom demands and we all stand in front of his quarters and give a cheer and throw our hats into the air. We don't hardly know what else to do. We feel as happy for the major like it was us that married her. John Cole says he never saw a woman to match her. He's right. Major hasn't said a word but the fort gazetteer says her name before she wed were Lavinia Grady so I guess there must be Irish in her anyhow. Major's name is Neale so I guess she's Mrs Neale now. I was surprised to note the major's Christian name because I don't believe I knew it rightly till that moment. Tilson. Goddamn Tilson Neale. Which was news to me. But that's how you learn things I guess.

Well the major is a new man now and he is as happy as a duck in the rain, I do not lie. It is good to see what marriage can do for a man like him who feels the world as a burden he must carry alone. She don't even come out the next day in a dress so I guess she must be intending to stick to the britches. I notice it is sort of a skirt divided into two pieces really. I never seen the like before, I guess the east is getting very forward and all sorts of new things are shooting up. Also she favours these little Mexican jackets, she must have ten of them because every day is a new colour. As a one-time professional girl I can't help wondering what her underwears may comprise of. In my day it was all frills and satinised cotton. There's something sleek about her, like a trout moving through the water. Her hair is glossy as pine-needles, pitch-black, and she wears a diamond-spangled net over it, like she was ready for business. She carries one of them new Colt guns in her belt. She's better armed than we are. Guess we think Mrs Neale is top-notch alright. It warms my heart to see how much she is kind to the major. They link arms about the place and she talks like a geyser. Every little thing she says has grammar in it, she sounds like a bishop. I seen the colonel meet her for the first time and he stammered like a schoolboy. I don't blame him. It's like being bathed in flames just looking to her, and I ain't even that sort of man would like to kiss her. It's like meeting a bit of sharp weather. Blowing against you. She's a peach among women, I guess. There's other officers' wives in the fort and even the sergeant has an old nag of a wife for his sins, but she ain't like that. There's leagues for everything, doubtless.

It's strange how close I watch her. But I want to find out something. I want to see how she wears her arms, how she moves her legs, little things no one else gives a damn about maybe. Guess I was fascinated by her. How she held her chin up when she talked. How she flashed her eyes without knowing maybe. Like she had candles in them. She has a bosom like a small earthworks. Smooth, defensive. Them Mexican jackets was stiff with stitchings all across it. Made her look like something soft and good was being armoured up. I had in my days of being a girl considered the phrase 'feminine mystery' because I had been obliged to try to turn my hand to it. Here was the sockdolager of goddamned feminine mystery.

Goddamned lady, says John Cole. Guess she is.

Caught-His-Horse-First must of gone down into Mexico or Texas raiding because we don't hear nothing about him for a long time. Things just go on. Lot of life is just like that. I look back over fifty years of life and I wonder where the years went. I guess they went like that, without me noticing much. A man's memory might have only a hundred clear days in it and he has lived thousands. Can't do much about that. We have our store of days and we spend them like forgetful drunkards. I ain't got no argument with it, just saying it is so. Two years, three pass by, and only change I can put a clock on in my head is the major's two girls. Babies that Mrs Neale pushed out. She pushed them out and then was going about the fort as usual just a day after like she was a squaw with work to do. Twin girls but they didn't look just alike because one had black hair and other sand-yellow like the major's. I can't even recall this moment what they called them, they was only little anyhow. The black-haired one was nicknamed Jackdaw later on account she liked to steal shiny things. No, I do recall their names of course I do. Hephzibah was the black-haired girl and the fair one was Angel. I couldn't forget Angel. Major would be on his porch cooing at them in the cot. Why shouldn't he, they was his.

Then news came in from our new scouts which was a good set of Crow Indians from over Yellowstone direction that Caught-His-Horse-First was seen riding north-west of Laramie. So they follow him up there and after a day's riding he enters all unknowing he is being watched into a new village, about thirty wigwams the Crows counted. Sergeant must of been waiting for that because he has a requisition order for a field gun already dated back a year so he furnishes this to the ordnance quartermaster who is a man more placid than Caesar without needing to bother the major and by dawn of the following day we are setting out in good heart to see if we can locate the village, the svelte gun making a sort of merry rattle along the way.

CHAPTER 8

The bow is drawn back and the bowman tries to hold it as taut as he can and then when he is satisfied with the position of his prey he can let the arrow loose. There is a fierce strange moment when the arm can no longer hold the pulled string, and nothing will do but to let it fly, so the bowman must know all the staging posts of his task, or make a bloody hames of it. I was just pondering along these lines as we went in fairly good order in the hoofprints of our Crow scouts. That Caught-His-Horse-First was a wily man and it would not be any picnic to find him and bring revenge to his soul. The sergeant thought it only right that as many of the old section who had found the killed men so many seasons before should go that day to find the village. Caleb Booth was there as the Jesus among us risen again. In the meanwhile Caleb had grown a big moustache and had a little baby son by a pretty Sioux woman, Oglala Sioux too, so I guess that was strange. I guess love laughs at history a little.

The year just gone had wore away at the sergeant and even if we were young and knew nothing we knew it was not only age was eating away at him. He is as gaunt now like the spike of a dead tree sticking up from the land and all his old measure of flesh and even his violent talk had withered away somewhat. The man I had took to be just something of a monster and even a wicked man in his way was grown different in my eyes. He was as rough as the Black Hills in his demeanour and his brain was full of nothing but orders, drinking, and tobacco. He never said a thing that wasn't pickled with cusses. But that were just the front side of him. Around the back was a differing aspect, I won't say roses and gardens, but a sort of queer quietness that I had come to admire. And relish even, so that I could quite easily find myself seeking out his company. He drilled us along the boiling summer ground as if he wished the American sunlight to burn us away like leaves in a bonefire. He was harsh and cruel when you mistook an order or wheeled right when you should of wheeled left. I seen him hit troopers with the back of his sabre and I seen him one time shoot at the heels of a erring trooper so that that man was obliged to dance and caterwaul to survive. But he was a handbook of war and war's actions and he had never led a company to their detriment. And even though he were not the culprit for the massacre of our companions a year back he took himself to be so by some degree and his thought of revenge was a calculation to put back things that was amiss in his estimation in their place.

That he was a filthy bad singer I have said before and only the memory of his vile tones forces me to say it again and I do pray that in heaven the singing will be confined to the angels.

A day and a night passes and the sergeant keeps us moving and is against sleep. Sergeant thinks we is crossing so far north-west the darned Crows must be bringing us home to Yellowstone. That is a strange country we often hear stories of. By morning of the second day we begin to move into forest and the land is rising and the sergeant robustly rebukes the Crows. You the craziest damn wolves I ever followed, says the sergeant. How you expect me to bring this gun over that pile of rocks? So the field gun is left to follow with a dozen men who will need to raise it foot by foot on pulleys and all kinds of damn hard work in the sun. There is a Negro called Boethius Dilward driving the mules that pull the gun and he is said to be the best damn mule-drover in the regiment, but still. Mules like flat ground just like human beings do. Boethius Dilward shakes his head at the Crows too. You do your best, Boethius, says the sergeant, and I apologise for this stupidity. I will bring that gun up, says Boethius, sir, never you fear. Just see that you go along quiet as a doe, you hear, Boethius? Yes, sir, and I will, he says. Goddamn, says the sergeant.

Just four or five hours later we begin to see a country whose beauty penetrates our bones. I say beauty and I mean beauty. Oftentimes in America you could go stark mad from the ugliness of things. Grass that goes for a thousand miles and never a hill to break it. I ain't saying there ain't beauty on the plains, well there is. But you ain't long travelling on the plains when you begin to feel clear loco. You can rise up out of your saddle and sort of look down on yourself riding, it's as if the stern and relentless monotony makes you die, come back to life, and die again. Your brain is molten in its bowl of bones and you just seeing atrocious wonders everywhere. The mosquitoes have your hide for supper and you are one hallucinating lunatic then. But now in the far distance we see a land begin to be suggested as if maybe a man was out there painting it with a huge brush. He is choosing a blue as bright as falling water for the hills and there is a green for the forests so green you think it might be used for to make ten million gems. Rivers burn through it with a enamelled blue. The huge fiery sun is working at burning off all this splendid colour and for ten thousand acres of the sky it is mighty successful. A stagger of black cliffs just nearby rise sheer and strange from the molten greens. Then a wide band of red striked across the sky and the red is the red of them trousers Zouave soldiers wear. Then a colossal band of the blue of bird eggs. God's work! Silence so great it hurts your ears, colour so bright it hurts your staring eyes. A vicious ruined class of man could cry at such scenes because it seems to tell him that his life is not approved. The remnant of innocence burns in his breast like a ember of the very sun. Lige Magan looks at me, turning in his saddle. He's laughing.

That's a sweet country, he says.

I'll say it is, I said.

Why don't you say that to me? says Starling Carlton at his other side. I can apply an appreciation of a view just as good as Trooper McNulty.

Ain't it just glorious though, Starling, ain't it? says Lige, like he don't know that Starling is coming at that one sideways. But he does know. Then Starling gives way and decides for the sake of friendship to follow Lige into that brand of easy talk.

Man, says Starling, it is. It just is.

Then Starling looks real happy. Then Lige does too.

Goddamn, says the sergeant, keep quiet back there, goddamn.

Yes, sir, says Starling.

It is approaching dusk and that same God is pulling a ragged black cloth slowly across his handiwork. The Crows return in a flurry of dust and haste, the village is only a quarter mile ahead, the sergeant bids us dismount and now we are in the awkward position of being clumsy-footed Europeans near a village of geniuses when it comes to tracking and vigilance. We got to be better men than we are for all that night, and the horses got to be quiet which ain't always in the rulebook of horses, and what's more we hope and pray that gun will come up in the darkness silent and not sound like the seven visions of Ezekiel. Cook parcels us out his dried provisions and we sit like a homeless people on our hunkers eating them not daring to light fires against the challenge of the night. No one says too much and what is said is only light-hearted and bantering because we want to preserve our advantage over fear. Fear like a bear in the cave of banter.

We're two nights without sleeping and now as the dependable orb of the sun makes a show again on the horizon our bones are aching and our minds are strange to us and cold. About four in the night by the sergeant's pocket watch the gun came creaking and crashing up behind us and the sergeant sent our full company back to carry it up into position. That was damnable crazy work. You got to dismantle the wheels and the carriage, take off the gun, and carry the weight of ten corpses through thorny scrub and rocky ground. Then the powder, the big bullets, and the percussion caps like Brobdingnag versions of what serves for our muskets. He brings the mules and horses back a mile, Boethius. It's just us on our pins then, Shanks' pony. We can hear the damn Sioux singing and calling like they was a hundred children bereft of their mothers. It just ain't a sound to make your mind easy. I would not be the only fella wondering what in hell they was doing there. Revenge of course, but was this any way to take that revenge? Damn foolishness whichever way you looked at it.

But no one says a word. We remember the sergeant standing alone at the site of the massacre and we remember him cutting off the noses. Caleb Booth no doubt remembers other things since he was there to see them. He lay alone in a tent with all his comrades dead nearby but he knew we would come. He said he knew we would and we did. Something binds us close in all that. So we work in the dark, stumbling about like drunkards, readying the gun, and the sergeant whispers his other orders, and how we are to form in a sickle moon shape so as to cover as much of the village as we can with fire after the gun has done its worst. Crows say there is a deep dark ravine behind the tents so we reckon we can cover the runaways left and right. The squaws will try to get the children away and the men will cover them till they reach some safety. If Caught-His-Horse-First is true to character he will fight as fierce as a mountain cat. There is no easiness in what we are doing. If the Sioux get the upper hand we are all food for hogs. There won't be no mercy anyhow because we know we ain't seen no sign of mercy beforehand.

Sergeant ain't no beginner and he has placed his gun on somewhat higher ground by using his good judgement even in the dark and that seems right when the weak golden light of morning fills the land. Its beauty now feels treacherous and our hearts are sick with fear. We can't seem to warm up none and yet we are moving about with vigour and the sergeant's skinny shape walks over here, walks back there, and he whispers some instructions, he makes signs with his hands and arms, he is never still. The smoke of new fires rises from the Indian camp and it is suddenly as if we are hell's men wandered into paradise.

So what is this sorrow then, this weight of sorrow? Pressing down on us. The gun is primed, rammed, and ready. The gunner is Hubert Longfield Ohio born. One half of his long thin face is blue from an old accident in the field. Guns blow up when they like, you never do know. He does all the work on the gun like he was dancing a queer old dance. He positions and pushes and opens and sets. He stands off with the firing string in his blue-mottled paws. Now he awaits the order, now he wants it. There's two gunners ready to supply again. Every face of the watching troopers is turned towards them, a lean long moon of men. Must be six o'clock now and all the babes and the children of the camp are astir, and the squaws are at the kettles. We can see clear as paper cut-outs two buffalo skins stretched black and stiff on wooden frames. God knows where they found those buffalo, they must of ranged far afield for them. Now the skins are drying at the pace of drying skins, which is slower than a little brook of time. The wigwams are mightily decked and there's none of the wretchedness you might begin to see in wigwams as you go back towards the east. Out here nothing much of us has touched them. The men will gladly take whisky if they find it, but they will drink everything they find in a sitting. A Sioux man will lie dead drunk for a day but the following day he will be Homer's Hector again. These people before us made that treaty with the colonel but once the sorry articles of the treaty was neglected they went back to what they knew. If they was waiting on government victuals they starved.

The sergeant whispers his order like the word of a lover and Hubert Longfield pulls on his string and the gun roars. It is the roar of one hundred lions in a small room. We would gladly put our hands over our ears but our muskets are raised and trained along the line of the wigwams. We are watching for the rat-run of the survivors. There is a stretch of time as long as creation and I can hear the whizzing of the shell, a spinning piercing sound, and then it makes its familiar thud-thud and pulls at the belly of heaven and spreads its mayhem around it, the sides of wigwams torn off like faces, the violent wind of the blast toppling others flat, revealing people in various poses of surprise and horror. There is murder and death immediately. There are maybe thirty tents and just this one shell has made a black burning cancer in the middle. Squaws are gathering up children of all sizes and looking wildly about as if they don't know what direction will be safety. Then the sergeant gives an order in full voice as our calling card has now been delivered and we fire the muskets off in a line and our bullets go viciously into wood, hides, and flesh. Straight away a dozen squaws go down and their children cling to them or try to flee. By now twenty braves are running about with their guns, and now Hubert is fixed to fire again and fires. A long segment of the camp is torn away like you might obliterate a painting. As if our bullets were only weary and weak we seem to wound twice as many as we kill. There's many staggering about, clutching their wounds, crying out, but now the braves seem to have done their calculations and try to bring off the squaws and children towards the back of the village. Fire, fire, men, calls our sergeant, and we reload like lunatics and fire. Powder, ball, ram, cap, cock, and fire. Powder, ball, ram, cap, cock, and fire. Over and over, and over and over Death at his frantic task in the village, gathering souls. We work in our lather of strange sorrow, but utterly revengeful, fiercely so, soldiers of intentful termination, of total annihilation. Nothing less will slake our thirst. Nothing else will fill our hunger. To this story of our dead comrades we are writing an end on the hot wind of summer. As we fire, we laugh. As we fire, we cry out. As we fire, we weep. Leap away, Hubert, pull the string. Cock an ear, Boethius, back with the horses. Raise up your musket, John Cole, fire and fire again. Blue line of men, look lively, for Death is a fickle friend.

Sergeant gives the order to fix our bayonets and forward we rush to strike through anyone that shell and bullet has gave deceitful quarter to. If the braves have made a stand we ain't hardly noticed it. Filled with revengeful force it's like no bullet could harm us. Our fears are burned off in the smelter of battle leaving only a murderous courage. Now we might be celestial children out to rob the apples in the orchards of God, fearless, fearless, fearless.

Our sorrow spiralling to heaven. Our courage spiralling to heaven. Our disgrace entangled in it like sorrow and courage was so much briars.

The Sioux men are hunkered down behind whatever will protect them but once we reach the limits of their village they rise up without hesitation and with bare breast charge against our approach. Each of us has one charge in his musket that must be preserved for a sure hit if there be ever such a thing in this kind of raggle-taggle battle. I see Caleb Booth in the corner of my eye fall in the Indian fusillade. Then they are pulling knives from their waists and hollering and there is a sort of mad joyous desperation in it that kindles a crazy fire in the heart. We are not lovers rushing to embrace but there is a sense of terrifying union none the less, as if courage yearns to join with courage. I cannot say otherwise. No fighter on earth as brave as a Sioux brave. They have their squaws and kindred sheltered and now at the last desperate moment they must risk all to defend them. But the shells have done terrible damage in the camp. Now I can see plain the broken bodies

94

and the blood and the horrible butcher shop of carnage that those bursting metal flowers have manufactured. Young girls are strewn about like the victims of a terminous dance. It is as if we have stopped the human clock of the village, that's what I were thinking. The hands have stuck and the hours will be no more. The braves come on like perfect demons, but I will allow magnificent, keenly storming. There's so much blood in our hearts they might be bombs also. Now we be wrestling and falling and rising, we are thirty soldiers against six or seven, all that our bombs and bullets have missed. These are fierce men with the bitterness of useless treaties in their bellies. Even in the flash and spark of battle I can see how famished they are, the bronze bodies long-muscled and scrawned. We kill these men by sheer weight of numbers. Now only the sheltering squaws and such remain. The sergeant, wheezing like a wind-broke horse, halts the ruckus of death and bids two men go down to the ravine and round up the women. What's in his head to do that we do not know for the women rush up from where they have laid in their forms of grass and with shrieks as sharp as blades charge against the startled soldiers, and they are engulfed in a frenzy of stabbing. Others of us rush over and kill those women. Now we have four, five of us dead, and all of them. Fearfully the lip of the ravine is broached. We look down into its sheer stony depths and there in a nest are a butcher's dozen of youngsters, their faces gazing up, as if they are praying to see their people returning for them. But this cannot be.

Now the sergeant is blowing smoke because the Crow scouts say that Caught-His-Horse-First ain't among the dead. What we done is we have killed his family, two wives included. Also his only son seemingly. The sergeant looks pleased at this but John Cole whispers to me he ain't so sure. Sergeant ain't always so bright about things, he says, but just to me. The sergeant is of a mind to throw the children into the ravine but Lige Magan and John Cole suggest it's just better to round them up. Bring them back to the fort where they can be tended. The little school will have them, they say. I know without any degree of doubt that they are thinking of the major and Mrs Neale. All that has passed has been without the major's say-so and the coming of Mrs Neale has placed a caution in every man's soul. I am only saying how it were. The sergeant can kill as many braves as he likes but there will be already a reckoning for the squaws. Sergeant can say Goddamn as often as he likes but it's true. Goddamn Easterners know nothing, he says. Goddamn. No one speaks, we're just waiting for orders. Starling Carlton don't say a word, he's kneeling on the ravine edge with his eyes closed. The sergeant's narrowed face looks sullen and angry but he tells us to round up the children. We're so tired we can't understand how we will return to the fort. The blood is intact in our bodies but we feel like we are bleeding into the earth. There's a few dead troopers to bury, couple of fellers from Missouri. A young feller from Massachusetts who was assistant muleteer to Boethius Dilward. And Caleb Booth. Sergeant rallies hisself and puts all vexation aside and doesn't fail to say a few uplifting words. That's why we still obeyed the sergeant. Just when you think he was going to hell by the highroad he shown he ain't the worst.

CHAPTER 9

But death were coming too for the sergeant. He laid up in the infirmary where John Cole thawed out in his time and you could go in and see him. At first he wouldn't say much but little by little he seemed to want to say more. The hospital steward which was all we had for a doctor that time did his damnedest but there wasn't much to be done asides from mopping up. All the tubes in his stomach were rotting and sometimes he had shit coming out of his mouth, like it had lost its sense of direction on the plains of the sergeant's body. He was still the sergeant, you couldn't just say anything to him, you had to tread carefully for fear of a savaging. Grizzled old bastard like him don't go providing death-bed transformations. But at the end what he said to me was, he didn't know what life was for. He just said that. He said it seemed very short looking back even though it had seemed long enough when he was getting through it. He said he had a brother in Detroit village but it was probably no earthly use writing to him because he couldn't read. Actually this exchange of words took place one evening late in the fall when the last of the year's heat was trying to hang on with failing fingers in the wind. The steward had just closed the window but nevertheless the breath of outside lingered on in the wooden room. The cold spaces of the yards between the buildings. The sergeant was now more bones than man. He looked like an old saint carved in a church but he still talked like the foul soul he was. I don't mean that unkindly. He was a queer sort of a man alright. Mostly cruel and thoughtless but there was the seam of something else unnamed. I was just alone with him looking at his shrunken face in the half-light. The thin eyes glittering yet. His disease had blacked up his face. He spoke about Caught-His-Horse-First and how he hoped we'd get him eventually. I said we sure would keep a weather eye out. I was thinking maybe now our accounts were balanced but I didn't say that. Then the sergeant seemed to go wandering in his mind a little back to the Detroit of his youth when his brother was beginning to come good in business and then he killed a man. Missed the noose by a mere shadow of words because there wasn't witnesses. Fell into melancholy, was what the sergeant said. He seemed a different man talking about his brother. Said his mother was a hard old woman and his father were killed in 1813 fighting Injuns along the frontier of those times, Kentucky. Said his only regret was he married a woman that didn't like him and that he never divorced the harridan and tried for a second

Mrs Wellington. The sergeant! Well all this surprised me, let me tell you. But a dying man can just say what he likes. It don't have to be true.

Then he dies. At least we don't have to listen to his singing no more, says Lige Magan.

Also at this time Mrs Neale had took in the captured Indian bairns into her school. Turns out Caught-His-Horse-First's daughter was called Winona which in the Sioux language means First-born Girl according to Mr Graham the interpreter. She might have been six or seven then but who could tell because their record keeping was about as good as my own crowd in Ireland.

Well I weren't the only soul thinking maybe the books was balanced between the chief and the blessed army. The sergeant weren't too long in his humble grave before Mr Graham received some sort of communication and we was told that Caught-His-Horse-First was wishing to give us a visit. The colonel and the major went into confab about it and it was decided to entertain this visit as maybe it might lead to better times between us and the tribes. Everything was awful stirred up and the colonel feared an out-and-out war on the plains, that's what he said. And the major maybe had his mind back in the time when the chief had saved us on our hungry march and although he was putting the massacre into the mix he was also mindful of the work of the late sergeant in slaughtering the chief's wives and son. The major in his heart always strove for justice I do believe and as he had a properly low opinion of man in the main he could allow a great margin of leeway when it was indicated. Troopers theyselves often when about the world were given to sprees and drinking, and there was oftentimes violent upflares even in camp that resulted in more than bruises and uproar. But just as the drear Black Hills were said to be speckled with gold, he believed that man was likewise. Also he had the mighty civilising medicine of Mrs Neale, a woman who might have been a preacher had she not been cloven. The mixture of beauty and religion in her could make troopers faint with what can only be reckoned love. Maybe lust too.

If the sergeant had been still overground it's not likely he would have stood for this occasion. But the sergeant were now tendering his name I should think with trembling hand at the Pearly Gates.

The day appointed was cold, sere, and dark. The river before our fort looked dank and sad, what John Cole called the 'hairless' ground all about us worried by stray smears of ice and snow. A goodly number of buildings had sprung up outside the protection of the fort. There was a saddlery premises painted in a dying green, and the office of the Indian agent was stuck up beside the fort wall like a piece of poetry amid the plain story of everywhere else. Plasterers and carpenters had come up all the way from Galveston, Texas for some reason to fit out that little palace. As for our fort it were fairly falling down in places but the colonel kept it shipshape as funds would let him. The big gates with its old arch of lodgepole trees seemed to hark back to forgotten times. First thing we knew, our much depleted cavalry troop was ranged in front of the major's quarters that is to say on the back end of the parade ground. We had our muskets primed but we was told to keep them slung on our sashes easy fashion. Boethius was told to set his two cannon behind the stable block to be brung up just in case but I do not believe the major for a moment thought this would be necessary. No, sir. Major believed he had read the soul of his man like an open book and could count on his interpretation of that fanciful bible. First thing was, the pickets on the wall above the gates called out their sighting of the Sioux horsemen, coming up slow and gentle in the distance and now stopping it would appear about half a mile off. Now Mr Graham was ordered to go out on horseback to them and see what was what and Mr Graham he mounts up and goes with two slightly trembling troopers through the opened gates. I noticed it was Starling Carlton held the gates for them and closed them tight behind them. On off they rode like chaps expecting Death sooner than Christmas. The far ground where the Sioux waited was just high enough for us to spot them there. There wasn't a man wanted to have goed with Mr Graham and his escort. Mr Graham was a bald little man so he was hardly a threat to anyone. The two troopers with him were black-eyed Spanish-looking men from Texas that no one would miss if they was murdered. Or so I was thinking. I guess I was amusing myself in the tension. So then Mr Graham duly reaches the band of Sioux and he must be yapping, as John Cole calls it, and the yapping goes on for a while, and then Mr Graham comes back as stately as a little king and the look of relief on the face of the troopers was a priceless sight. The chief wants to come in alone, he says, as a proof of his good intentions, and talk to the major. I hear then some of the troopers laughing because they're thinking maybe we can just shoot the desperado then. But they don't know the major and maybe Caught-His-Horse-First knows the book of the major just as well as the major knows his. It's the sort of arrangement stirs the heart rather. You got to admire a man that will ride forward from his armed comrades and come on to the gates of a whiteman's fort. Starling Carlton has left the gates wide after admitting Mr Graham and we can all see the chief approaching. In the distance we especially note the exuberant beauty of his head-dress and his flowing clothing. He wears a metal breastplate made of whiteman's alloy doubtless but you feel he wears it like a great jewel rather than as armour. Now he coming closer and I see something else. Given that it is dank winter and game is so scarce as to be only rumour I am hardly surprised to see his face gaunt and perished as the goddess of winter herself. His legs are only queer sticks about his pony and the animal itself is bone-struck and ill. Famine has come into the heart of this man. At the gates he dismounts neatly despite his lack of stirrups and hands over his gun and his knife to Starling Carlton. Then with one hand he smooths down his face and strides forward onto the bleak parade ground. A little flurry of snow has come from the river and a nasty wind snakes into the fort and makes a whine between the buildings. The major for his part goes forward also unarmed with Mr Graham who any blessed person can see is overborne with worry and dismay. His wretched little face is sweating like a cold wall. The chief sets out his stall and Mr Graham translates the lengthy speech. Seemingly what it all boils down to is the chief wants his daughter. Mrs Neale as it happens is standing in the porch of the school with all the faces of the Indian children ranged at the dark windows within like so many moons. The chief talks again in his highflown way and things are referred to like love and dignity and war. Indians always talk like Romans for sure. The major answers again and it looks to me like he is inclined to give him the girl. There must be a bargain brewing and it ain't nothing to the troopers either way. They got to see how thin the chief is, he don't look much like a fighting man anyhow. It's all kinda sad, I am thinking. I reckon it's sad. We know cold brutal war and how it be waged there on the plains because we been waging it. There's no soldier don't have a queer little spot in his wretched heart for his enemy, that's just a fact.

104

Maybe only on account of him being alive in the same place and the same time and we are all just customers of the same three-card trickster. Well, who knows the truth of it all. The major turns his head and calls to his wife and tells her to let the little girl out of the schoolhouse. Mrs Neale bangs her hands on her legs but she clumps back and does what he bids pronto. The little girl comes out like a piece of brown fire and darts across the compound and stops beside the chief. He is very quiet and stoops to her and then lifts her up onto his right hip. Major Neale concludes the meeting as they say, and starts to come back towards us and the chief and his burden starts to go the other way. Starling Carlton he's standing there with the musket and the knife like the Negro doorman at the old saloon in Daggsville. The snow storm is just a thing of threadbare veils, we can see everything. We are tensed up like we should be shooting but there ain't no reason. It's just a solitary Indian with nothing to shoot back with. We may be black-hearted men when our turn comes but there is a seam in men called justice that nothing burns off complete. Caught-His-Horse-First goes back to Starling Carlton and Starling Carlton says something to him. Of course the chief ain't got no idea what he is saying so Starling repeats it louder. He is saying something like, that a better gun than mine, maybe you could give it to me. What the hell is he saying, says John Cole. Says the chief got a better gun, I say. What the hell, says John

Cole. Then Starling seems to calm down a little and the major sets out towards them maybe to settle the matter but he stops when he sees Starling hand over the gun. The chief takes it in his left hand and rests it up along his upper arm because he got no choice with the girl in the way of his other hand. Then just in that instant Starling Carlton unsheaths the old Indian knife and runs at the chief. There's no force on earth could withstand Starling Carlton running at you because he's the weight of a buffalo calf. By Jesus he just drives the knife into the chief's side. The little girl screams and falls from her father. The gun just seems to go off then and Starling Carlton is hopping around and roaring because the bullet has struck his foot. He will limp on that foot for the rest of his born days, I reckoned. With the knife still wagging in its wound like a Mexican bull in the bullring the chief gathers his daughter back up and throws her and himself onto his pony, and dragging the animal's head around, kicks like the devil and rides away in a frantic gallop. You can see the pony is as surprised as we are. A couple of troopers think to fire after him but I guess the chief ain't in the business of being hit so easy and anyhow the troopers are firing through the gap of the gates. Starling Carlton is hollering out for them to stop. He already got a bullet in the foot, ain't that enough? In the distance you can see the Sioux braves churning about on their horses like so much butter. Then our sharpshooter Lige Magan runs

106

up the parade ground and up the nearest ladder and onto the wall and draws a slow bead on the galloping Sioux. The major is shouting for Lige to desist but maybe suddenly Lige don't speak English. You know in your heart he has no chance to hit nothing. Then the strange thing happens. Caught-His-Horse-First seems to stop in mid gallop and turns his pony half-beam to our sight. Something's been hit alright but it ain't the chief or the pony. Mrs Neale screams and starts to run out towards the gates and the major goes sideways at her to catch her waist and detain her dash. It's as if all time stops and the storm is stilled and nothing will go forward. Forever more the major's wife will be caught in her run and the chief will turn his horse side on and look back at us holding the dead body of his child. Forever more Starling Carlton will keep hollering like a fool in pain and Mrs Neale be wailing and forever more the black clouds of evening will be stilled in the firmament and God yet again retreat from us.

What breaks the spell is Boethius running round from the back alleyway to see did he miss his cue.

Major seems to decide to let the question of what the hell Starling Carlton was doing lie and he acknowledges next morning on parade that nothing much good could of come of that plan anyhow. He sees that now, too late. Snow falling like bread of heaven that won't feed no Israelite. Maybe the major is feeling that old days are dying and new days are coming. Lige says he was only trying to get a shot in for Caleb Booth and he didn't mean to kill no girl. Everyone understood that. Major seems intent on leaving it then. But that don't stop John Cole asking Starling Carlton a few nights after in barracks what in hell he was doing. Starling Carlton is a friend so he must feel obliged to answer. He says when he seen that the chief's gun was one of them new Spencer carbeens he just got a choler in his head like a storm. He was sudden mad as a brushfire. He couldn't see how he had to tote his goddamn musket in his goddamn sash and this Indian go about the place with gun royalty. That's what he said, gun royalty. And so on. So, why'd you go stabbing him, says John Cole. Weren't it obvious. Goddamn it, didn't John Cole see the chief raise his carbeen to him? Goddamn, did he not shoot him with it? What you saying? Ain't it a fact, Handsome John Cole, that you got Indian in you somewhere? I guess you feeling sorrow for your own kind, god-damn it. Then John Cole is confused for a moment and so am I. I can't remember if the shot came before the stabbing or after. I am trying to get back to the vision of it in my head. I reckon it was after but my mind's not so sure. Oh Jesus. Then John Cole is looking like Starling Carlton stabbed him too and then Starling Carlton comes over close and says, look see, I ain't angry with you, John Cole, don't you be angry with me. Alright, says John Cole, and only myself can see his eyes are damp. John Cole will cry if you do right by him. Then Starling Carlton puts him in a kind of bear hug. I'm thinking, I bet John Cole can smell the stink of that man now. It don't last long but it happens. Then I guess we think we can be going on from there as usual.

CHAPTER 10

Next part of my story happens about two years later. Only thing that happens meantime out of the general going on of things is one of the Indian whipper-snappers takes a shine to me and as she learns her English from Mrs Neale I begin to learn about her. Her history as it was contained in her own language I guess she starts to discard out of her head because all her talk is of Mrs Neale and how things be with her in the fort. I guess she must be a cousin of the late Winona and as I can't get my tongue around her Sioux name despite being the only few words I am obliged to acquire I beg mercy of her and ask if I can call her Winona. She don't seem to mind. There's a lot of giving of names in that old world of her people so maybe it seems natural to her that I give her another. Starling Carlton got angry and said I shouldn't be friending vermin, that's what he said. He was trembling as he spoke, his chins vibrating like the breast of a bird. He says Irish was bad enough and far as he's concerned you can take all the Africans and put them into a great feed for hogs but he says Indians is the worst, according to Gunter. I can't tell if he's serious because his face don't move when he says all that. John Cole says that Starling Carlton ain't all there no more. Probably end up in Old Blockley, meaning, the famous lunatic asylum. I say Winona is only eight and she ain't vermin, not a bit. Starling Carlton kept referring to this matter for half a year and then he shut up about it.

But Handsome John Cole weren't right in his body and it was decided by the major that he should not take up another signing when his present time was done and he should release himself from the army. As John Cole and me had signed up together for the same term of service I would be free to leave with him. A passel of two soldiers, he calls us, and smiles his pleasing smile. We'll get our pay and some dollars for the journey east and keep our hats, our trews, our shirts, and our linen pantaloons. Major said the best thing was to get out and then if a cure was found to come back in. He said we was excellent dragoons and ought to be in the army. But he couldn't feed a man through illness time and again, regulations and sense forbid.

Now through all this while he's talking John Cole is looking at him with ghostly face. Don't think John Cole can imagine the world without the army suddenly. Feels like he is being cast out of paradise, he says. Won't ever find a berth so good from Dan to Beersheba, he says. Major says he knows this well and it pains him to have to bring the news. Colonel thinks so well of him especially in the matter of engagements where he was obliged to fight.

111

I go over to Mrs Neale and ask for Winona as a apprentice servant and Mrs Neale says she'd be ready for that alright. Girls go out to be put in work around nine, she says, and Winona speaks well and has most of her letters. She got numbers too. I taught her all the plain cooking I know myself. She's quite the dab hand with a bain-marie. You like white sauce, don't you? she says. We are talking in the dark front parlour of her quarters and Mrs Neale knows me well enough but even so she squares to me and asks me the hard question. I don't think any other woman in creation except her would ask it but she does which was a measure of her. I ain't going to be easy in my mind, she says, unless I ask you. Men do think they can take a Injun maid for their own solace and I ain't about to countenance that so you better speak truthfully now, Trooper McNulty, that you only want this girl for a servant. Why, I says, in the whole history of the world you can take my word that that is a yes. I will protect her like my own child. And how you so sure? she says. Well, I just am sure, I says. If I hear otherwise I will send men to punish you, she says. And I feel again that fierce strange heat off her like someone was burning logs in her bodice.

When we got to Missouri a letter catches up to John Cole to say his father is dead but he don't know what to do with such news as there ain't a farm or nothing to claim on it. I guess he just thinks his father is dead and there's an end to it. He says he would sure like to have seen him before he died and he is surprised to learn that his father died in Pennsylvania and he don't even know who is sending the letter, it don't say. It's more than ten years since he seen him and it weren't a fond goodbye then either. And who was your mother? I say, surprised at myself I never asked that before. I never remember a mother, says John Cole, though he looked like he would've liked to remember one. How old was your father, I says. Well, I don't know, he says, I must be twenty-five or nearly. Maybe he was forty-five, fifty maybe.

It's not like we got no money so we rent a house in Lemay along the river just a few miles outside St Louis. Curious to relate John Cole feels as fit as a hare and wonders if it weren't the damn water at Laramie was poisoning him. John Cole says he's cooking a plan and writes to our old friend of fond Daggsville days Mr Noone. That letter swirls around the country like his own letter bearing news of his father and it's a month and more before he gets an answer. We know from Mr Noone's faithful saint's day letters that he has left Daggsville when too much civilisation come into it. But we can't remember for the damnable life of us where he said he was going. Turns out Mr Noone he has a new place up in Grand Rapids running minstrel shows and he says he just might have work for Thomas McNulty if he ain't lost his pretty looks fighting. That night as we lie chest to chest in the old doss and Winona purring in sleep in the next room we feel the lure of the unknown future distil into our bones.

Guess you ain't lost your looks anyhows, says John Cole, staring at them in the half-light. Look pretty good to me.

You reckon? I says.

I like the way you look anyhows, he says, and kisses me.

It's still new to be in a house and not slipping about the barracks like ghosts. It's naught to Winona to see two men in a bed considering you might see that in any posthouse or boarding house when beds is scarce. I don't even know how many beds she seen as such, she slept on the floor at Laramie. She got her own little bed now. She never even seen a town before and she likes to walk with us down to the river and take the ferry over to the store. Plain cooking just as promised is at her command and she speaks quite good and I don't know why but she don't get too many insults on the road from the cruder sort. Maybe we look like we'd box such a person and we would. John Cole must be six foot three so you don't rile him in a casual way. I'm a little man right enough but maybe the best dagger is a short one sometimes. I always wear my Colt conspicuous on my trouser belt. I guess Winona don't have too much to do and I bought her three dresses in St Louis as we came through so she has a wardrobe to her name. Nice flouncy pink dress is my favourite. I guess I like dresses just as much as she does. The girls in the shop put her underthings together without me looking because they said to look away, and we got her shoes and all too. There's a Negro washerwoman nearby does the washing weekly. She'll even starch. She says the Negro prayer house in St Louis used to be burned regular but she don't hear it was burned recently. Got Winona's straight black hair cut nice and bought her combs and a brush, she brushes it all the time at her vanity mirror. Winona. She don't got a family name that anyone can pronounce so we ask her does she like Cole or McNulty and she says Cole sounds better, and maybe it does.

So when we go and buy train tickets for the new line to Grand Rapids, we give her name as Winona Cole. Seems natural as spitting in a spittoon.

We get to Grand Rapids by way of Kalamazoo and put up for the night at Sweet's Hotel and in the morning our old friend Mr Titus Noone come in to view us. The whole way on the spitting puffing cranking train Winona was sat upright and sleepless as if she were in the belly of a demon and was soon to die. The folding and unfolding picturemaps of the beauties and terrors of America outside the window was as nothing to her. Old lakes like seas, old woods as dark as childhood fears, and sudden towns all swank and mud. Mr Noone he still ain't so old we find. He is as dapper as a mackerel. His black coat shines with strangeness because it is made of the furs of black bears, his bluebird-blue cravat flashes also with birdy life,

115

his cufflinks has been fished out of rivers in Australia he tells us, dark emeralds like poked-out eyes. His barber has shaved his face-hair so that it is all straight lines, black patches, and immaculateness. His skin is made of the aftermaths of smiles. Most likely Titus Noone has come into his heyday. John Cole looks at him and looks at me and laughs with that laughter that denotes delight and relief. Mr Noone gazes on us and claps his gloved hands like the feller who does the three-card trick but he ain't no trickster and he laughs too. I guess we remember what he done for us in Daggsville and he remembers maybe that we did not let him down. Things like that sure is a basis for ongoing business. Fagged though she be by the long journey just the day before Winona still has the heart to join in. No exaggeration to say she got a laugh like a freshet in a summer meadow. When he first come into the hotel room Mr Noone had bowed to her and took her hand and shook it gently and said how do. I do well, she said, in her best Boston English learned off Mrs Neale. Just a moment of something that didn't mean nothing. It gave me heart to see. Things that give you heart are rare enough, better note them in your head when you find them and not forget. This is John's daughter, I say, without thinking much on it, and never having had that thought before exactly in words I knew about. John Cole didn't talk against that. He beamed. Well, says Titus Noone, I guess her mother was a beauty, and he bowed his head as if to intimate sorrow at her possible passing, and he ain't going to ask about that unless we say something more. So we leave it there like the last note of a ballad.

A little maid as black as a whetstone brings in tea and whisky. As if we was a creature with one head our eight eyes alight on the tea-pot and the cups on the tray and break out into laughter again. God knows why. I guess we're giddy. Mr Noone says he got a big enterprise going in a fine hall on Grab Corners. Nicest bunch of blackface minstrels between Timbuctoo and Kalamazoo. Well, he says, they're all pretty straight-up except one, his big knock-down star called Sojourner Wrathall. He does all the wenches, he says. Riotous goddamn genius. Cunt of the first water, no pun intended. What do you boys intend to do up here, he says? Well, says John Cole, a little abashed, we was just up here to talk to you. Of course you were, of course you were, he says. See, says John Cole, I had this thought come into my head last year. We was in this Indian camp up near Fort Laramie and there was these Sioux men dressed as women and the effect was very strange, some of them was so good-looking, and it made your knees a bit soft to see them. And I been thinking all this while that since Thomas ain't no girl no more we could put him into women's dresses and see what effect that had, I was just thinking you know it might have just the same effect as I was feeling there on the prairies. Well, says Titus, he could do himself up minstrel fashion and play the wench parts? He could well, says John Cole, but I been nursing this thought, I guess like a preacher nurses a vision of revelation, you know, of Thomas in his dress, and being as ladylike as a lady, only more so, everything done just so, and aiming for beauty, you know, and he is a beauty, ain't he! So, says John Cole, after a break for laughter, I was thinking it might bear a try-out up here, in your hall, since you know us, and know we ain't no fools. And is he going to sing, or dance, or what? says Mr Noone, leaning in now with great interest, all his show-man's antennae waving like a big desert ant. I thought, says John Cole, maybe he could be in little plays, maybe, or come on as a handsome young man, go behind a screen, and have some dancing from others and such, and then come back out as an out-and-out killer beauty, and just see what the audience thought of that. Or, she could be in her boudoir or such, completing her corsage, and maybe I come in as her beau and we have talking then, or singing – well, I can't sing, so – you know? Okay, and what will this little lady be doing, he says, nodding at Winona. I don't know, says John Cole. I never thought of having her. Could be the child part, says Titus Noone, does she sing? You sing? says John Cole, not knowing one way or the other. I can sing, says Winona. What can you sing? says Titus Noone. I can sing 'Rosalie, the Prairie Flower', she says, Mrs Neale taught me. That a dead child song, says Titus

118

Noone, nodding his approval. We can black up Winona, he says, and she can be the maid, and sing goddamn 'Rosalie, the Prairie Flower'. Bring the house down. Meanwhile, Thomas in the dress, and you the beau, and swanking round, and Thomas ladylike and lovely just like you intimate, why, yes, why, yes, I think it might go. If it go, I pay you twenty-five dollars a week, for the three of you. How does that sit? That sits just as pretty as a robin in a bush, says John Cole. Well, says Titus, I have high hopes. I remember so well how much the miners took to you both when you was girls. Let's drink to it, goddamn. And we do, we drink to it.

Mr Noone says they have miners too in Grand Rapids working the gypsum seams along the river. Something about miners makes a good audience. We're hoping anyway. Then, with a bow and a sweep of his slouch hat, Titus Noone goes off and John Cole and me and Winona go out next morning and put all our savings into our stage gear. John Cole says he got to get the best dress we can afford. Got to be top notch. He ain't aiming for no comedy skit. Wants me to be as splendid kitted as a high-born woman. Alright. We have the tricksy task of getting the full kit in a ladies' haberdashery but the girls there ain't so bad. We tell them we're working in the minstrel show, they think that be very grand, so we have a good spiel to give them.

It's evening in Grand Rapids as we trail back to Sweet's Hotel. We are as weary as Indian fighters.

The lights come up in the taverns and the eating houses and the sidewalks make their little bang under our boots and the shopgirls is affixing the shutters and the colder night air crowding into the roads. We ain't even got the cost of a cart to carry our purchases so we are on Shanks' pony. Could be lead in the bags the amount of stuff a lady needs. Beauty hasn't come cheap and we are all bets on now with the 'act'. We're going to be seeking urgent employ if it don't go. God took but a week to build the whole world, says John Cole. We can do it, I say.

We get back to our room and light the wick in the oil lamp and pull off our boots and we don't dare to send Winona down for eats and so we will have a hungry night. Winona sets everything to rights then beds down on the little divan pushed agin the foot of our bed. We'll be chaste as real travellers tonight. Soon her little shipshape form is caught in sleep, rising and falling with every small breath so that the bed feels like there must be a troubled brook running through it. In the darkness as we lie side by side John Cole's left hand snakes over under the sheets and takes a hold of my right hand. We listen to the cries of the night revellers outside and hear the horses tramping along the ways. We're holding hands then like lovers who have just met or how we imagine lovers might be in the unknown realm where lovers act as lovers without concealment.

CHAPTER 11

On the great night the stage doorman Mr Beulah McSweny opens the stage door as anyone would expect and allows us in where civilians cannot go. Mr McSweny were a black man from Toledo eighty-nine years old. All week we was going over our little act and Mrs Delahunt from the starving Kerry hills has overseen the painting of the flats and Mr Noone hisself he has mapped out our footfalls on the stage and sitting back in the haunted darkness of the hall has decreed where best Winona might give her song while we do our dumb-show in front of the footlights. The biggest confab is about does John Cole touch me or no or even kiss me and Titus Noone says best play it by ear and be ready to run off into the night if it blows up. Soon we are in the long dressing room at the rear and we are just one atom in a ruckus of a dozen characters daubing the black onto their faces and the little costume mistresses are sewing fat girls into costumes and there is a wondrous blather of laughter and moiling talk. The two real Negroes in the troupe – Mr Noone does call them Africans – are painting black on their black faces and daubing white mouths that make the singer clearer they do aver in the foggy yellowness of the footlights. The wicks be floating in the oil and make a mist like you might find along a morning valley in the sweet land of Yellowstone. Winona gets her black mask too. She looks in the mirror at herself with delight. Who am I now? she says. Singers warm up by singing. Gobs of spit are vacated from tobacco-y throats. The comic girls sit before their mirrors and practise their faces, pulling them into queer states. Out on stage soon we hear the first skits going over the footlights like crates of delicious apples. We can hear the roar like a river from the crowd and the sudden pitch into silence and then the roar again like the river was plunging down a falls. What surges into us is that elixir that do come from putting a danger in front of yourself like people intending to leap down into those falls and survive them. John Cole dandies himself up till his cheeks is shining like a lamp. He never did look so handsome. Our dresser comes behind my screen and assists me in the dark challenge of my underwear. What goes on first, what is added like a riddle next. The stays and the corset and the bosom holder and the padded arse and the cotton packages for breasts. And the soft under-blouse and the petticoats and the dress itself as stiff as a coffin-board. The dress as yellow as water in moonlight. Rich stitching, brackets of lace, and tucks, and crosshatched sides. A fog of flower-printed muslin before and behind. All good in the light, we trust. Stagelight, that will conspire with us, and make us into creatures not ourselves, wonders of people. Then the manager of the acts gives us the nod. We stand in the wings listening to the act that goes before us. Our suppers greatly desire to travel back up our throats. We are tense as fencing wire. It is a riotous song and dance, with all that quick Negro lingo and happy uproar. The crowd is pushed up from zephyr to gale. The stage clears and we hear the music that Mr Noone has assigned us starting softly on the piano. For a violent moment in my inner eye I see my father lying dead in Ireland. The flats are set in place and John Cole goes on with Winona. She walks down prettily to the lights and sings her song. We have heard the song sung while we did practise but now it is sung with a new force. There is something else crept into it like a mouse. There is applause and laughter, there is simple delight. I step on the stage and find the lights blazing against me and yet in the same instance pulling me forward. I am like something left over after a storm. Slight, a waif. It is like I am underwater in a pool of brightness. Slowly slowly I walk down towards the watching men. Something strange has happened, the hall has fallen into silence. Silence more speaking than any sound. I guess they don't know what they are seeing. I guess it is true that they are seeing a lovely woman. Soft-breasted woman, like something off a picture of such dames. Now there rampages through me a thrill such as might be got otherwise only from opium. I might be one of the footlights, with a burning wick for a heart. I don't utter a blessed word. Winona trips about as if putting a boudoir to rights. John Cole all spit and polish approaches from the far side of the stage and we hear the men draw in their breath like a sea tide drawing back on the shingle of a beach. He approaches and approaches. They know I am a man because they have read it on the bill. But I am suspecting that every one of them would like to touch me and now John Cole is their ambassador of kisses. Slowly slowly he edges nearer. He reaches out a hand, so openly and plainly that I believe I am going to expire. The held-in breath of the audience is not let out again. Half a minute passes. It is unlikely any of them could of holded their breath like this underwater. They have found new size in their lungs. Down down we go under them waters of desire. Every last man, young and old, wants John Cole to touch my face, hold my narrow shoulders, put his mouth against my lips. Handsome John Cole, my beau. Our love in plain sight. Then the lungs of the audience giving out, and a rasping rush of sound. We have reached the very borderland of our act, the strange frontier. Winona skips off the stage, and John Cole and myself break the spell. We part like dancers, we briefly go down to our patrons, we briefly bow, and then we have turned and are gone. As if for ever. They have seen something they don't understand

and partly do, in the same breath. We have done something we don't understand neither and partly do. Mr Noone is over the moon. He is trembling for joy in the wings looking out into the hall with a light-drenched face. The crowd beyond the curtains now are clapping, hooting, stamping. There is a craziness in it all that betokens a kind of delicious freedom. Notions are cast off. If only for a moment. They seen a flickering picture of beauty. All day they've laboured in the beds of gypsum crystals, hacking and gathering. Their fingernails are a queer white from the work. Their backs are sore and they must troop out again in the morning. But for a minute they loved a woman that ain't a real woman but that ain't the point. There was love in Mr Titus Noone's hall for a crazy foggy moment. There were love imperishable for a rushing moment.

Next day we feel some remorse about working Winona and John Cole brings her over to a Mr Chesebro and asks him could he take an Indian girl for his school if she be a half-caste and his own blood. The gentleman has a little stone school in a lane the back of Pearl Street. He says to John Cole that the town would not stand for that and so John Cole comes back with Winona and says he would like sometimes to kill just for the sake of making his point plainly. He never had no schooling himself of course. Maybe I was thinking myself a great scholar because I was a few years schooled up in Sligo. I guess I was thinking that.

So, says John Cole, do you think you could teach her something that she ain't learned off Mrs Neale? I said I don't reckon so. There ain't no Indian school hereabouts because the Indians were drove out years and years ago. Looks like the Chippewa were the big cheeses round here one time. Goddamn it, he says, how come there ain't no place for Winona? Then he's talking about this that night to the elegant Beulah McSweny and he says he'll teach Winona. He says his nickname is the poet McSweny and he has wrote maybe three songs used in the minstrel shows. No, by God, is that right, says John Cole. Yes, he says, and I can school Winona three mornings a week because I only works evenings. That's just the best, says John Cole, how did you get to be such a gent, Mr McSweny? My father was a free man, he said, on the Mississippi river. Ferrying every damn thing between the English and the Spanish. Where your father now? says John Cole. My father gone so long, says Beulah, there was a seventeen in the date when he was overground. God Almighty, says John Cole.

Thus we inaugurate the best time in the little kingdom we have pitched up against the darkness. Seems to be a law that if we get a house it's going to overlook the water. We got a riverside house of four rooms and we got a porch on the street side and it ain't the best part of town and that's where we fit like gloves. Like gloves. No one can best imagine the motley crowd that go to make a

126

American town. First you got the have-nothing know-everything goddamn Irish God damn them who will live under leaky steps and count themselves in palaces. Then you got the half-breed Indians mixed with God knows what. Then you got the blacks, maybe they came up from Carolina or them places. Then you got the Chinese and the Spanish families. Where we are is where all these folks come home at night to roost when they've done working, mostly at the gypsum mines or doing for the Dutch the other side of town. Our landlord is the poet McSweny. After all he been saving his money for seventy-five years so he got a half dozen properties.

But that ain't the point. The point is we living like a family. John Cole know he was born in December or seems to remember that month and maybe I remember I was born in June and Winona says she was born during the Full Buck Moon. Anyhow we roll all that into one and on the first of May we have assigned our birthday for the three of us. We say Winona is nine years old and John Cole has settled on twenty-nine. So that must make me twenty-six. Something along those lines. Point is, whatever ages we be, we're young. John Cole is the best-looking man in Christendom and this is his heyday. Winona is sure the prettiest little daughter ever man had. Goddamned beautiful black hair. Blue eyes like a mackerel's blue back. Or a duck's wing feathers. Sweet little face cool as a melon when you hold it in your hands and kiss her forehead. God knows what stories she seen and been part in. Savage murder for sure because we caused it. Walked through the carnage and the slaughter of her own. You could expect a child that has seen all that to wake in the night sweating and she does. Then John Cole is obliged to hold her trembling form against him and soothe her with lullabies. Well he only knows one and he does that over and over. He holds her softly and sings her the lullaby. Where he got that no man knows not even hisself. Like a stray bird from some distant country. Then he lies on her bed and she pushes in tight against him like you might imagine bear cubs do in the winter hide or maybe even wolves. Tight in, like John Cole was that bit of safety she is trying to reach. A harbour. Then her breathing slowly lengthens and then she is snoring a little. Time to come back to bed and in the darkness or the helpful dim of the candle he looks at me and nods his head. Got her sleeping, he says. You sure do, I say.

Not much more than that needed to make men happy.

After a few months of doing our damnedest for Mr Noone it just seems natural to be not always changing garb by the hour and there seems to be greater contentment in it for me to wear a simple-hued housedress and not be always dragging on the trews. Outside is one matter, in another. Winona never does say nothing about it. Never seems to see me only as what I am in my face.

Whatever that be. I don't know then and I don't know now. But I am easier in the dress, that's all I can say. Well I would almost attest I say funnier things or things that make my man John Cole laugh like a donkey. Winona makes her plain cooking and we sit the three of us in the dim light and in the summer we have the windows covered against the violent heat and in the winter likewise against the rats of cold that creep in anywhere you leave a finger's width of a gap. At home Winona don't sing minstrel songs but those other songs that carry her back to where she begun in the innocence of her youth. We are racked to think we don't know who even her mother was or maybe it was a woman that we killed. God knows that feels like a colossal-sized crime betimes and if you was counting crimes on a abacus maybe it won't be the only one we done against her. She could slit our throats in the night with justice, spray out our blood redly on the linen pillows. But she don't do that. She sings and we listen and all three are returned to the prairie in our heads. She to her guiltless haunts and us to those moments when in truth we stood gazing out onto all that lonesome beauty.

We alter and cut and stitch our act till it is ten jackets in a row rather than just the one. We learn to listen to the house and take our tack from the humours and rapids of particular nights. The stalls is cheap and oftentimes men come in three times a week and the great change to the houses is the women of the town are coming in too. Fine flamboyant lower-type girls and shopgirls and fishgirls and the girls that bag the gypsum. They're looking to see this strange dame that is as womanly as a woman like them. They want to peer at it, scope out the mystery. I want to show them it. It makes for wild silences and queer plummeting moments. Where things pitch down into bright darkness. Where my stomach drops to my neat and gleaming shoes. Strange business in Grand Rapids and I never do learn the plus and minus of it. Only drawback is we are obliged to get me into civvies real quick instanter after a performance and I ain't able now to leave by Mr McSweny's door but John Cole got to take me out through the theatre saloon as two anonymous Joes and out along the alley with the heaps of bottles and spittoon slops. Pistol in his trouser belt snug as a squirrel. Because a few of them Johnnies fall in love with the shimmer and downright strangeness of the act. Guess they want to marry me. Or have me. Meanwhile John Cole says he loves me more than any man since the apes roamed. All the news in the *Grand Rapids Courier* is that a man was once an ape which John Cole says is no surprise to him considering.

John Cole asides from declaring his love gets Winona to write to Lige Magan in Fort Laramie to see how he is getting on. She got a good hand now from Mr McSweny. Lige Magan writes back to say all is dandy with him and that Starling Carlton is also dandy. She off her own bat writes to Mrs Neale because she got warm memories

130

there. The Post Office faithfully carries these flimsy items back and forth along the perilous trails. They don't seem to lose one link. Mrs Neale writes to say she is missed at the fort and that the other students have been moved on to Cisco where they have found their niches in domestic service. There is a great furore building on the plains she says and Winona has done well to remove herself and asides from that she says the major believes there are other kinds of war brewing generally. I am wondering what she means by that and I write to the major direct to find out. He writes back and says he is hearing dire news from the east and what do I hear where I am and it's only then I realise what's gathering. Guess we were heads down in our own business, the act and just living and loving and such. Fierce stuff fermenting all around right enough and new regiments being formed on every side to defend this that or the other. I never even heard the word Union till I read it in the *Courier*. Guess that was our lot because I guess we took our tune from Mr McSweny. Ain't going to be any America unless we fight for it, he says. I ask him that night to fill me in. Suddenly I am all filled in and filled with fervour what's more. That queer tenderness of heart that rises to fine words. He talks about slaves and the true and proper love of country and the call of Mr Lincoln. Now we're dizzy with patriotic feeling and desire. John Cole sitting there wide-eyed.

Soon the whole thing goes up and our audience

is petering out. Guttering out like a used candle. The buggers is joining volunteer regiments. Flooding into barracks spirited up in fields. Scraps of great speeches in Washington reach our little district like the bits of things dropped by feeding birds. Mr McSweny allows that he is too old to fight. I'm just too old, he says, though everything still working, mind.

Then the major writes again and asks will we join his new regiment that he is raising in Boston where he hails from. Says he is leaving Mrs Neale and the girls in Fort Laramie for safety and heading east hisself and if we present ourselves in a week's time he will induct us. Now he signs hisself Colonel which is a mighty big handle and I guess that's what he is now but John Cole says we'll still call him the major for convenience. The poet McSweny undertakes to keep Winona in bibs and biscuits and we give him some dollars we have kept aside. We lock up our goods in big boxes like coffins, my dresses and John Cole's stage finery, and all, and we kiss Winona and set off. Surely, says John Cole, we'll be back soon. If you don't come back I will set off to find you, says Winona. John Cole laughs and then he cries. He holds Winona and kisses her forehead. Mr McSweny shakes my hand and says not to worry only don't be gone too long on account of my great age. I says I have noted that. And off we go.

CHAPTER 12

Spring comes into Massachusetts with her famous flame. God's breath warming the winter out of things. That means something to a thousand boys heaped into camp at a spot called Long Island outside the old city of Boston. Except the endless yards of rain as thick as cloth that falls on us. Battering the tents. But we got new business with the world and our very hearts are filling with the work. That's how it seems as we set out upon our war.

Mostly muskets and only a few of them Spencer carbines that so put anger into Starling Carlton when he saw it at Caught-His-Horse-First's side. Pistols and a few of them famed revolvers. LeMats and Colts. Swords and sabres. Bayonets. That's what we got to bring against the Rebels. New kinda bullets we ain't seen to shoot Indians with. Not round like the old ones, but the shape of a arched door into a church. The major in his present guise of colonel takes in a whole ocean of Irish out of the Boston reeks. Stevedores and shovel men and hauliers and rascals and big-mouths and small mousy lads. Whatever's going because we got to swell into a huge army, that's the main task. Me and John Cole is corporals for the stint because we're actual soldiers that done soldiering. Major brought in Starling Carlton too and he's a sergeant and Lige Magan. And Lige Magan because he getting older now is made colour sergeant and will carry the flag. Must be fifty years old is Lige. Everyone else is just privates, volunteers and loyal men and chancers. There's a thousand faces and the ones we know best will be in D Company. We sign up for the three years and everyone believes this war will take no more or we ain't Christians at all. Most of the privates sign for ninety days. Want to do their duty and then go home proud men. We're drilled up and down our scraggy parade ground and the sergeants try and teach the new boys how to load their muskets but by God they ain't a quick study. Lucky if they get one in ten balls out. Sheridan, Dignam, O'Reilly, Brady, McBrien, Lysaght, a line of Irish names as long as the Missouri river. A few of the boys been in Massachusetts militias right enough so they ain't so useless. But God Almighty. Maybe Mr Lincoln better start worrying, says John Cole, looking on bemused as all dickens. Making a hash of simple drills, says Starling Carlton. He come in the day before all bluster and friendship and he hugs John Cole and I swear he nearly kissing him for the joy of the reunion. Sweating like a damp wall. Lige Magan shakes our hands and says it sure is a how-do-you-do this new war and how have you been, boys? We say we been good. How's that Injun girl? says Starling. Oh, she's good enough, I say. The major he's as busy as Jesus at a wedding but he come over anyhow and smiles on us in his way and says Mrs Neale sends her compliments to her old soldiers. That has us laughing. Starling Carlton thinks it's a bigger joke than it is and can't stop guffawing face-up into the clouds. Major takes no offence whatsoever and Starling Carlton don't mean to give none. He's looking around now blinking and knocking the sweat off his old forage cap. You'll do your best, boys, I know, says the major. Yes, sir, says Lige. God damn it, I guess we will, says Starling Carlton. I know you will, says the major, in his nice colonel's uniform. You follow your captain, now, boys, he says. Captain Wilson he means, a quiet red-haired Irish. Then there's Lieutenant Shaughnessy and Lieutenant Brown. Seems like decent Dublin men enough. Sergeant Magan. Two corporals, me and John. Stew then of Kerrymen and other western seaboard starving types. Fellas with faces like old black bog-oak. And the younger ones all smiles and frowns, listening. Eyes and noses and mouths of all descriptions. Mothers' sons. Seen already the death of their world and now asking pardon of the Fates so that they can fight for a new one. All the faces. Captain Wilson gives a fine speech just the day we setting out for Washington and I still can see all those faces staring up at him on his saddle-box. God damn it, you could weep at the memory if you had a mind. We only ask, says the captain, that you keep the Union in your heart and by that star steer your course. Your country desires of you something beyond any man's capacities. It wants your courage and your strength and your devotion and all it might have to give in return is Death. Maybe he got it out of a manual. Talks like a Roman, says Starling Carlton, looking dazed as a damsel. But somehow it hurt us into an understanding. Soldiers fight mostly for dollars which in that case were thirteen. It weren't like that then. We could of eaten the head off our enemies just then and spat out the hair. Nice Wicklow man with a musical Yankee voice.

Then happy to be freed from camp we march down to Washington in a noisy blue river of four regiments and are mustered in and inspected by the lofty toffs who are but black specks in the distance and we can't hear a blessed word of speeches. Most like the same old nonsense, says Starling Carlton but any fool can tell he's proud anyhow. The whole goddamn seething army is ranked about there and the field guns shone into an ecstasy of sparkling glory not to mention the men spruced up and shaved as best they can manage. Twenty thousand souls ain't a sparse party. Just ain't.

Nice boy called Dan FitzGerald falls in with us in a card-playing capacity so it's very like old times at Laramie except we're bivouacked under slightly shifted stars and it's a city of blue-coated gents all around. We got wives churning uniforms in the wash-churns and we got great boys for singing and even our drummer boy McCarthy who is only eleven years of age is a card. Name sounds like an Irish but he a black boy from Missouri. Missouri don't know if it's Rebel or Union so McCarthy he leaves while they decide. There's big tall men in the next row of tents that are gunners in charge of mortars. You never seen such wide thick arms on men or wide thick barrels on guns. Look like cannon that been eating nothing but molasses for a year. Swole up like a giant's pecker. They say they'll be needed under the walls of Richmond but Starling Carlton says there ain't no walls. So we don't know what that rumour means. Our company is mostly Kerrymen and FitzGerald he comes from Bundorragha which he says is a filthy poor part of Mayo. I ain't met many Irish who will talk about those dark matters but he does easy enough. He has a tin whistle does other kinds of talking. He says his family was killed in the hunger and then he walked to Kenmare over the mountains and he was only ten and then over to Quebec like the rest of us and by a miracle he didn't take the fever just like me. I asked him did he see anyone eat another in the ship's hold and he says he didn't see that but he seen worse. He says when they opened the hatches in Quebec they drew out the long nails and the light came into the hold for the first time in four weeks. All they had gotten on the journey was water. Suddenly in

137

the new light he seen the corpses floating everywhere in the bilge-water and then the dying and then everyone to the last a skeleton. That's why no one will talk because it's not a subject. It makes your heart ache. We shake our heads and deal the cards. No one is talking for a while. Goddamn corpses. That's because we were thought worthless. Nothing people. I guess that's what it was. That thinking just burns through your brain for a while. Nothing but scum. Now we've girt our loins with weapons and we'll try and win the day.

There are hard fights sometimes in the camp already but it ain't with the yellowlegs. Some of those native-born soldiers fear the goddamn Irish since in a bad mood they might knock you down and stomp on your head till they feel better but you won't. Irish boys all stuffed with anger. Bursting into flame. Who knows. As corporal I am trying to bluster them into peacefulness. Ain't easy. I can throw them into clink if they don't come off the boil. They carry a grudge like hunting dogs carry the bird so I got to be fair as Solomon. But then an Irish might be the gentlest man in Christendom too. Dan FitzGerald he would feed you his arm if you was hungry. Captain Wilson he only come out from his home place last year. Says the place still going to hell by the highroad. But he is a tip-top character. He was a major in the Wicklow Regiment of Militia. It seems like his people must be swells but he ain't high-handed and the company is content with him. Looks like if he says to do something we might do it. Starling Carlton says the trouble with the Irish sodger, the trouble with him is he thinks when he is bid to go do a thing. He turns it over in his mind. He gapes at his officer to see if the order pleases or don't. That ain't a good trait in a soldier. Every Irish thinks he be in the right and he will kill the whole world to make a proof. Starling Carlton says the Irish is just ravening dogs. Then he clasps my hand and laughs. Goddamn Starling Carlton, fat as a grizzly bear. He's a sergeant so I can't punch him as I would wish.

Dan FitzGerald and the drummer boy McCarthy has sprung up a friendship between them and Dan is schooling McCarthy in the matter of Irish tunes. Made an Irish drum out of the dried skin of a mule and a spliced barrel-stave. Whittled him a striking stick and he's all set. The two of them go running at these dancing tunes and it puts a lick of enjoyment into slack times. Not many of them now. We're poured down slowly into northern Virginia and we was hoping to hear that tracks had been laid but no hope of that. We're walking.

Lige Magan's little detail carries the colours and it's a sight. Nice banner sewed by nuns somewhere, they say. I got to keep my men fore and back in good order and John Cole has his own bunch and it has to be allowed Starling Carlton knows his army business and we don't feel too bad with the captain leading our company. In fact must be said all the men are in devilish high spirits and want to be running at Rebels as soon as can be arranged. Starling carries weight but even without a horse he's strong as the centre of a river current. He bulls along mightily. We don't miss our old sergeant's singing but McCarthy beats out the march on his drum. Left right, left right. Eternal soldiers, it don't ever change. You got to get from one point to another and the only way is the old forced march. Otherwise you get dawdling, fellas peeling off to drink from a stream, taking an interest in the farms we pass in case some good woman has baked cakes. Can't be having that. And then we are stomping down into that two-faced country, it's north Virginia, we don't know where allegiances may lie. Could be death to find out. Got to say Virginia appeals. Great mountains stand to the west and old forests there are not thinking about us, not for a minute. They say the farms are tired worn-out places but they got the look of plenty. Four regiments is a noisy river but still the songs of birds pierce through our din and local dogs come to the edges of their domains and bark their fool heads off at us. That pack and the musket and the rough uniform got to be borne gaily. Or else it start to crush you. Best think your way into feeling strong, best. No man likes to fall out because he can't manage a little jaunt down into Virginny, as Dan FitzGerald calls it. Anyhows aren't we going down to show the Rebs where they went wrong. Error of their ways. We got a nice deal of ordnance and it is our wish to show them what it can do. It's not our lot to know the orders that drive us on but that ain't needed. Just point us at those Johnny Rebs, says Dan FitzGerald. Sometimes we sing big songs all together as we go and we don't offer the birds of Virginia the versions on the printed sheet as you might find in Mr Noone's hall, but new versions with every stinking word we know stitched in. Every lousy stinking low brothelly word.

Before we leave I send a letter to Mr McSweny hoping Winona is going on well and I hope he gets it. We was not paid the first two months and then we were to general rejoicing and then it was possible for men to send money to their families and we was no exception. The Catholic chaplain carried our wages to the postal depot and sent our put-together sum up to Grand Rapids under army wrap. He never asked no tricky questions about wives. John Cole's daughter was a handle good enough for him. But he's one of those sociable easy-hearted Italian pastors and all ranks like him and all religions. A good heart carries across fences. Fr Giovanni. Small man wouldn't be much good for fighting but he good for tightening those screws that start to come loose on the engine of a man when he's facing God knows what. A few nights into the march I'm on sentinel duty and relieving Corporal Dennihy and it's clear to me the man is shaking. Even in the moonlight as we exchange our words I can see he ain't good. So it ain't everyone looks forward to the fight. But Fr

Giovanni creeps over to him and starts to buttress him up. Looks better for it in the morning anyhow. So, Corporal, he says to me, you send any other man gets windy. I will, Father, I says.

Sense of ferocious danger then descends when we reach the spot where we must deploy. News is the boys in grey are beaded into the great line of woods that seem to rush down that country. Three long great meadows rise to a bare and blasted headland. Deep three-foot grasses such as would make a cow hurry on to partake. Our batteries are ranged in expert wise and by afternoon our section's positioned and good. Something building in the hearts of the soldiers, if you could see that thing it might have strange wings. Something fluttering in their breasts and then a great clattering of wings. Our muskets are loaded and where we are a line of fifty men kneels and another fifty stand behind, and then a loading line, and then men there anxious and silent ready to step forward and fill the gaps. The field guns start firing into the trees and soon we are marvelling at the explosions such as we ain't ever seen before. Fire and blackness bursts in the tree-tops and then you might think the green of the forest washes forward and back to close the destructed place. All this a quarter mile off and then we see the grey-coated soldiers appear at the ravelled margin of the trees. Captain is peering through his glass and he says something I can't hear and it's spoken back in a relay and it sounds like he is saying there be about three thousand men.

That sounds like a great number but we're just a thousand more. The yellowlegs group on the top meadow and our batteries are trying to get a pin on them. Then they are getting a pin and then the Rebels are moving down because there ain't nothing joyous in receiving well-served bombs. The Rebels run down towards us in a fashion never expected at least by me and then when they come in range the officers steady us and then call out to fire and then we fire. Those crazy Rebs go down in numbers and then just like the forest seem to close with green courage over the gaps of deaths and then they keep coming on. Each line of us reloads and fires, reloads and fires, and now the Rebs are firing, some by standing for a moment, some on the hoof as they hurry down. It ain't the slow march we were taught at all but a lurching wild gallop of human creatures. You wouldn't think so many could be killed and it not stop them and then all round us we are falling with a bullet in a face or a bullet in a arm. Those fierce little minie bullets that open in your poor soft corpse. Then the captain screams out to fix our bayonets and then we are bid to stand and then we are bid to charge. Of my little bunch of men one still kneels in dazed conviction so I deftly kick him to his feet and on we go. Now we are one heart running but the grass is tufty and thick and it is hard to run nobly and we are stumbling and cursing like drunkards. But somehow by fierce tuck of strength we keep our feet and suddenly it seems desirable to lock with our foe and suddenly the grass seems no obstacle at all and one in the company cries out *Faugh a ballagh* and then there is a sound made in our throats we have never heard and there is a great hunger to do we know not what unless it is stick our bayonets into the rush of grey ahead. But not just that because there is another thing or other things we have no names for because it is not part of usual talk. It is not like running at Indians who are not your kind but it is running at a mirror of yourself. Those Johnny Rebs are Irish, English, and all the rest. Canter on, canter on, and enjoin. But suddenly then the Rebs swing right and turn their charge across the meadow. They've seen the great swathe of our men come up behind and maybe seen a engine of death complete and whatever it is we can hear the officers calling out in the chaotic uproar. We're stopped in our charge and kneel and load and fire. We kneel and load and fire at the side-on millipede of the enemy. Our batteries belch forth their bombs again and the Confederates balk like a huge herd of wild horses and run back ten yards and then ten yards reversed again. They greatly desire to reach the cover of the far woods. The batteries belch behind, they belch behind. Some bombs come so low they want a path through us too and many fall in our lines as a missile forges a bloody ditch through living men. A frantic weariness infects our bones. We load and fire, we load and fire. Now in the burgeoning noise dozens of shells hit into the enemy, sharding them and shredding them. There is a sense of sudden wretchedness and disaster. Then with a great bloom like a sudden infection of spring flowers the meadow becomes a strange carpet of flames. The grass has caught fire and is generously burning and adding burning to burning. So dry it cannot flame fast enough, so high that the blades combust in great tufts and wash the legs of the fleeing soldiers not with soft grasses but dark flames full of a roaring strength. Wounded men fallen in the furnace cry out with horror and affront. Pain such as no animal could bear without wild screeching, tearing, rearing. The main body of soldiers find the mercy of the trees and their wounded are left now on the blackened earth. What is it causes the captain to halt our firing and by relayed message halt the guns? Now we are merely standing watching and the wind blows the conflagration up the meadow leaving many a howling man and a quiet man in its wake. The quiet are in their black folds of death. Others where the fire hasn't touched are just groaning and ruined men. We are bid retire. Our surge of blue draws back two hundred yards and boys go out in gunless details from the rear and there are the medical boys and the chaplain too. Out from the Rebel trees come similar souls likewise and a truce is struck without a word. Muskets are thrown down both sides and the details charge up now not to fire and kill but to stamp out the black acre of lingering flames and tend the dying, the rended, and the burned. Like dancers dancing on the charred grasses.

CHAPTER 13

Nothing too tricky about dying for your country. It's the easiest item on the menu. God knows the truth of it. Young Seth McCarthy he come up from Missouri to be a drummer boy in the Federal army and what does he get only his head took off by a Federal shell. We seen that on the morning after when we strode the field looking for papers and the like we could send home. Seth there with his drum still roped to his young body. But he didn't have his head. It wasn't the only or the worst sight of the aftermath. Let's put the charred corpses first on the list. How come God wants us to fight like goddamn heroes and then be some bit of burned flesh that even the wolves don't want. Burial detail told to bury grey and blue alike and say the prayers. Fr Giovanni tells his beads and we hear him muttering in his Latin. The boys that never seen battle afore some of them were not cheerful. I don't know what those bad sights do to a person. A few soldiers just shaking in their tents and no amount of beef jerky or even whisky can pull them straight. They got to get sent back to some place but the battlefield ain't right for them now. Couldn't hold a spoon let alone a musket. John Cole is very concerned in his nice-hearted way and two of his privates is dead as poked-out winkles. Took the fire from their own hind firers. That's how it goes oftentimes. Just comes home to me how curious dark is battle. Does anyone know what in tarnation's going on? Well, not this Christian. Me and John Cole thank God and old Lige Magan and Starling come through and also Dan FitzGerald. Else how we going to play cards God damn it.

When my sentinels is set up that night I pull away alone to a little copsewood. Alone there a while. Moonlight pouring down through the scrubby oaks as if a thousand dresses. I am thinking man is something of a wolf but also ain't he something stranger too. I am thinking of Winona and about all her travails. I couldn't say who in that while I was myself. Sligo seem a long long time ago and only another brush of darkness. The light is John Cole and all the copiousness of his kindness. Can't get that drummer boy out of my inner eye. He's stuck in there like a floating thing. I guess he should a got more from living than he did. Brave lad out of Missouri and cheery and not expecting nothing. His head rolling about a lonesome meadow in Virginia. Bright eyes and now they put him in a hole. By God it wouldn't even be good enough to weep for him. How we going to count all the souls to be lost in this war? I am shaking like a last dry leaf on a branch in winter. Rattling. I don't guess I have met two hundred souls in my time and knew their names. Souls ain't like a great river and then when death comes the souls pouring over the waterfall and into the bottom land below. Souls ain't like that but this war is asking for them to be. Do we got so many souls to be given? How can that be? I am asking the gap between the oaks these questions. Got to go now in a minute and relieve No. 2 post. Relief, halt! Arms-port! Relief, support-arms! Forward-march!

It is so silent you could swear the moon is listening. The owls are listening and the wolves. I took off my forage cap and scratch my lousy head. The wolves will come down after a few days from the mountains when we are gone and start to dig through the stones we've piled up. Nothing more surer than that. That's why the Indians put their dead on poles. We put them in the dirt because we believe it to be respecting. Talking about Jesus but Jesus never knew nothing about this land. That's how foolish we are. Because it just ain't so. The great world lights like a poor lamp because the snow begin to come down into the clearing. Dimly illumined over in the east corner is a huge black bear. Guess he just have been there the whole time, nosing about for grubs and roots. I hadn't even heard him. Maybe he too was respecting the queer silence. He saw me now and swung his heavy head in a slow arc towards me to get a better view. He was considering me. His eyes looked clever and calm and he sized me up for a long time. Then he swung his whole body as if hanging from ropes and went crashing away into the forest.

The snowfall grows heavier and I am wending my way back to camp. Giving the secret response of the night to the sentry. Nosing along E Avenue between the tents. The colonels and the majors and such are in the big officers' wickiup. The shroud of canvas glowing dimly. Indeed they have real lamps burning within. The officers are sitting in silhouette and their backs are turned blackly to the opening. The picket standing mute outside in the new issue of snow. I can hear their low voices. Talking of family or war I cannot tell. The night has plunged into proper darkness and the pitch core at the centre of everything is in command. The whippoorwill calling over the tents of the sleeping men. Short note, long note. The whippoorwill will call forever over these snowy meadows. But the tents are temporary.

We're moved up towards the river and are bound to establish winter quarters. Guess no man knows who hasn't endured it the wretched boredom of those times. You'd rather risk a battering of canisters and grapeshot. Alright or nearly. Me and John Cole is mighty amused when evenings of blackface is put together for amusement. It's knowed we've worked the halls but here we sing together as two boys and give an Uncle Tom or Old Kentucky Home and leave it there. Union boys in blackface maybe strange. Kentucky got both toes in the war so we have to tread softly there. Dan FitzGerald goes innocent into a dress one night and though he's blackface he sings an Irish Colleen song and by God but the proclivities of a dozen men's aroused. Starling Carlton says he wants to marry her. We leave that there too. Otherwise can't get your damn feet warm and since there ain't a scrap of news getting in the world could of ended and the last trump sounded for all we know. Messengers come pushing through only when the cold lifts its hand. Cases of fever plague the men and some of them go clear off their heads. Even the bad whisky runs out and if the supply wagons ain't made it you is going to be eating your boots. Paymaster never comes neither and you're wondering are you still a living man or has Death converted you till you be now a shivering ghost. When spring comes the ground is still hard and yet we are turned to digging out long rifle pits and redans for the guns. Seems this part of the river hides a ford under the present flood. When it shortly reappears we will be tasked to guard it I guess. Starling Carlton says he's glad he's a sergeant now and don't have to dig. Says he wonders why he ever came east and sure misses Fort Laramie and killing Injuns. Don't you wish to help the black man, sir? says Dan FitzGerald. What you now saying? says Starling. Help the black man get his freedom and keep the Union, sir? says Dan. What's this about niggers, says Starling Carlton, I ain't doing nothing for niggers. He looking clear bemused. Don't you know why you fighting? says Lige Magan, by God,

I don't believe you do. I know, says Starling Carlton. In the tone of a man who don't. Why you fighting then? says Lige. Why, because the major asked me, says Starling, as if this were the clearest fact in Christendom. Why the hell you fighting?

Here come back the warblers and the goddamn butterflies and now also the high-up officers who just the damn same as the warblers went off at that first hint of snow. Can't expect toffs to sit in camp like cabbages. Colonel Neale he tried to get west before the most awful of the snows but he only got as far as Missouri he says. Worried now about the twins and Mrs Neale. Gets some reports of trouble over yonder but expects the army will handle it. The war has thinned out troops in the west and citizen militias took their place somewhat. He don't like citizen militias, Colonel Neale. Confederate militias the worst, roaming about and shooting ducks in barrels. He says wherever a gap opens you'll find trashy men to fill it. General news seeps into camp. The war is widening everywhere. But the clock of the day turns just the same. Bugle and barked order. The big supply wagons dragged by oxen hove into camp. Well we was nearly eating bullets. Got a little boneyard full of the winter's haul. Fr Giovanni likes his brandy but he always does the honours. The bugler with his frozen lips sticking to the mouthpiece. Raw with little wounds he don't have time to give to healing.

Soon we hear tell that the big army's coming

south and will cross at the ford. Our captain opines they want to go on to a spot called Wytheville and cross the Blue Ridge Mountains. Bring grief to the Rebs in Tennessee, Captain Wilson says. That might be true and that might not be true. But the water has dropped and the two-foot shallows are yellow and brown from the stones below. New recruits arrive in a batch to fill the empty places, Irish just the same as always. City dregs, says Starling Carlton. But as they come in we give them a cheer all the same. Good to see new leaves and new faces. Everything's astir and we ain't feeling so bad now. Sap rising in men too.

Guess the Rebs believe if they can wipe us off the bank they can hold the ford and stop the Federals pushing through. Now we know there be a huge force of them approaching up the right bank of the river. Ten miles off a blind man can see the dust and ruckus of men. Must be ten thousand. At least a division of those hole-in-the-trousers boys. We're only four thousand but we're dug in like prairie dogs. Rifle pits galore a mile wide and all set in devious vees and on each flank full batteries and we got so much shells they rival the pyramids of Egypt. We got a regiment to hold a line behind and we have a nice rabble of compa-nies on the right flank. Starling Carlton says two to one only fair to the yellowlegs. Lige says Starling can't count. Starling says Lige is a lying Tennessee traitor. What you saying now? says Lige. Ain't you a Tennessee boy? I am. Well, why ain't you fighting for the Rebs since you smell the same as them? My pa'd shoot you dead hear you talk like that, Starling, says Lige, guess you don't know nothing so you can't say nothing about Tennessee. I know a back-stabbing turncoat when I sees one. Then why don't you step over here and say that to my face? says Lige. I am saying it to your face. Your face is two feet from my mouth. Goddamn it, Lige. Then the two burst out laughing as is their wonted manner. Just as well as up to that point they was looking like assassins.

Colonels lurking on the holding line behind and sergeants coming down with orders. Getting to be all business and here we go. Lige has a piece of paper with his name and farm wrote on it and he always pins it to his chest before battle. Don't want his body going in a pit nameless and his pa never hearing. His pa is eighty-nine year old and must be teetering on the brink of life, who knows. Then Lige falls back and tends to the colour detail. Gets our flag up with the shamrock on it and the harp. Green as an April leaf but dusty and torn too. Takes the river wind and shows its shape. There's a huge noise being made by the approaching Rebs and it must be allowed we is nervy now and sick even. The faces are turned to the south to see what it all looks like. There's all these little humpy hills and stands of scrubby trees and then the full dark river pouring south on our left. Friendly, protecting river. Colonel Neale appears now on his horse and talks down a few moments to Captain Wilson but no one can hear what they saying. Sounds humorous anyhow. Then the colonel goes trotting along the ranks and he's nodding to the men. We got a big company of cavalry on our right but they're back in the trees and you can't say if they'll be used. Might have to rush down if the Rebs break through some place. We don't intend to let that happen and we're full of salt pork and hardtack and we ain't wanting any story of defeat going north. These are little simple things that sit in your head. There is also that queer terror that begins to swell in your belly and men sometimes suddenly need a shit and the sinks are too far back. You're belching and the food comes up your gullet like it wants to say hello to the world again. Let's not forget the pissing into your trousers. It's a soldier's life. Now we can see the Reb troops better, we can see the regimental banners here and there and they got cavalry too coming up slowly with them, and now they are spreading their forces wide and you can imagine the colonels trying to keep a hold on all this. The first cousin of an order is chaos. Cousin chaos himself. We can nearly feel the ground under us trembling and poor Starling Carlton though he is making sure men are in the right position throws up his pork in a violent expectoration. He don't lose a breath though and he don't care much who sees it. He wipes his grimy mouth and don't miss a beat if he can help it. Terror is just the cousin of courage too. I hope so because I feeling it. We

154

are watching the Rebs and by God ten thousand might be a short sum. More like a goddamn full army. We can see the horses cantering the guns up on two sides and we can see the battery men getting range and then it don't seem like two seconds later the first of the shells go whining like God's screaming infant over our heads. They're going to throw about four thousand infantry at us in a terrifying wodge of men at centre and here they come. Before we know what is going on we have range on them with our guns and off go a hornet cloud of shells towards the Rebs. Blooms and sudden trees of smoke and fire appear among the myriad troops coming on. We can hear above the din our gunners shouting orders and sergeants and captains are barking words and you can feel your whole corpse gathered up into one tight fist of fear and fright. Holy mother of the Jesus good-natured God. A rich black fog of blown ordnance drifts out across the river like a river fog. Starling Carlton since his breakfast is gone is standing laughing beside me. Why he is laughing not even he knows or he least of all. The captains give the order to fire and a thousand muskets give voice and fling their round shot towards those walking demons. Johnny Reb with his skinny legs and his butternut rags and all he thinks about and thinks good carried under hats of all descriptions. South don't got uniforms, grits, or oftentimes shoes. Half of these fierce-looking bastards in bare feet. Could be the denizens of a Sligo slum-house. God damn it, probably are, some of them. On they come. I can see the regimental banners now better and this damn one at centre coming on has shamrocks and harps just like ours. Usual crazy fucking war. There's at least ten colour details I can see. That's all the orders a simple soldier needs. Once you can see your banner you'll go. Not going to leave that to the blasted foe. Other things I see are how thin these boys are, how strange, like ghosts and ghouls. Their eyes like twenty thousand dirty stones. River stones I'm thinking and I'm getting crazier by the second. I'm so frightened and crazy the piss runs down my army-issue trews freely. Bursts forth and floods my legs. God damn it. Like a mare staling in a field. Well, polish my boots. Our first round drops maybe two hundred men. Johnny Reb going to have plenty of burials. We see some cavalry come down east of our barricades and five hundred horse go running at the left flank of the Rebs. God knows whose guns are dropping some of them. Shells not finding range and so much smoke now and shouting and screaming the whole vista is erased. Goodbye Virginia and hello only ruckus and turmoil. We're reloading as fast as our fingers can let us. Bet Starling Carlton wishes he had that nice Spencer now he wanted to kill Caught-His-Horse-First for. Wish I owned it myself. Takes two three minutes to ready your musket. God damn it. Fire again and make it count. Fire again and make it count. Now the advance is broken and the Rebs are pulling back.

156

They can't take fire just in that way from the breastworks and the redans. Can't shoot enough of us and can't get near enough to o'erwhelm us. Engulf us like a river flood and drown us in death. Can't do it. The cavalry now veers to centre running at the retreating men. They're slashing at backs and heads with their sabres and now their own cavalry is running at ours. Holy good Jesus. They come together like writhing devils, turning and raising the sabres, and firing off pistols into faces as freely as you please. Dozens and dozens falling. Such a blather of terrified runners and horses rearing up and throwing riders and God knows what else of perils. Then the cavalry galloping back and let the damn Rebels find the little hills. God damn it, no. They have another regiment of cavalry running up through the retreating men and they almost got to turn again because they'll be trampled by their own. Here they come on again. We're firing like lunatics possessed. Firing and firing. The whole sea of them turn again and you'd swear old Canute must be working the miracle he could not of old. The tide of men goes back. We seen them go for about a quarter hour and a cheer goes up among us and we are standing and kneeling, panting there like waterless cattle. God burn the world but Starling Carlton leans on the parapet and rests his big face wholesale on the earth like he was kissing it. But he is exhausted as a hunting dog been hunting for a day. He's run his big form so heavy he's fallen over like a killed man. I can hear him muttering into the earth, his mouth and face plastered in mud. The day is as dry as a furnace but his sweat makes mud enough to throw a pot. John Cole come over from his detail and kneels at my side. He leans his head against my right arm at the top and seems to sleep for a moment. Seems to fall into a sleep. Like he was a baby after a lullaby. Suddenly the whole body of men seems to be sleeping. No force will ever rouse us again. Our eyes are closed and we are asking for our strength returned. If we got Gods we're praying to them. Then it seeps back. No thankful speech of any captain could be so deep as the relief of it.

CHAPTER 14

Towards twilight the buggers come on again. The breeze has swung round to the east and now a million small waves appear on the river. Lace from a million seamstresses. The old heralds of the twilight are a slow blindness across the land and a long high colour the colour of apples seeps into the sky. The mountains that were faint blue in the distance darken and slowly blacken. The lead drops in the glass. Maybe we are not so ready as we were and afterwards hard words are spoken about the defences along where the sinks are and the field hospital. They must of been creeping up just like that red colour in the sky. Though the first thing that hits us is the cavalry again but they must of scoped out a weakness and through the right yards and supply dumps they pour and they are trying to throw the horses at the stronger rear line. Past the line is the damn colonels and the rest. All the same soldiers pour over against the invading horses. We can see all this while stupidly standing on the breastwork. The dimness of the evening makes us stupid. We can feel the approach of slaughter and in aiming to avoid it we put ourselves before it. The first cohorts of the darkness is a enemy too. The very world and its natures is against us. The hundreds of men repel the cavalry best they can and the horses wheel east again and pour away into the smudges of new night. The colonel must guess the next and we are ordered over the breastwork and down into the wild fields and are to meet the coming Rebs if they are coming. There ain't a heart among us wants to leave the breastwork. Didn't we dig the damn thing and why leave it now. The bundles and wastes of shadow do not beckon us. Dan FitzGerald looks at me for orders and I say nothing. Are we to go or what? he says. I'd rather not, I say. But maybe we ought, I say. For the honour of Bundorragha, he says, laughing. What did Bundorragha ever do for you, Dan? I says. Not a thing, he says. So, I says. Then we scramble over the ditch, then we all scramble, let's say a thousand men, and luckily enough the Rebs ain't sent their army this time but only a scattering of companies. Maybe feeling out the way. Maybe all they could hide along the little hills. So we are ten steps out on the fresh grasses of Virginia and the river goes along in its silent majesty all fringed with its little waves and by chance the company coming straight to meet us is that rabble of Irish we spotted before. Just by chance in that chancy way of war. Lige Magan has our banner raised and comes along in the centre of our companies. We are walking down the grasses at a steady pace and our bayonets are fixed and our guns sloped. We won't do nothing till the other crowd comes quicker. We see a new canter in their step. Captain Wilson orders us on and we break into a run. No one wants to do it and everyone does it. Now we hear the first crackles of the Rebs firing and in an instant the field is aflame with noise and returning fire. No time to be reloading now and on we rush with bayonets borne forward. A small cry begins in my throat and seems to grow and then this same roar alights in the other throats and now the roar is the roar of a thousand and the captain is roaring the worst. It would scare the Archangel. The roar is bigger than any wind we know and in it is a sort of queer lust and something akin to cruelty. The Rebels before us have expended their guns and they throw down their muskets and unlatch their bayonets and now they come on against us with a bayonet in one hand and a knife in another. We ain't never heard of this. Now in the further darkness comes rushing a streaming confusion of horses and we pray it is our cavalry. The slashing and hacking of sabres and firing of pistols. Horsemen stoop down to cut away tendons and muscles. All this in the gathering darkness. Was it madness to attack at twilight or genius? The Irish Rebs are shouting too, shouting filthy things in Gaelic. Then we reach each other and it is all wrestling, punching, and stabbing. These boys are big and afterwards we learn they are railway workers and dockers from New Orleans. Big boys and used to murder and mayhem. They don't run over this darkness to love us. They want our lives and to cut out our hearts and murder us and still us and stop us. I have a big sergeant trying to get his Bowie into me and I am obliged to run his stomach with the bayonet. The noble adversaries fight on for ten minutes and in that time hundreds are tumbled on the ground. Dozens are groaning and calling for assistance. The darkness is nearly complete and the Rebs turn again to withdraw and the cavalry lets them go because you can't see a damn thing now in the soupy night. Reb and Federal alike lie bleeding in the blackness.

Then there is a curious lull. The wounded are making the noises of ill-butchered cattle. Throats have been slit but not entirely. There are gurgles and limbs held in agony and many have stomach wounds that presage God-awful deaths. Then the moon rises quietly and throws down her long fingers of nearly useless light. We trudge back to the breastworks and we get the details into action and the wounded are carried up into camp on the new ambulances. The dressing station has survived the Reb cavalry and the surgeon is inside with his saws and bandages. There are more bullet wounds than expected and though in all truth I heard no shells throughout our charge many have missing arms and arms hanging and legs. The helpers light the big oil lamps and the sawing begins. There's no hospital yet further up the country so it's now or never. Anything that can be bandaged is wrapped tightly. At the end of the surgeon's table the pile of arms and legs grows. Like the offered wares of some filthy butcher. The fires have been stoked and the irons is pushed against the wounds and the screaming men are held down. We know in our hearts they can't survive. The old rot will set in and though we may bump them back north they won't see another Christmas. First the vile black spot and then all hell to pay. We seen it a hundred times. Still the surgeon works on just in case. He's sweating like Starling Carlton. Too many, too many. Some may be lucky, we pray. Here's Lige Magan with a knife in his neck. He must of been knocked clear into Monday because his body is loose and sleeping. Maybe they gave the bugger ether. The blood-soaked surgeon wraps Lige's sloppy wound and then he's laid aside. Bring on the next, bring on the next. Aye, but Doc, save old Lige. He the best. Clear this fool out, says the surgeon. Can't blame him. He'll work another seven hours. God guide his bloody hand. Our comrades. Poor ruined lengths of paltry men.

When his wound heals they try to return poor Lige to the ranks. But turns out he can't turn his head. That New Orleans Irish Bowie knife was a spanner in his works rightly. Anyhow since he ain't no spring chicken he gets an honourable discharge in the midst of war and he tells us he will likely go back to Tennessee to tend his pa. Says they can be two old bastards together. His pa still runs three hundred acres so he might be needing fresh hands for that. Lige looks excited saying all this but also in me there is a natural sorrow. John Cole holds Lige in great affection and so do many. Only Starling Carlton looks scowling and says hard things but that's just the same as him saying good things. Starling won't be half of what he is without Lige, we know. I guess folk become joined at the hip over time. Can't have a thought about Starling without Lige being in it like a squirrel in a tree. Big sweaty Starling going to have to find another buddy. That ain't going to be easy in prospect. What Starling says to me is he's worried that if Lige can't turn his head he won't see robbers creeping up on him. Seems to bother Starling mightily. Also he says Tennessee ain't a peaceful country now. How can a bluecoat go back to Tennessee? Good question. Only, he won't be wearing a blue coat. They give him some weary civilian clothing for himself as Lige goes off. Don't look like no three-hundred-acre farmer in them. Looks like the robber Starling fears. We shake hands with Lige and he goes off and he has to walk to Tennessee more or less. Says he guesses there must be a road across the Blue Ridge. Must be. No one knows. Off he goes anyhow. Write us a letter when you can, says John Cole. Don't forget now. I'll keep in touch, says Lige, ain't going to let you go. This makes John Cole very quiet. John is a tall man and thin and maybe he don't have much painted on his face. He like to make his decisions and then do a thing. He has my back and he wants the best world for Winona and he don't neglect his pals. When Lige Magan intimates his seeming love for him, John Cole does show something on his face though. Maybe remembers the old sick days when John Cole couldn't move a muscle and that Lige danced attendance. Why should a man help another man? No need, the world don't care about that. World is just a passing parade of cruel moments and long drear stretches where nothing going on but chicory drinking and whisky and cards. No requirement for nothing else tucked in there. We're strange people, soldiers stuck out in wars. We ain't saying no laws in Washington. We ain't walking on yon great lawns. Storms kill us, and battles, and the earth closes over and no one need say a word and I don't believe we mind. Happy to breathe because we seen terror and horror and then for a while they ain't in dominion. Bibles weren't wrote for us nor any books. We ain't maybe what people do call human since we ain't partaking of that bread of heaven. But if God was trying to make an excuse for us He might point at that strange love between us. Like when you fumbling about in the darkness and you light a lamp and the light come up and rescue things. Objects in a room and the face of the man who seem a dug-up treasure to you. John Cole. Seems a food. Bread of earth. The lamplight touching his eyes and another light answering.

That Reb army has made an awful mess of us and we are relieved and moved back a ways north.

Colonel mighty pleased though that the Rebs was repulsed as he calls it. Guess they were, at a cost. At a spot called Edwards Ferry we crossed over and it were a strange and excellent feeling to reach Union land again. Shoes a terror though and John Cole got a raw underfoot from the mud and gravel living in his boots. I take ten moments to pull them off and wash his feet in the river. We never seen farmers all the trail up through Virginia. They flee away and hide every scrap. Now the farmers ain't so chary and we get fresh food as we pass such as we ain't pleased our gobs with for a long time. Pies still warm from the oven. If in heaven this be the cooking I'm game. We go into camp with a main army and there must be twenty thousand men shitting in the same bowl. Like a great strange city rose among the little hills and farms. If Maryland ain't pretty country God's a girl. We're tired in our marrows and Captain Wilson wants to hone us back up. Draws the line when Starling Carlton finds a cherry orchard three hills over and thinks he'll be best living there. We got to go over with a rope to bring him back. Find him sitting up in a cherry tree. What the hell you doing? says the captain's orderly Joe Ling. I ain't talking to you, says Starling, you just a private. So Joe Ling goes back to camp and the captain come out himself and he's standing under the branches picking cherries almost by accident and chewing them and spitting out the stones. Good cherries, he says. Well got, Sergeant Carlton. Thank you kindly, says Starling, climbing down, I tries to do my best. You want me to tie him? says Private Ling. Tie him up? says the captain, no, I want you to take off your caps and fill them with cherries. So back we wend well laden. Starling Carlton very easy and go-free then, walking along beside me. There's said to be storms coming over Maryland but just this day the day is one of those given to the earth as a reminder to what it can be. Pleasant and steeped in a kinda heat you can't take against. And the fields and narrow roads verdant and pleasing and the cherry trees laden with those little red planets and then the promise of the apples and pears later if the storms don't destroy them. Makes a soldier want to farm and stay in one place the rest of his given days. In plenitude and peacefulness. We're going along well and Starling is talking about the country round Detroit in the summer and how as a small boy he wanted to be a bishop. Then Starling stops on the dry road and is staring down at the dryness and I think he won't move again and maybe it is best to fetch the rope after all. I guess Starling Carlton is as mad as two puppies. I guess you're a good friend to me, he says then, real quiet. Then the captain just a few yards ahead calls back, you coming on now or what? We coming on now, I say.

Every month if the paymaster's iron cart finds us we send ten dollars to the poet McSweny for Winona Cole. She's back working blackface for Mr Noone so she got her own fortune if three dollars a week be ever a fortune. Our fortune is twenty-and-some letters from Winona tied in a shoelace. She sends us all her news in her nice handwriting. She hopes for our return but she don't want us to get shot by a) the Rebels or b) the colonel, for desertion. She says she hope we got victuals and that we get a good wash once a month as she always insisted. Guess a king couldn't hope for better. Mr McSweny says she's blossoming. Prettiest girl in Michigan bar none. I'd say, says John Cole. No surprise, ain't she Handsome John Cole's daughter? I say. Well. John Cole laughs when I say that. John Cole is of the opinion that we don't got so many days of life but that one day on the old Bank of Time we draw the last one. He hopes he sees her again before that. That about as pious as John Cole gets.

It was ourselves heaved over to Tennessee then. We wrote a little missive to Lige Magan before we shipped out telling him to look out for us and got back a sad letter itemising the death of his pa. He was took off his farm by the Rebs and hanged for a bluecoat and all his pigs slaughtered. Didn't even requisition the pigs. Guess they wouldn't eat Federal pork. Goddamn fools and murderers. His pa had freed his slaves and had put them to sharecropping so they wouldn't starve. Rebs said this were treason to the Confederacy. That's right. Lige said he walked the whole way home from Virginia because he couldn't use the railroad through Big Lick. I never looked back, he said, which was his little joke. Since his neck was fixed hard. Rebs were keeping the railroad to themselves, he says. His farm was in a place called Paris in Henry County but all he found there was bones and sorrow. We was saying all this to Starling Carlton since we reckoned he might like to hear the news but Starling got agitated and didn't want to hear no more. Stormed out of the tent like he needed a big shit urgent. What the hell's the matter with him? said John Cole.

Colonel Neale was pleased with us but the high-ups weren't so pleased with him and he been replaced and Captain Wilson been bumped up to major and we got a new colonel who don't know us from a hole in the wall. Colonel Neale is now again the major and he has gone back to Fort Laramie and Starling Carlton wanted to go with him but he signed and won't be released from happy servitude for another month. Colonel said he would be glad to have us again at Laramie so that was very pleasing. John Cole says we could just go pick up Winona when all this was over or our three years was up whichever come sooner and skedaddle over there. Why not? Well, first thing, you and something there don't agree, I say. Maybe the water. Anyhow what about the dresses? Well, says John Cole, we could go on all the damn way to San Francisco. Find us a theatre there and put riot into the hearts of simple men. Or stay put with Mr Noone, why not? I say. World's our oyster, says John Cole, looks like. So we making plans

169

like honeymooners. Our service up in four months or thereabouts. No one thinks the war will be over then and some say we will never see the end of it. The Rebs are stronger than they ever were and their cavalry is like a flashing fire of death, they say. They ain't got proper provisioning, they ain't hardly got food, their horses are skinny and their eyes are aflame. It's a mystery. Maybe they all ghosts and don't need nourishment.

Month's up and our old pal Starling gets his papers and tucks them into his sack which is just two square feet of gunny cloth. It is a burning hot morning in early fall and his heart suddenly opens as he is going. We have come through a deal of slaughter together and everything we have done adds up to a sum of regard right enough. Starling Carlton is the strangest man I have called friend. The book of Starling Carlton no man can read easily. The letters all cluttered and lots of smudges and blackness. I seen that man kill other men without much regret. Kill or be killed. All the things he says he hates are the things most dear to him and maybe he knows it and maybe he don't. John Cole gives him a horn-handled Bowie knife as a keepsake and Starling stares at it like it were a bejewelled crown. Thank you, John, he says. Off he goes after his beloved major and maybe that was the measure of the man called Starling Carlton. That in essence he were true.

CHAPTER 15

Those of us still indentured to Mr Lincoln are being force-marched into Tennessee but then for many days we can't even find the enemy. That's pretty queer since Johnny Reb is told to be everywhere. But not where we looking. We're knocking round woodland and goddamned sore-looking Tennessee fields and we don't see no fresh-baked pies now. It's one thing to go on a forced march but it's another for the supply wagons to come behind. Walking and walking like goddamned marionettes. Major Wilson is in command of three companies, A, B, and C, but maybe he in command of the whole regiment because all the new colonel does is drink rum. Where the hell he gets his rum is a question. But he gets it and he drinks it. Spends most of his time asleep in the back of the colour party's cart and it ain't a pretty sight. Guess Major Wilson can cover it well enough but still. This colonel fella is called Callaghan so that might explain it. Feel like lighting a candle to Major Neale next church I come to.

After many such confounding days cavalry detail

rides up and has orders for the colonel so Major Wilson takes them and reads them quick so the irregularity may feel less. All ahead we can see a great pall of smoke rising and we can even hear the clump-clump of shells like giants walking over hard ground. Guess there's a mighty battle up ahead and now we are to put ourselves in the guise of a relieving corps. We aim to do it. Dan FitzGerald nods to a gaggle of recruits to his side that never seen battle. You all ready? he says. Good lads. Now Dan not even a officer, not by a long gap. Guess they are going pale in the face from wondering what the hell happening now. Scraggly beards like frocken bushes, farmboy faces. You get your muskets loaded now, boys, says Dan, easy like he was their own brother. That's how the new boys will live through. Someone showing them when to be brave and when in the name of the good Lord to run like thieves.

We got to move up quick because the boys up there been holding a line for three days. Looks like we are the succour long awaited. Dark fields and troubled crops, the big sky growing melancholy with evening. Doubt they'll light the candles in the small farmhouses tucked into woody corners. Don't want to be attracting no demons of soldiers along with the big moths of Tennessee. Wake in the morning and your tent be speckled with the beggars. Our few thousands climb the last picket fences and go on up into slowly rising country. You can feel the new effort in your limbs

172

and the faces of the new men look strange and affrighted like they was running against their will. It's the corporals' task to make it all seem righteous. Got to put a sense into them that this is manly work. They been trained six weeks in sticking bayonets into sacks and loading on their backs. Digging breastworks. If they run now they will be shot anyhow by the captains coming up behind. Best keep going, boys of Massachusetts. In due course of things we start to meet our bluecoats coming back down. Guess they got the order to fall back now we are racing up. Man they look like weary boys and the wettest soldiers in the history of the world. Rain up here in the hills be like swimming in a creek. Who you boys? one asks as he stumbles down. We the Irish, says one of the recruits, in a squawky henlike voice. Very glad to see you boys coming up, he says. I can see straight off the heart it puts into our new men. John Cole appears at my side and says, who was that man? I don't know, John, I says. Didn't you recognise him? says John. No. That was Trooper Watchorn, to the life, he says. Trooper Watchorn dead, I say, we shot him.

On we go. We got many soldiers now coming back. Hot up there, boys, watch youselves, they say. *Faugh a ballagh.* Men coming back down on the backs of other men, wounds dripping blood on the quiet ground. Soon the sound of gunfire and shellfire is closer. We break from the trees and all before us on a rolling hill without trees we see the front line massed and firing. The Rebs not far off deep in long lines of rifle pits. Much better safe than us. How'd they get their artillery up this far? Must have come by another way. Our blue-coats loading and firing. Now we see we got at least rough breastworks for a shield. That's something. Our arrival prompts a mass exchange of places. Boys with exhausted and reddened faces or strange whitened faces greet us. Thank God, they say. Their order's given to fall back through us. As they go on they give a scattered cheer. Thank God, thank God.

The day swaps sight for darkness and now the fierce firing ceases. The Reb lines go quiet and likewise us. Can't see a blessed thing. The night's so dark with clouds that even when the moon rises she can't find a fingerwidth through. It's like we was all struck blind by sudden catastrophe. Holy Jesus, says Dan FitzGerald. Was ever night so dark? Then we thinking we ain't eaten nothing all the livelong day and is there any chance that salt pork come up with us? Gotta feed these crouching souls. But looks like not, all told. We set our pickets and our sentries as thick as a fence. Don't want them snarling yellowlegs creeping up. Their guns still have a distance so they still lobbing shells for a while anyhow. We have batteries right and left it seems, likely on flatter ledges, and for a while also in duet with the Rebs our guns reply. Then in that vast murk of night it all stops as if a performance was now at a close and the players taking off their face-paint to go home. Major Wilson marks the trouble of this place. Worst thing looks like we don't have no advantage of neither height nor numbers. Horrible stalemate and no doubt the suffering and the casualties have been great these past days. We hear that maybe two hundred been carried down. Dead as rabbits mostly. We taste in our mouths the terror of this place like it were bread of a kind. I sense in my bones we don't got enough men to hold. It's a queer instinct comes from long service. Like we was two plates of a scales, the Rebs and the bluecoats. Each man a grain of corn. Seems to be the scales banging down their side. Situation is such you're not keen for morning because morning will bring back the war. We ain't sleeping now though we might try a while. You got to stop your hands gripping your musket so tight you strangling it. Try to breathe easy and pray the moon won't show. All the black night we think our private thoughts and then at dawn light touches everything in its kingdom. Tips against leaves and strokes the faces of men. Who can we blame then when the Rebs come at us from both sides surprising the bejesus out of us? Pour over the verdant hill in front for good measure. Feebly we fire in disarray but it's as sudden and absolute as a flood. No one knows the numbers of the Rebs. There must be thousands upon thousands. We thinking we looking at two brigades at most but Captain Wilson now opines we gazing upon a corps entire and he gives the order to surrender.

Surrender! Tell that to the yellowlegs sticking us with bayonets and busting their muskets into our faces. If they ain't got time to reload they turn the musket and hammer it onto our heads. We'd fight for two cents but all up the line the majors and captains are concurred in surrender and now we lifting our arms like lonesome fools. Otherwise we going to be no one left. In a half hour of slaughter we lose a thousand anyhow. Ten thousand demons fallen on our bones. God help us but I don't reckon He does that day.

Johnny Reb he's happy then and all the ruckus slowly ceases and then we got the curious pleasure as a man might say lying in his teeth of seeing their faces up close. Well truth to say they don't look too devilish. Some of them laughing at us, pointing their muskets to round us up. If ever a man felt like a goddamn errant sheep it was then. Flocks of sad-looking bluecoats gathered in. God damn it. We feel shame and hurt much worse we find than bullets. Maybe a tincture of relief that we ain't been butchered straight. They say Rebs like to kill their prisoners in harsh country but these cold-looking boys don't do that. We never do hear no good story about the Rebs and we don't like to be so close. Seems these boys be a division out of Arkansas, some place like that. Speaking like they got acorns in their mouths. God damn it. Dan FitzGerald says something to his captor and he gets a full box in the mush. Dan goes down and then gets up again, keeps silent.

One of our companies is a bunch of them coloured boys and these is unpicked from the weave of prisoners. We got guards all thickly about us and looks like we being prepared for a march. Orders are given in their queer Southern voices. To take an order from a Reb. Most holy Jesus. We still have the hearts of free men though now we're prisoners and those hearts are bursting with a wretched force. The Rebs line up the coloured company, faces to an old field ditch. About a hundred boys. They don't know what's happening no more than we do. An order is shouted and fifty Rebs are firing into the blacks and then those not shot start to run and cry out and then fifty other Rebs step forward with loaded guns to finish the task. The soldiers fall into the ragged ditch and then the job is ended with pistols and then the Rebs step away like they been shooting birds. John Cole looking at me with wordless amaze. Maybe here and there a doubtful gaze. But also a grimness here and there and here and there a glaze of satisfaction. Job that needed doing and it done, the Reb faces seem to say. Then the rest of us is told to form ranks and then we are told to move and then we move.

Andersonville. You ever hear tell of that place? Five days it take to march us down and if ever a spot weren't worth the walk that's it. All we got for our strength along the way is filthy water and soggy lumps of cornbread as they call it. Neither corn nor bread you ask me. A regiment of yellowlegs to guard us and they don't have nothing either but the same foul fare. Worst-looking lot of soldiers I ever seen. Some of them got the shakes and some goitres and worse. It's like being herded by ghouls. Hundreds fall on the trail and those with wounds must seek a surgeon in heaven. Bodies kicked away into ditches like the blacks was. Guess there must be many a poor bluecoat sleeping the eternal sleep in the ditches of Tennessee and Georgia. Feet swole up till you can't keep your boots on or fear to take them off for never getting them back on. Hunger in your belly like a growing stone. The weight of hunger weighing you down mile by mile. And such a sick heart and a drenching fear. Third day a big thunderstorm and it only a huge song singing of our distress. Hard to get the darkness out of your head. Full ten thousand acres of dark blue and black clouds and lightning flinging its sharp yellow paint across the woods and the violent shout and clamour of the thunder. Then a thick deluge to speak of coming death. Tramping on and on, barefoot or clacking boot. Our faces round and sere and bleached like the seedpods of the flower honesty. If we had hidden knives we would fillet out these Rebels' hearts. That the first day and the second. Looking about wanting to rend and ruin if we given a chance. John Cole says he keep seeing floating in his mind the drummer boy McCarthy who done his utmost and died. And then he seeing over and over the coloured men dropped foully into the ditch. Keep your thoughts quiet, John Cole, I say. Then the third day in the thunderstorm we suffer a change. The sun of Death burns our innards and the moon of Death pulls at our blood. Our blood slows and youth is cancelled and we feel like aged men full of years. Dejection and despair. Such weariness as was never recorded in the annals of warring men.

Well we come into this wide compound and see a great horde of poor bedraggled men. Union soldiers as once was. We got maybe a thousand tents Sibleys and A-frames. That's our city. Avenue of dirt between making two halves and fifty paths into these curious residences. Must be three thousand prisoners maybe more. Hard to make out. Forlorn and ragged trees also look like prisoners of something beyond the high log fence. Watchtowers looking down on us. All we Irish troop in. Guards everywhere standing with muskets sloped and Confederate boys sitting by their propped guns maybe waiting for the order to annihilate us. We don't know. A stench like it were coming from the arse of the devil. Heavy crust and smear of filth everywhere that has killed every growing thing. We can see soldiers taking a shit at the sinks as open as a field. Bony moony arses. Then we sit in thirteen to a tent, me and John and Dan among the rest. Dan keeping close to us because his mind be dark with remembering. He seen all this before, he says, at first I can't catch what he means. The journey's not been good to Dan, his feet are leaking yellow water looks like.

If there's a surgeon he must be on furlough, we don't see them. Goddamn guards puts in two blacks with us, seem to think it's humorous judging by their grins. One of them got a hand falling off where he took a swipe of a sabre and he's missing some toes. This boy needs a doctor and he groaning all day and night on the filthy floor. All I can do is watch him. His friend tries to clean him up but everything's too sore I guess. His friend says his name is Carthage Daly and at first he looks at us to see if we haters. I guess we ain't because he tells us they been fighting now a year. Seen action in Virginia and also was under the walls of Richmond as the saying goes. Seems like a decent man and he tries and helps his friend who he says is called Bert Calhoun. Young Bert Calhoun needs a damn doctor is my opinion but there ain't one. The whole prison camp full of this need. The Reb in charge of our little merry lane of tents is First Lieutenant Sprague. Any question you ask him he laughs, as if to say, you filthy bluecoats funny boys. We amuse him greatly. I ask the guard is there something to be done for Bert Calhoun and he laughs too. Guess we must be one of them comedic acts of Mr Noone. Probably could tour the South judging by the laughter. That boy's hand is hanging by a thread, I say. Can't you get someone to do for him? Surgeon won't attend no nigger, says the guard. Private Kidd is his handle. Ain't you got to tend a man so sick? says John Cole. I don't know, says Private Kidd. He should a thought of that afore he thought to fight us. Goddamn niggers. There's another dark-haired boy in the tent with us wants us to stop asking to help Bert Calhoun. Says they shoot anyone that helps the niggers. Says the niggers put in with us to find out where we stand. Says he seen just yesterday a guard shoot a bluecoat sergeant because he asked just the same question John Cole did. I'm looking at John Cole now see how he taking this. John Cole nods like a sage. Guess I understand, he says.

Bert Calhoun dies but he ain't the only one. The winter drear with her icy soul's come in now and there ain't a stick of wood. Half the prisoners don't got shoes no more and all of us is missing bits of clothes. We ain't got a coat between us being summer and fall soldiers. That's the cold then eating your skin like rats. They've opened a wide long pit in the east corner and every day the dead are tipped in there. Maybe thirty a night. Maybe more. We ain't got no goddamned food except that lousy cornbread. We get three fingers of that a day. Swear to the good God no man was ever conceived could live on that. Week after week go by and we praying Mr Lincoln will exchange for us. That's how it used to be done. But Lieutenant Sprague delights to tell us that Mr Lincoln says he don't want no skeletons back. That's us. He don't want to exchange Reb prisoners all plump with Northern grub for no Union skeletons. No good to him no more, says Homer Sprague. And he laughing again. We such a source of fun. A river-source of fun.

We lying there week after week. No point moving about except to drag your sorry backside over for a shit. The sinks. Such a stink you never could imagine. Nothing ever cleared out. I swear you could read the long dread history of cornbread in them sinks. Now the nights drop far below the limit of the gauge. We all sleep like a nest of slugs tucked tight together. We take turns on the outside of the pile. You might die in the night from the frost against your heart and many do. Over to the pit with them. After six months we don't care as much as we did. We're trying to live but we have a sneaky care to die. Handsome John Cole, Handsome John Cole. Dan FitzGerald's a man of bones. John too. Myself too. It's nearly crazy how thin a man can get and still breathe and move. In the south corner are Reb prisoners in a special hut and these boys are tried and taken out and shot. Their own boys so what chance we got. Mr Lincoln, please send us news. Mr Lincoln, we done beared arms for you. Don't leave us here. Lieutenant Sprague must of been spawned by the devil because he laughs and laughs. Maybe he laughing because otherwise he would tear out his hair and go mad. I guess maybe so. They got precious little to eat theyselves so it's skeletons minding skeletons somewhat. They ain't withholding food, they ain't got any. I swear I see guards han't got no shoes either. What crazy war is this? What world we making? We don't know. I guess whatever world it is is ending. We come to the end time and here it is. Just like the goddamn

Bible says, says John Cole. How come we lying here and guarded and inside four walls and the camp lying within this wooded land and the dogs of winter biting and scraping at our limbs? What in tarnation for? John Cole just for eternal badness keeps an eye on Carthage Daly. He don't speak for him and he don't speak against him but he inclined to share his cornbread because the guard don't give Carthage one tiny morsel. Not a crumb. John Cole sharing a moiety of nothing. Tears his cornbread down the middle and when no one seeing passes it to Carthage. I watch this day after day for three four months. Got to say it is a marvel how the mortal bones stand out. I can see his hip bones and his leg bones where they thicken at the knees. His arms just whittled branches from a dried-out tree. Long hours we lie close and John Cole lays his hand on my head and leaves it there. John Cole, my beau.

CHAPTER 16

The coldest winter in the history of the world they say. I guess I believe it. John Cole says if something don't happen very soon by the good Lord he going to die. I say that John Cole will never die and he signed the dotted line on that so he must oblige. But I can see he ain't good. He's shitting water and we have to crutch each other when we trying to go east to the sinks. But we are two boys among thousands. No one gets a ticket to the ball. Noble boys that won in fierce battles and maybe cowards too with their coward's deeds hid in the dateless mists of war all equal under the sun and moon of Andersonville. Homer Sprague who I guess is the king of this demented compound he famishing too. Queer to see. All the guards and the Rebel boys on picket skinnying up. By God. There ain't nothing in the South they say. Union burned every crop in the fall and burned the land and burned the shelters of these folk. And yet they tell us fallen men of great victories and Richmond han't fallen like Vicksburg did. They could tell us any damn history and we wouldn't know the truth of

184

it. They seem to believe all the words in their mouths. It hurts us to hear of such things.

But has this fair world ever seen this long tally-stick of suffering? We got boys here from all corners, mostly eastern men but also some of those states that rub up against Canada. We got farmers, coopers, joiners, settlers. Merchants and sutlers that served the Union cause. They all the same citizen now. Harrowed by hunger and ploughed through by sickness. We got splendid examples of dropsy, scurvy, and the pox. We got ailments of the chest, of the bones, of the arse, of the feet, of the eyes, of the face. Huge vicious rashes of redness mark a hundred faces. Bodies painted with ringworm, lice bites, and a million bugs. Men so sick they are dying of death. Strong men to start that are hard to kill. When you get your scrap of food you got to stuff it down your throat quick march or it will be stole. No cards hardly, no music hardly, only silent stubborn suffering. Men lose their sense and they are lucky. Men are shot for wandering over the death line which is just a row of white sticks near the boundary wall. They don't know where they are. Men stand mute and crazy looking in the mouth of tents with long beards and whiskers. Just stand all day for weeks and weeks and then lie all day. The blacks, Johnny Reb just clean hates these boys. Forty lashes on a wounded soul. Just walk up and shoot them in the head. John Cole he starts to speak but I hushing him time after time.

Then Abe maybe he get a rush of guilt I don't know and a bunch of Rebs was let out in Illinois and flushed back south and we in a batch of equal number sent northward. Mr Lincoln right about something because we just rags and bones. Thousands left behind in Georgia glimmer in our dreams. Dan FitzGerald don't get his walking papers and we are obliged to shake his hand in farewell. A boy that come through seven types of slaughter. All those faces never rescued and consigned to death. We lie side by side in open carts and feel our leg bones knock against each other like some strange music. Once we get to Union country they put us in ambulances that clop-clop north. The destitution of the war marks everything. Looks like we want to rub out America. Farms in ruins and blackened towns. Guess the world ended while we was away. John Cole's quiet face looking out through the flaps of the ambulance. His black eyes like river-stones. Those ain't constant tears just rheumy eyes. I guess that's it. What we was seems broken on a wheel but still we long to reach Winona. That's what we got. Mr McSweny's moved further up the river because the gypsum mines are taking land. He got a place on four poles on the riverbank. Two rooms and a porch to watch the day. Winona she is twelve maybe more and she say nothing when she see us and her face say all she needs. The boys carry us in and put us in our bed. John Cole's face so thin you can see quite clearly how he will look in the

186

grave. We're sorta dead men looking to come back. There are six doors of mercy they say and we are hoping to find one open to our touch. We got the strength of eggs. Mr Noone come in and looks at us and by God he cries. Right there by the filthy waters. John Cole he laughs then and says, Titus, it ain't so bad. By God, says Mr Noone, I know, I cry easy. All the blackface men and women pledge pies and cakes. They going to spoil us into strength, that's certain. Maybe you can show us in an act, says John Cole. The Incredible Skeleton Men. I ain't doing that, says Titus Noone, I ain't. Of course you ain't, says John, abashed. I ain't, says Mr Noone. Major Neale he writes and says he reads we got out and sends his best wishes. Says he found Mrs Neale and his girls all well back a year and they send their best. He says the war has took the spancels off the west and it's all a great ruckus of trouble. Starling Carlton back in harness and going on well, made sergeant now in what the major calls the real army. Guess there's the real and the unreal right enough. Everything like a goddamn dream there by the river in Grand Rapids. Months where Winona strives to haul us back. Day comes when we pull on clothes and John Cole laughing at how we flap. It's comical. Slowly we build back to men and not ghouls to fright a child. More months and then we're sitting at the eating table and then out on the porch in healing sunlight. Beginning to feel the proper itch of life. Turning our heads to plans. One morning we walk slow as turtles to Ed West's barber shop to shave our beards. Man, we don't look like John and Thomas, no. Not the ones we knew. Look old and strange though we ain't even thirty far as we know. Any man in his rights to curse this world but we find we don't so much. Looks like we be stitched at our sides me and John Cole for a start. That's plum. How come we got Winona from the storm of life and she says the same and says she's so glad to have us home. That's better music than leg bones knocking in a cart. We set to go on. Why not.

A man may judge by this eating of the riverbank by the mines that Grand Rapids doing good so long as the drear war rages. Day comes when arms are laid down and then there is cheering in our narrow city but then also we know that hundreds will never come back and there ain't no call for what the place was making formerly. There is a silence like a peopleless forest such as was found one time along the old Missouri river itself now so clogged with human matters. Everything makes a mighty pause, the little stores are still, the streets become the walkways of the old. Mr Noone must close his doors and his sparkling tribe disperse. Titus Noone looks puzzled, hands deep in his pockets. Surely he loves his players most of all and it pains him to his marrow to give them their marching orders. But no citizens no cents.

There's a half-blind preacher in a temple called Bartram House and I don my best dress and me and John Cole go there and we tie the knot. Rev. Hindle he says the lovely words and John Cole kiss the bride and then it's done and who to know. Maybe you could read it in their holy book, John Cole and Thomasina McNulty wed this day of our Lord Dec. 7th 1866. In the euphoria of war's end we reckon a craziness is desired. God don't mind we know because that day of deep winter is clement, clear and bright. Then as if a token of God's favour we get a letter from Lige Magan. We been sending missives back and forth while we putting meat back on our bones. He's struggling with his farm. The men that his pa freed been killed by militia long since but two. His whole country ruined by war and like a waste of ghosts. The coming year lies heavy on his mind and how he to burn the land alone in January? Been set in grass six years and now it ripe for baccy. If we not otherwise engaged could we come and help him in his hour of need? He says all his cold district is a swamp of mistrust and he trusts me and John. Going to be hard years but maybe we could feel there were something to win. He got no *kin* but us. If we come he hoping we got good pistols and also further states that rifles would be wise and a hundred rounds per soul army-style. Fact is that they calling him just a scalawag like his pa and fact is he is. John Cole reads the letter to me on the porch by the river. We muffled to our eyes with old sack coats and our heads encased in old bear-skin hats. Our breath is flowing out like lonesome

189

flowers that die on the air. The deep river runs cleaner now the mine is halted. Winter birds sing their wise old songs on withered river posts. Winona in her winter dress and she as glad as a rose. Old Father Time seems to be looking on with his scythe and sand-clock. Mr McSweny listening while he smokes his seven-cent cheroot. This Tennessee baccy, he says. It good.

We cast an imploration on Beulah McSweny to come with us but he says he ain't testing the patience of the South towards his kind just now and anyhow how would Mr Noone thrive without him? John Cole treks up to Muskegon where the army unloading ten thousand mules and horses now the late war is done and buys four mules for nothing. We have wrote back to Lige and he is mighty pleased we coming and he says to bring mules for ploughing if we can get some. Says horses being eaten now and Tennessee starving. Going to take a week get down there. Maybe two. Depending what we find. Beulah gives us ten two-dollar Erie and Kalamazoo notes he got saved. Can't take that from you, says John Cole. John, he says, you might as well. We also got five gold coins and two five-dollar bills which is everything we got after army service and a little bit owed by Mr Noone when we left to go to war. It ain't no Yankee fortune. The fourth mule will take our slender stuff. Winona's spare dress and my private dresses except the moths been into them some-what. The dress I were married in goes back to

Mr Noone's prop-master. John Cole asks the seamstress Miss Dinwiddie to sew the gold coins into the fancy bit below the bodice of Winona's daily dress. It's to keep them hidden but Winona smiles and says her grandfather did just the same in the long ago when he were riding out to war. Mighty medicine, old Spanish coins sewn into his war dress.

That night we drink more whisky with Mr Noone and company than was wise. It was a sweet time. Mr Noone makes a speech about the old days and new days to come. Farewells and promises of eternal friendship pass our mouths and make our faces sombre.

Looks like we're ready to go south. You could drop a plumb line from Grand Rapids and it would pull down straight to Paris, Tennessee, so we going strict south by the compass through Indiana and Kentucky, says John Cole. Mr McSweny nodding now like we are talking about something he will never have to think of again. He says the best thing is take care of Winona. Mr McSweny be a hundred years old maybe but he ain't too old to feel the pain of parting. Guess Winona rooted deep into his heart just like she done with us. Guess Winona feels like something special in the world. A sort of boon and award for being alive. Beulah McSweny holds out his grizzled brown hand and shakes her smooth hand as brown as polished pinewood. Thank you for everything you done, Beulah, she says. The poet McSweny looks down. I guess you don't need to thank me, he says. No, Beulah, I do, she says.

Since we got them cheap mules we ain't going to be able to catch them trains in a Memphis direction. Can't put four mules on a stagecoach neither. But we don't mind it. We'll go along easy and not bust their wind. Be glad to show Winona all that country, John Cole says. Guess we discover that the worst roads in Christendom go down through Indiana. Ain't they got shovels? says John Cole. Dire mud to put boots of black on the mules. All the same they look busy in the Indiana towns, astir with themselves. New-looking places. And all to us a nameless country though I expect everything has a name but we don't know them. Sometimes we ask a name of a river as we cross just for the hell of it but it makes no difference since we passing through. Our business is going south. Folk look out at us under the hatbrims like we was not very desirable creatures. We traipsing down main street of a dozen podunk places and in one or two Winona gets filthy words thrown. One big boozy red-faced charlatan soul one place laughing at us and saying looks like we travelling with our whore. Ain't that unusual. John Cole not being easy with talk like that stops his mule and slowly dismounts and starts to walk over to the great galoot. Well, he runs like a fat rabbit and squeals too. You just got to answer a bully, says John Cole. That will do it. Then he comes back to us and swings his leg again across his black mule. Nods his head and we go on. Maybe we go a little faster just in case that brave boy got friends. Winona though looking proud like John Cole did the right thing there. Guess he did. Lot of what they call civilisation in Indiana we notice. Theatres. Which makes us sad that we ain't lookers no more. Old men afore our time but we still have a hankering for the work we done before. I still feel the sadness of not donning no dress. Always remembering the strange silence in the crowd and things without words hovering in the air. Crazy nights. Queer way to make a living but we made it all the same. I'm wondering if Lige Magan grows good eats could something of the bloom of youth return? It might. Mr Noone never said a word about it but we knew what the trouble was. Beauty lives in the faces of youth. No going round that. Never was a hag yet that men desired. I don't mind being a matron now if that's our fate. Guess it comes to every woman by and by.

Out between the towns among the December frosted woods and the cold farms Winona some-times sings a song the poet McSweny taught her while we was away. It's a useful song because it's as long as ten miles hoofing it. There ain't a person alive could tell you what the song means. The song she sung was 'The Famous Flower of Serving Men'. But she sings it as good as a linnet. I guess if anyone's a loss to Titus Noone it's her. Such a sweet clear note she keeps in her breast. Pours out like something valuable and sparse into the old soul of the year. Makes you see the country with better eyes. The distant country melting into the sky and the crumbs of human farms scattered over the deserted commons. The road just a threadbare ravelled sleeve between these usual sights. Like three thundering buffalo ran through long ago and that was all the people of Indiana craved for a path. Farmers just that bit easier with us than the town folk but still in this thrumming after-music of the war there's caution and fear. Guess the human-looking bit is Winona but there again we find that Indians ain't much favoured despite the name Indiana. Otherwise we snake down through swamp country and river country. We come to a broken-down old place at nightfall and a man there says he can ferry us over in the morning but he won't do nothing in the dark or we'll be sitting on sand for sure. He has an easy-going way about him. Don't seem to fear us none. He pickets up our mules just like he knew them as his own and says we can throw our bedrolls down in his hut. I can't understand why he so friendly and then it comes clearer. Says after we smoked a while with him and eaten some things he has mostly those mussels that he's a Shawnee. Joe's his whiteman name. Shawnee country here he says but most of the others gone years back. Still a few he says but the government want them gone too. Ever heard of Indian Territory? he says. Anyhow he's sitting tight just at present and fishes the mussels in the river for pearls. Make shirt buttons out of them in the town over yonder. He don't make much. Well he was a dark-faced man right enough though the summer makes Indians of everyone in Indiana. Then he asks Winona where she from and she says she's John Cole's daughter but before that she were Sioux in Nebraska Territory. He tries to say something to her in Indian but it's not her old language. Me and John Cole sitting there and time raging past the little window. All he got for glass is the skin of a cow's stomach stretched tight and dried. He said his wife was killed a while back by men he reckoned were renegades. Country ill at ease and at first he thought we might be killers too but then he saw the girl. Girl in a nice dress and her long black hair plaited nice. Made him think of the old days when he were young and things were better. Looks like we ain't going to be around much longer. He wasn't too sad when he said that. He were just shooting the breeze. Passing the time. Just an old widower Indian man by a river whose name we didn't know.

CHAPTER 17

All night the mosquitoes eat our ravaged forms and we enjoy but a fitful sleep and in the later small hours a deluge wakes us. Joe's hut don't keep much of it out. At daybreak the swollen river has a new and violent aspect and great branches from some unknown riverbank ride down the flood like hornéd bulls. Still the rain pours down and the river rises to touch the foot of Joe's hut. It's cold as a gentleman's icehouse and Winona is trembling like a little cat. Was human kind ever as wet. Joe gazes on the river and says this bank is Indiana and the other bank Kentucky but it might as well be heaven's shore as far as reaching it goes. Then the rain clouds batter off and seem to be rushing towards the east as if with business to do there urgent and then the sky opens its vast skirts and a pale chill light seeps everywhere and a weak sun retrieves dominion. All day in sodden clothes we wait for the river to fall and the hoarfrost stiffens our clothes. Then in deep afternoon John Cole and Joe pull Joe's fishing skiff down to the water and the skittery mules are asked to broach the torrent and we sit in like strange travellers and Joe pushes off. The pack mule has the worst of it. The long muscle of the river rocking him to and fro. And Joe rows mightily as if he were duty bound to risk his life and reach the other bank. He cannot find footing there for his boat and we are obliged to clamber off and into the icy boil and haul on the mules' ropes and bring them on towards land and so here's Kentucky. Joe breaks away and lets his boat run down in an angle to the current and there he floats and then finds the lee of some old rock and pauses and raises his hat to us in farewell. Lucky I paid him in Indiana, says John Cole. Soon we settle our mules and before too long enter a cold hushed wood of pines and John Cole has Winona change to her dry dress and throws my own dress to me since there's nothing else. He pulls on his old army trews and jacket and he got a Zouave shirt he took as a battle souvenir long since so now he looks like a half a gypsy. We been sure to keep our pistols dry in the tar sack we keep for that purpose and so now I stick my pistol in my skirt. John Cole puts his pistol in his boot. The wet clothes are draped about like the flags and colours of some crazy regiment. When we emerge the other side of that wood I don't know hardly what we look like.

Two days we enjoy the beauteous aspects of Kentucky if we can so call them and John Cole reckons we will gain Tennessee the day following. The road is firm and good under the tamping iron of the cold. We go on famously. Truth to tell the dress appeases me and I don't change back though my other clothes is dry. John Cole is talking about the few things he knows about Kentucky which ain't much. The towns we pass look quiet and clean enough and ragged smoke rises from the chimneys of farms. By God if that ain't a milkmaid milking her cow. There's men clearing fields of stubble with buckets of fire. Birds work at the last seeds in the remnant grass before them like another sort of fire. Black fire washing back and forward as their sense of danger bids. Wagons and carts clip by us and neither pay us any heed nor molest us. A better sort of man in clerical clothes doffs his black hat to me. Guess we're just another family heading somewhere. It's a kinda happiness. Then we pass into a district of bigger farms and fences going away over a turmoil of hills. Fences with the queer aspect of white grave markers. Sure enough coming down by a stately line of trees we see hanging there by the roadside about thirty blacks. Two girls amongst them. We ride past while the swollen faces look down on us. Every corpse has a note pinned to it and the note says *Free*. Someone wrote that in charcoal. The heads are bowed by the ropes in such a manner as to make the men seem humble and meek. Like old wooden saints. The girls' heads is just big boils of blood. There's a little breeze with a cargo of deep cold and the bodies all sway an inch towards us, an inch back, one after the other as the breeze chooses through them. Winona's asleep in her saddle and we don't say a word for fear to wake her.

We're even kinda glad to cross into Tennessee but that only shown how little we knowed I guess. We're soon a day in and we're beginning to wonder how much of a cook Elijah Magan is. Wondering will there be beds or straw. Either way we're thinking it will be nice to have this sitting on mules business over. We ain't just got Trooper's Back we got Trooper's Leg, and Arse too. Never once has Winona complained and she's been a meal for mosquitoes and I never seen a nose so red and raw from cold. You could think she relishes the journey.

Well we're just ambling along when these four dark-suited men appeared on the road. Early evening and there's just the black trees and the ten million acres of red sky. December twilights seem made for apparitions. Here are some. Seemed to come up sideways from the bushes out of nowhere. Quiet boys with good horses. Got glistening coats. Boys theyselves not rough neither, sorta well turned out but maybe was sleeping in the wilderness a while. One of them has a short light-blue jacket under his bear cloak. Looks like bear anyhow. They all got hats of not too large vintage and all in all they present a familiar military aspect. But they ain't soldiers exactly. The man with the Rebel jacket badly hid he also got black whiskers hanging down and a black beard in a cone. Looks like a half-dressed colonel. The horses stamp a bit in the margin of the road and huff out big flosses of steam and go *huff* the way a horse is ordained by God to do. Each man has a decent rifle at half arms of the sort Starling Carlton envies. Looks like Spencers. We only got a musket behind John Cole's leg. Lucky I ain't got too far to go in that skirt to fetch the pistol if needs be. John Cole already drawn his pistol from his belt and has it laid easy and friendly you might say across the mule's mane. Like it lived there some-times. Normal. The whiskered man laughs and nods at us. The other three faces stare, looking us over, trying to understand Winona maybe, the way all white men do. Where you heading? says Colonel Whiskers. John Cole don't reply, he only just cocks his gun as if he were scratching his finger with it. Where you heading? he says again. Paris, says John Cole. You've a ways to go yet, says the dark man. I know, says John. This your woman? says another of the men, a smaller, hungrier-looking individual, with a patch on one eye. He got about two dark hairs falling from his hatbrim. He looks dirtier than the other three. Then there's a fat man as heavy as Starling Carlton but with a handsome visage. The fourth man's hat is sitting on a froth of russet hair. Mr Patch asks his question patiently again but John Cole has decided he don't want to answer that one. You Northerners? the red-headed fella says. I guess so. Guess they're Blue-bellies, wouldn't you say? Now he's asking this question of his companion Colonel Whiskers. I don't doubt it, says the colonel, pleasantly. That pleasant tone ain't good, we know. Trouble is, them Spencers. John Cole got one bullet for someone and I've got another. Maybe while I'm killing someone John Cole can get the musket up and then that's a third. If we ain't just dead as crows by then. It would all have to be done so quick. But they won't be expecting a wife to fire maybe. Anyhow something must be done because we know clear as the Latin mass that they going to do more than ask questions. It sure was nice talking to you, says John Cole, as if he were intending to spur his mule on. What you got on the pack mule, friend? says the colonel. Just clothes and such, says John. You got gold maybe? he says, as simple as a child. John laughs, we ain't got gold. Union dollars? No, not even, says John Cole. Well, we don't tolerate no beggars in this county, says the colonel. Then no one says not a thing. The horses snort and their breath blooms. A fitful wind plucks at the leafless bushes. A robin flies down onto the track in front of the men as if he was hoping the hooves had turned up grubs. A robin is a quick-eyed bird. The robin is the labourer's friend. Just in the moment I'm spotting the robin John Cole decides it's time to fire his gun. Two of the horses heave back in surprise and a degree of terror. The bullet tears into the colonel's right hand and God knows where then and I ain't thinking much about that but fetch into my skirts and draw the pistol and try my damnedest to put the ball into the patch on

201

that other man's eye. It's a good target anyhow and I can't have missed by much because the man drops from his horse as if dispatched from a scaffold. Then John Cole fires the musket at Mr Red. All this in three seconds and both the red-haired man and the colonel get off shots but I don't know where they go in the ruckus. Don't reckon they thought John Cole would fire so reckless. Me neither, but here we are now. The colonel has fallen from his horse because I reckon that bullet went on through his hand. Mr Red looks dead enough and the man with the patch got a bullet *somewhere*. That leaves only the fat man and he fires in the same hand of seconds but a bullet hits him too so as I think for a moment one of our mules must have a gun. No it ain't a mule it's Winona. She got a little lady's pistol all squared and pointed and she just fired it at the fat man and he just fired at her. Little Dillinger gun with a bullet you wouldn't think would kill salt. She goes back off her mule like a branch struck her in a gallop. The Lord Christ I leap down and throw her up with John and remount myself in a flurry of skirts and we kick on our mules with fearsome desire. The colonel sits against the gravel bank and stares like he been assaulted by the Holy Family. On by we rush and thank God for mules that will run when bid. We never asked them to move quicker than a trot the whole way from Grand Rapids and now we ask them to be gazelles. They oblige, by God, the pack mule and riderless animal deciding it were best to come with us.

Somehow we expecting pursuit and capture so we keep those mules a-clattering on as best our spurs can urge them. The terror in our hearts. John Cole has one hand driving on and the other arm is holding round Winona. Some two miles on the mules is almost beat and by chance then we reach a decent wood and don't mind how we canter in and blood our legs and hands with brambles. In a clearing then we tie the mules. It's gotten real dark. John Cole bids me reload the guns in case we're catched and he lays Winona on the frozen ground just like you would a corpse. He expecting it's her corpse. Her eyes fast closed. He could bear all the deaths in the world but not this one death. He sees where the bullet torn her dress and he pulls the rip bigger. He's looking for the hole in her skin so he can tend it somehow. The twilight's agin him. He seen ten thousand bullet holes but never in Winona. Face blank as night too with sleep. She look so dead but she ain't since you can see her breath rising. He shakes his head. There ain't no sign, he says. We got to save her. She all we got, we got to save her. He's gotten the top of the dress open now. Then he seen the gold coins that Miss Dinwiddie sewed and there's one with a savage dent. God Almighty, he says. God Almighty.

It's our good fortune that them mules ain't at all mulish and come with us because now I must take off that dress and put on trews again. Still I'm finding a man can wear trews and be womanish still. Oh, a person sure may need a deal of nonsense in his head to make way in a life. That's what I'm finding. The mules we bought in Muskegon are just the same way. Boethius Dilward would not have to lay the stick across these rumps. Supposed to be stubborn and they as faithful as hounds. Nature ain't all, that's clear and certain. John Cole look like he'd kill you easy and not think much about it after but the way he tends to Winona says volumes otherwise. The big thing is she been shot by a rifle which is a mighty hard-running bullet even if the bullet was took by the coin. She going to have a big bruise across her belly and anyhow she still out cold. We got that ratlike feeling that people might be creeping up on us so we got to go either way. Looks like that whiskery gentleman was shot bad enough maybe even in the stomach which will hopefully halt his gallop for good but we don't know that for certain. If I was him I would be watering in the mouth wanting to get back at us. Could be coming up like a dark alligator now through the vicious underbrush. Goddamn brambles and poison weed and I'd say rattlesnakes and cottonmouths too only it's so icy cold. Goddamn dark and drear Tennessee with its killer boys. We got to make haste and get to Lige. Lucky then Winona come to. Is I dead? she says. No, not yet, says John Cole.

Winona says she can sit her mule again and I

guess she won't feel the pain till later. Like sticking an invisible spear in her, that thwarted bullet. Going to be sore soon enough. Winona a girl of maybe thirteen, fourteen years, so why she so brave? Where you get that gun? says John Cole. Beulah gave it for going away, she says. If Mr Lincoln had her he'd a won his war easier. Goddamn filthy goddamn war but I guess you got to fight them. Everything bad gets shot at in America, says John Cole, and everything good too. Much-lamented Mr Lincoln the goddamn proof. John Cole leads his mule and Winona's out and I take the pack mule and my own. Going to be oats for these mules if we make it. We come down on the dark road and the moon has rose up a ways and he shines his light along the frozen way. The frost picks up the silvery illume. You could feel you was in an old storybook it's all so strange. We mount up gingerly and John Cole casts a glance at our good girl Winona and he tells her to ride in front so he can see if she falls off in the darkness. I be all right, she says. Hey, Thomas, you keep looking back just in case, he says. I will, I say. So we ride on the whole night and we ain't going to even dream of bedding down and sleeping. The night sky clears the way it does all of its choosing. Just the moon now high and bright like a lamp seen through a dusty window-glass. You got to wonder how things are up there? Some say the moon is like a coin, the very coin that just saved Winona. Big disc of silver like that might be

205

worth a bit. Some say you could catch it if you could reach that far. Must be some ways off anyhow. The cold is creeping under our hatbrims and down our collars. The cool cold light of the moon. The trees go silver before it like they was followers of the silver moon. Kentucky with all its critters and scattered souls sleeping, even the trees maybe sleeping. The moon is wide awake like a hunting owl. We hear the Kentucky owls screeching over the damp cold marshes westward. They trying to find each other in the tangled mess of trees. I feel of a sudden lighter than I were. I give thanks fierce and quick that Winona is alive. The mules treading along so mulish graceful and only their choosy footfall sounding. Otherwise the usual full sounds of night. Something cracking through the wood, bear or elk maybe. Maybe the wolves come hungrily through the brush. The sky is just beaten silver now too and the moon alters his light a shade to make sure he seen. Now has a coppery yellow tinge. My heart is full of Winona but also John Cole. How come we got to have Winona? I don't know. We been through many slaughters, John Cole and me. But I am as peaceful and easy now as I ever been. Fear flies off and my box of thoughts feels light. I'm thinking, John Cole looks big for the mule. I'm thinking of all the cities and towns I never been to and I don't know who's in them and they don't know me. Yep, he sure looks big for that mule. Like the mule and him ain't in the same world exactly. Then he pulls his hat down tight. Ain't nothing in it. He pulls his hatbrim down, under the moon. With the dark trees around. And the owls. Don't mean nothing. Be hard to be in the world without him. I'm thinking that. That part of the country you see two or three shooting stars a minute. Must be time of year for shooting stars. Looking for each other, like everything is.

Winona bent over further and further and then grew in hardship and her face were blanched by pain and at daybreak I cut two poles and braced them with a third for a travois and tied what we had spare between and covered her with my dress and pulled her along on that. She was so slight it were like drawing a leaf. She never moaned once though she could of moaned free as she like considering. I'd a moaned good let me tell you. Strike from a bullet's like Death's brother. I'll say.

Lige Magan's letter it said to pass quietly around the town of Paris by means of a sheltering wood to the west and when we come out the other side we would reach a creek and then to follow the trail along the bank of that creek westward so we did that.

CHAPTER 18

We can see Lige's need straight off even as we move along the trail. Beautiful creek running like an endless frosted beard. Field upon field of worried-looking land. Tall blackened weeds and some festering crop half won. This yellowed land and then the frighted-looking sky stretching away to heaven and all on the horizon the stubs and spikes of unknown black trees. Then hills heaping away into the distance and stubborn forest and even further maybe mountains with their Jewish caps of snow. But not enough hands to make good these fields that's clear. Don't have the spruced-up spank of work. Ain't in army order nor shipshape neither. We come slow up to the house and there's old Lige with his crown in blessed white and his smile cutting open his mouth above a long white-speckled meg. No hat and the hair a fume of smoke. Queer to see him in civilian garb that's certain. Colour Sergeant Magan. That bore the colours of the regiment. Come down his steps onto the tamped sand and took our hands in his. By God his eyes are shining. Hey, Lige, how is it? It's good, it's good.

Then we telling him about Winona and the man with the whiskers and Lige says he knows that man. He ain't no colonel but was something in the yellowleg army right enough. Those boys with him was boys of his command. They been ranging round doing mischief and hanging blacks. We said we seen his work along the way. That's it, says Lige. You might expect to see that man again if he live, he says. Tach Petrie is his name. Tach Petrie, I think they call him, says Lige.

Man we got a lot to do other than worry about Tach Petrie and his possible demise or resurrection. Lige got a nice woman called Rosalee that tends Winona. She fetches in and lifts her to the house. My dress kinda lifts in the breeze and slides onto the ground. Whose dress that? says Rosalee, that Mrs Cole's? Where she? We don't have an answer for that. That Rosalee sets Winona on a trestle by a big long fire. Trying to think back when I saw Lige so happy. Guess he's mighty relieved. Rosalee got a brother works with Lige. Tennyson Bouguereau. They's freed Negroes and Tennyson works five acres for a share. All they had before us was a winded mare to plough. A mule worth three times a horse up here, says Lige. Mule like gold. He's so happy to see four. I say these the best mules ever lived in my opinion. Told him about the pack mule and Winona's riderless mule running with us. Hot damn, says Lige. Who'd a known a thing like that was possible. We ask him has he heard from Starling Carlton and how's he

209

doing. Lige says he hears everything west of the North Platte river and the plains in general all gone to pot. Sioux rampaging. Caught-His-Horse-First been seen and has a new band. All going to hell in a bucket. Says he heard Dan FitzGerald come home from Andersonville and is topping trees in Alaska. That real good, I say. Surprised to hear that. Thought he was a goner for sure. Yup, says Lige, he made it.

We kinda settle in like settlers. Find the tune of Tennessee. At this time I got a wounded mourning dove put by accident into my keeping. John Cole finds it in the woods with a bent wing. He is as close as ever man was to a vole for creeping round. There are days when no sound is heard. When veins of long light to the solemn earth descend. Sometimes it get so still and quiet I hear no one and it's like the world is over. God damn it John Cole steals in one soundless noon with a wooden box. He sits with me a while and all the while he is chattering I am hearing this rattly hemming and hawing in the box. I am looking at it. It's amusing John Cole to catch me curious. John Cole was talking about the new opera house in Memphis and how we should go down and see it. John Cole got such a big beard these times he look like he was on the Rebel side. Could of fought at Appomattox under Lee or something worse. He looks like a goddamn yellowleg colonel but I don't like to say so immediately. Because he beautiful anyhow. Time goes by and he's waxing about the singers that tour about the country like queens and such and then he spreads his arms and sorta cocks his face as if to say, well, I guess you was wondering what I brought? Well, I was, a little. So then he opens the lid and up pops this head, all curvy beak and beady eye. He says would I like to nurse her back? I said I would like, mostly. What mighten you want to call her? he says. Well, I'll call her General Lee, since that's what you kinda look like these days. You ain't kind, he says. General Lee hops out of her box and takes command. Then she's shitting on the old table.

Then we go burning land for Lige all January. Labouring at seed beds for his tobacco and then covering them with long linen rolls against the cold. Then snow beds us in and Tennyson sings old songs and Rosalee proves a lunatic on the washboard. Lige got a fiddle and you never heard such stomping. Winona heals and she the worst crazy of us all, whirling and stepping like a bronze flame. Lige got his salted beef and the mules are battened in the big tobacco barn which is caulked so good they must think they are in Typee. We tell them about our act for Mr Noone and then I'm obliged to don the frilled knickers and valise shoes and show them what we done. I don a straw dolly for a wig so it's all in fun. That's a two-candle act, says Lige, and lights another so he can see. Light from the fire makes my shadow big against the walls. I don't know if they feel the effect but maybe Tennyson looks shook and stunned. I ain't got the looks now but the light is kind. Guess a stranger peeking in would be mighty thrown. Two Negroes and a ancient farmboy gazing on. Inexplicable dame for sure. Gives me strange joy.

Snow goes then we're ploughing like our lives depend which they do. Now the four mules are hitched and show their worth and plough forty acres back and forth three times. The land is lined for plants and then the little plants is brought into the fields and one spikes the earth with a peg and another plants a plant and another gives it water and a feed. And Tennyson sings his African songs and when we're stooped in the trees for midday dinner Lige oftentimes plays the fiddle so that the notes go into the woods to twitch the sleeps of birds. Never work so deep and hard and never sleep so deep. Then we harrow the earth between our growing plants and walk along day after day topping and pinching flowers and cancelling sports. Winona the merciless killer of the hornworms. Fat green boys. The summer comes and blows the land with heat. Then it's thin shirts and dirty hands and sweat abounding. And we grow in friendship like proper army boys. Lige's pa sent Rosalee to school and she wise as Socrates on many things. She and Winona thick as thieves and I don't know but we could of done with Tennyson in many a fight. I never saw a man shoot good as him except Lige. He sets a twig up on a fence pole then splits it from fifty feet. That can't be done. Then weeks of harvest leaf by yellow leaf and leaves tied to sticks and sticks brought into the barn and the stove lit till the mules think they're in hell. Bushels of sparks fly out the door and more wood goes in. Like the barn were a great steam engine bound for someplace. Then when the leaves are proper sere the doors of the barn is oped and the good heavy air of fall let in to plump them. Then they is bound in layers and flattened and bound in bales. Then down to market in the town of Paris and the big carts carry them down to Memphis. And Lige gets paid and then we try the small glasses of whisky as pure as salt. Go running down through Memphis town as alight as any stove and then do things that none remember and then home. Then we do praise the world for having good things in it. Lige buys a few horses. And now we're November yet again and no crop needing more care and giving more back never known as tobacco. Lige's paid in gold because that's the only thing will do. The South is rank with notes. Might as well stuff them in the stove with wood.

Flowers draw bees and gold draws thieves. Guess that's a rule. A law. Guess they know when you're drawing home with pay. So we keep our guns primed and Lige obliges the succour of his fear by keeping two rifles just in case. We're always armed and ready. The frost has crisped the farm again and the long weeds hang down black into the creek. Bears looking for winter houses. The birds that don't crave winter disappear and the robin holds his ground. Half of our pride is in

Winona and the other half in our work and in ourselves. Maybe me and John Cole restored. We're strong and hard. Our faces cleared as if two fields by fire.

Oftentimes in that goosedown bed we talk of all our days. Lie side by side staring up at the spider-webs in the roof. We go back over things that occurred and talk them back into the present time. We believe we seen a fair bit. One way or another. John Cole wondering what we can do for Winona. Says she needs a skill. Blackface ain't the thing. Got to be colleges somewhere for her kind. One thing he did in early fall was try to get her into schooling but the school in Paris wouldn't take no Indian girl. And she a better girl than any living in America, John avers. Goddamn bitter-hearted world. Goddamn pig-headed world. Blind souls. Can't they see what she is?

Tach Petrie comes in his own good time. Guess that's how it was. Guess he had wounds to heal. One morning early waking we seen him standing far out on the farmland just outside a covert of old trees. We're standing in Rosalee's kitchen drinking coffee. Yesterday hail fell in great rocks that would kill a dog but there's no sign of them now. He looked alone there in his black clothes and his gun laid across his arm. The stalks of the baccy plants still sticking up waiting for new flames. Going to be doing that job shortly and all the long work to start again. It don't daunt us. I remember it as thinking I known it was Tach Petrie but at that distance how could I have known? Memory don't like nothing but itself. He came on and now far to his left and right arose two others. Suddenly were there like ghosts. Testing the ground maybe. Could have snuck up from the land along the creek but chose this instead. It's early and we maybe sleeping but still he stops just out of rifle range. He knows that range like a measuring rod. Bullet would hit him and fall off his jacket like a acorn. Lige says his reputation were for a coward but he don't look like a coward this bright cold morning. We got two rifles and our two muskets and Rosalee and Winona are detailed to reload them when needed. Rifles just quicker and a store of shots. Lige and Tennyson take them and draw a bead along the barrels and they sitting in old chairs and from behind they look like children asleep on a father's shoulder bent like that. But they watching Tach. Lige as all the world knows is a sharpshooter and there ain't a trace of doubt in him. Three men going to die and it ain't going to be anyone he loves or likes. Goddamn foolish yellowlegs, is what he says. Lost the war and going to lose this too. Then up from behind Tach Petrie somewhere rises after all about half a dozen more men. This makes Lige raise his head from his gun. He don't say a word. Best check out back, he says to Rosalee. Stick your head out and make sure we not cooked on both sides. Rosalee clatters back through the house. Now fear creeps in like a hungry cockroach. Pit of the stomach troubled by it. I think I just might throw up that coffee. We got muskets trained on the two flanking men but we don't have no troops in reserve to serve death to those new men. We still got the shelter of the house. Guess they'll be happy if they can kill us today. Guess that other evening must have rankled. Crazy thought jumps into my head that I should don that dress. Crazy head thinking crazy. Tach Petrie comes on. It got a kinda military feel to it. Now the men go down and start to work along fallen trees and fences and woodpiles and whatever shelters. Now they maybe in range. Rosalee comes back and says she can't see nothing sinister. She put the bar on the back door. Shutters fast on the windows. There's been rain and floods so great just recent the ground between the house and the creek be only a quagmire. No man would try that slope. That's true, says Lige. But this no man, this a devil and killer of men. Rosalee Bouguereau puts a hand on her bosom. Even so, even so. Now the wide land in front of the house looks empty. Where those boys? It's cold just waiting and the fire ain't lit. We got the windows up for firing and here comes the frosty wind crowding in. Porch keeps our place in shadows and hopefully the front looks just blank and black. Then you see a man running like a jackrabbit to make a new hide. Down he goes. There's another. Creeping up on you like a childhood game. Lige has his snout down on his gun muzzle now and his head cocked sideways and he's still as a painting. No, he won't want to fire till he sees at least three men and then he'll be happy to let them know we're awake. Probably don't have a God's clue. We hope. But anyhow then Lige fires. Beautiful long clean shot that tears the hat off a running man and top of his head too, you can see far off as it is the big splash of blood. Man falls heavily and then Tennyson got a bead on one and fires. Man that can split a twig at fifty feet ain't got no trouble shooting a running man. That's two, we're thinking. Fire's returned and they're just hoping to pot a rabbit blind. Everything quiet for a little and then I see three men reach the tobacco sheds. Get in behind the gable. A long cloud of dark unhelpful rain takes the pitch of colour off things. Brown and black world suddenly with the old smear of red paint across the sheds. Weather and time a good stripper of paint. We know straight off someone's going to have to go out and head them off. This creeping up and waiting no good. Got to make a new vantage. Looks like the other four keeping well spread apart. But the three at the sheds ain't peering out so that must mean they're snaking round the back. That's got to be down to me since my brain thinking that way. John Cole knows what I'm doing. He gets it without a word. So then I'm stooping and cross the floor and I lift the bar on the back door and Rosalee puts it back behind me, I hear the loud scrape. Just got a little ways to go in the open. I'm going to make my way round the big barn and then expect to see those creepers. I got a musket but also Lige's repeating pistol, I ain't naked. Feel cool and calm like I was going quiet for trout. Trout lying under a dark rock and don't make a noise on the bank. Go, go, go. I hear firing behind me, a big clatter of firing, and bullets whining, both from the house and from the field. That puts vinegar on my cuts. Where are these lousy sonsabitches? Lousy sons creeping up and why didn't their mothers tell them it were wicked to kill men? I inch my face around the barn gable. I see the three now, faced away at ninety degrees. The rain suddenly falls and steams down on their heads and my head. They're more in the wind's way and the wind burns against them like an ally. Only one has a long black coat and the rest look cold as orphans. I shoot the back man with the musket, drop it down, and pulling out the pistol fire on the second. Think I only wing that man and then I got to rush the first man or the deal is done. Still the big firing from the house front, but I can't see. I don't have no contract with no God and I ain't God's soldier nohow but I'm praying He will guard and keep Winona. You in the middle of a gunfight all you will think about's Winona. John Cole can watch hisself. He's canny. Lige and Tennyson. Rosalee she grown and wise. But Winona a flower of a girl and she's our task. This man I'm bearing down on I see him clearer now. One of those ragged blear-eyed wandering types. Looks like a man might have walked out of some old life. Irish, God knows where. Walked out of some old life to here, with some crazy man he don't know running at him. I get off two shots but my wanderer he quick and gets behind a trough. Then I'm the duck in the window and I got to throw myself through the air to make a shelter. Big old lump of iron was the case of some old boiler. The man's bullets strike the iron, one, two, and make a sort of chord of noise. The Tennessee rain stops short and anyone would swear that Mr Noone or his celestial brother raised a great curtain from this stage of death. Big light of Tennessee dropped down. A flood of white and silver. The house is firing like a great corps of men and between the sheds and the barn I spot that Tach Petrie running, and waving his hand at his men out of view. Ain't going to hit with a pistol from where I am. Going to have to storm that damn trough and the pig behind it. Well, God help me too in this endeavour, I'm thinking. I make my play. Here is the one big card of Life thrown down. God assist me, won't You? Up I leap and try to make the gap. I feel a bullet tear across my shoulder. Or maybe my ear. I can't tell. Or maybe my head. But down I go. Goddamn fool. The pistol bursts from my hand and goes skittering across the ground. My foe jumps out and runs at me back-bent. Don't move, don't move, he says. All hisses and curses. Stands on my hand and says, you move, you dead. Just move that hand one inch, you dead. I believe him. I look up and his dark and bitter face looking down. Strange eyes and face all puckered with scars. Looks like the world's worst tailor stitched him. Still the guns blasting away and then suddenly silence and then voices. You move, you dead, the man says again. I'm surprised even by his mercy so far. Why don't he just kill me? But men are strange and killing men are stranger. Then the big shooting starts again and I see flashing in the gap the running men, maybe Tach Petrie and his men are trying a rush. Firing and firing and men calling out. Queer to be there at the back of the barn with the new sky rearing like horses and as if we was breathing in a puddle of quiet. Me and that squinty man. This where it going to end then I don't want to live without Winona and John Cole. Great clatter of bullets again and then silence again. My man looks left quickly to see what's what. He don't know the outcome no more than me. Hey, Tach, he calls, Tach Petrie? He don't get no answer back. Tach Petrie, God damn it? But then a miracle occurs. There's another man comes stepping round the sheds. Another man, not ours or theirs. A big solemn hefty man with sweating face. Heavy staring oxlike eyes. I know that face. My foe don't even see him. The fat man fires. Takes off half my new friend's face. The blood falls on my head, mingles with my blood. Jesus holy Christ. Where did he come from? Starling Carlton.

He don't even say hello and he goes to the gap between the sheds and barn and starts shooting there. I'm wiping blood out of my eyes and the world is a ringing bell but I drag myself along and stand at his big back and peer out and see Tennyson standing straight up on the porch with his rifle ranged and firing out across the fields at figures running for the scrubby copses. Rosalee standing with a box of bullets and Tennyson only pausing to reload his Spencer. Then firing like a veritable trooper and also Starling firing and maybe Tennyson thinks it's me. One foe man nearly made it to the house but he's splayed in death and another further back has fallen and is just a black brushstroke on the frost. The rain that fell has frozen on the earth and that's the tale it told. Then curious peace descends and the firing echoes in your brain and it's like we taste the moments ticking by for Death but Death retreats. I yearn to know what's happened in the house and why is John Cole not took his share of firing on the porch? Why our old galooting friend's sprung up might be another question. My ear is spouting blood and the bell of time is queerly tolling and maybe then down I fall. Before I fall completely Starling stoops and drags me up and hoiks me against his shoulder. Goddamn Irish, he says, never could abide them.

CHAPTER 19

M e and Starling go back round by the barn because we don't want Tennyson killing us for good measure. So we come up the back of the house. Inside we got Lige Magan kneeling to John Cole. First I think he's dead but he just had his eyes closed the moment I come in. Then he opens them and sees Starling. Jesus, he says, what you doing here, Sarge? He just appeared like a angel, I says. If that's a angel I ain't going to heaven, says Lige Magan. Where in the name you sprung from, Starling? Lige says. There's a pour of blood coming out of John Cole's thigh. How he got a bullet in a thigh beats me. Must of shot him through a chink in the log wall. Jesus, John Cole, I say, you hurt bad? I see Winona over against the kitchen wall. She's pale as a summer sky. Now Rosalee comes back in and Tennyson must be keeping a weather eye open still on the porch because he don't follow her. I rummage around in the wound with the horseshoe pliers to get that bullet and then Starling and Lige sit on John Cole and I give the wound a poke with the smoky poker and there's a smell of John Cole burning. He lets out a roar wouldn't shame a donkey. Holy merciful God, he says. I hope those killer boys don't come back, Lige says. They ain't coming back because we killed too many, says Rosalee. I think we got the most of them, says Tennyson, just come in. I shot Tach Petrie anyhow, he says. You did good, says Lige.

An hour later we're just looking at the coffee Rosalee's prepared. No one drinks. Well, Starling, says Lige, what the hell brings you here? Starling ain't a man for a slow story. He tells it. I here on different business, he says. I weren't here to save you sorry boys. I is surprised you living such reckless lives with murdering thieves and such creeping up. Now, Starling, what this other business? Well, I'll tell you, he says. Then he tells us. Caught-His-Horse-First has took Mrs Neale and her two girls. Then he were seen over in Crow country. That a mighty big country but the major and two hundred men ride for days. Not a trace of the Sioux. Next day come into the fort a German trader with a message from Caught-His-Horse-First. Says he killed the woman and the child with black hair. He wants his sister's child and he'll give the other white child in barter. Then, he says, he will make another treaty and then there will be peace on the plains. Starling says the major's face look like someone painted him with whitewash. Never saw a human person so white and strange. And who's his goddamn sister's child, Lige Magan asks. That that Injun kid there, Starling says. So, says Starling, the major wants to know where to find her and I says I know, she's with John Cole and Thomas McNulty in Tennessee. Well, go down to Tennessee and ask them to bring her back, the major says – please God they will. John Cole's groaning on the bed. It's the worse idea I ever heard! he cries. Goddamn it. Then Starling Carlton is shouting things and John Cole shouting back. Something in my stomach lurches. Then Winona steps in close to him, touches his hand on the ragged sheet. I got to go back, she says. John Cole's staring at her then and don't say nothing. I guess he feels the force of some strange justice in her words. He's white as a apple core. I ain't letting you, he says. Mrs Neale was kind and good, she says. I owe her. You're a good girl, Winona, he says, God knows, but you ain't going back. No, but I got to, she says. Well, you ain't.

The whole thing decided the next morning when Winona and Starling Carlton gone. She's took a horse from the field. Must have left in the small hours. John Cole can't shift so I get another horse from Lige and set off after. Can't be but six hours ahead. I'll catch them. I ride like a devil for a bit but then can't risk winding my horse. It's deep December and this ain't no season for a trip to Wyoming – that what they calling that country nowdays. Three days later I come up into Nebraska. Guess I'm seeing the signs here and there, hoof-prints in the thin snow, or think I do, but it could be anyone. I asked every farmer I passed in

224

Missouri did they see a fat man travelling with a squaw? Starling's pushing on hard for sure. After four days I know I ain't going to catch him and it irks me now when night falls, but I got to sleep too. Only human nature. I got to kill what I can on the way but it mostly birds and jackrabbits and at least I got dried beef. One afternoon way off in the distance I see a vast low pancake of smoke rising off what seems to be a visitation of blackness. It's a herd of buffalo that strangely lifts my heart. Must be in their thousands but too far south for me to try my good fortune. The big Platte river sits somewhere north of me and I know there was an Irishman for every buffalo digging out the railroad in these late years. They say the Pawnee in ferocious temper all round here and I am nearly afraid to strike my lucifers to make a fire but in the night the glass falls to the positions of death. I hope Starling finds water and food if only for Winona's sake. Then it's a blizzard comes. A woeful blizzard with wind so sharp it would shave off your beard. All I can see is the moon of my compass. The blizzard blows five days and when it stops I ain't no wiser. Surprised to see scattered farms and houses in western Nebraska where once there was only the strange sea of grass. Onto the big trail now but no one runs oxen this late in the year. If they even come this way now. The new railroad rolls on into eternity but the rails as silent as the rocks. The land all silver white and the sky high and loathsome dark. Ain't a soul to see. Snow lies two feet deep and the poor horse don't like it. I come through a little patch of graves where Irish and Chinee buried. Just a little scrap of ground with a wooden fence in all that winter-hampered silence. That night there's a great jamboree of lightning and noise that makes the far hills stand out black as burnt bread and then I got to hobble my horse and hunker against a rock. Thunder so loud it frights the dreams out of my head. Memories flying out. Just wanting Winona. Something about the major's loss gnaws at my heart. But I'm wanting Winona.

When I get to the fort at last I am inclined to feel some relief. The picket lets me pass without a word. I go straight to the major's office without even searching for Starling. I got to go where the decisions is made. That's how it is. I go in and I see the major. His face is thin and white. He don't look like the man I knew. He comes straight over from his table and takes my right hand in his. He don't even speak. In the creases of his sere face there is what looks like redness painted. It just don't look right. He looks like he swallowed a live rattlesnake and it's biting him from the inside. Striking again and again and he don't flinch. He says something about his gratitude. He says it's all set for tomorrow and messages been sent. If I want a ninety-day signing he can give it and rescind it when it's done. I can't find the damn words to tell him why I came. He must think I came up with Starling. On his table is a daguerreotype of

Mrs Neale that was likely taken about the time he married her. Maybe old Titian Finch hisself it was who took it. He catches me looking at it. In his eyes I see a glimmer of his old self. He says something about Angel his daughter and then I say I can't credit that Mrs Neale is gone. Mrs Neale is gone right enough, he says, and Hephzibah too. That's it, he says, you are quite right. That Captain Carlton was going to fetch you was the only thing that kept me breathing. Please God tomorrow we'll have Angel back. We've put a drummer boy's uniform on Winona, he says, to show what we think of her. I just can't find the words that John Cole would need me to find. I'm staring back at him and then I am saluting and going out. The return to the fort bathes me in past times. Strange shadows and voices eddy back. Troopers that once I knew and the horrible singing and bitter character of Sergeant Wellington. Every life has its days of happiness despite the ugly Fates. I seen plenty men pass in my mind from something admirable to something you don't care about. But not that whittled major. That's what I'm thinking I guess. That straightforward man that never could bear injustice.

Next business is to find Winona and find out how she fares. Two weeks with Starling Carlton would wear out St Paul. I'm so hungry I could eat the head of John the Baptist but first I go searching. Starling is captain of A Company and that's where I find her. She's sitting by the stove in her new attire and by God for a second I think she's a boy right enough. She got her shining black hair stuffed into her forage cap. But up she springs and rushes over to me. The most affectionate drummer boy in the history of the army. How that Starling treat you? I says. He never spoke the whole way, she says. He never said a word? Only gived me orders, where to sit, to lie. Goddamn strange and blighted soul, I said. Then Starling hisself clumps in making the wooden floor bounce. He stops to gauge what I'm about and he draws out his revolver. You step back from her, he says, or I shoot you now, you filthy Judas. Holy Christ, Carlton, I says, hold your horses. I ain't gainsaying you.

It's with strange and darksome tread that I go over to the requisition depot and draw my corporal's uniform. I dress right there among the shelves and the quartermaster's clerk does his best as always to fit such a wren-sized man and he gives me my belt and accoutrements and I keep my own shoes. Ain't going to suffer in a pair of army brogues. The armoury issues a rifle and a gun. And as I'm tying my shirt and tucking in my balls I don't know what gets into me. The years fall away and it's like the first day in barracks with John Cole. St Louis a thousand years in the past. And in my mind's eye too I see him lying in bed in Tennessee with the hole in his thigh. I see him just a ragged gossoon the first moment I met him under a hedge in

228

Missouri. I am dizzy with visions of John Cole. I wonder am I betraying this man most dear to me. Maybe I am, maybe I am. But I'm also praying for things I don't even have names for and that sit in the dark of my mind unknown.

That German trader's been busy as a dung-fly. He's going to lead us to the meeting place. Don't know where the dollars are in it for him but he's a little cross man with no hair and a foreign-looking hat. I'm told he got shares in the new railroad town of Laramie a hundred miles to the south but I don't credit that. He's donned a white striped suit that wasn't washed since the Flood receded. Someone says his name is Henry Sarjohn which don't sound very German to me. Mr Sarjohn likes his tobacco anyhow and chews it in a big wet froth in his mouth. When he talk to the major he keeps turning his head and spitting. We're going to be two days riding and we ain't bringing cannon that I can see. There's five regiments full-brimmed with men in the fort because fear of the Sioux has made inroads on government hearts. They went into another treaty in '68 but the rail-road beginning to bust out the land. I could fancy riding with five thousand. But only two companies are allowed by Caught-His-Horse-First for this fandango. That's two hundred soldiers and his band is said to have growed to three hundred. Doesn't bother the major. He's going to get his daughter. Maybe he thinks if he don't it don't matter how many soldiers in the field. He'll be happy to die. He got that look to him. Desperate and gathered. Like a man on a high bridge thinking to jump. You'd nearly be a-feared of him. Starling Carlton is mounted on a big grey horse and it's the coldest day yet in the year and of course he's sweating. Pouring down into his collar and it hangs on his eyebrows in tiny icicles. He surely is the most unnatural bugger in Christendom. We ride at the back of the companies and Winona's tucked in close to us. You sure, I say, you sure? I can run us out of here easy, just give me the signal. I sure, she says, and gives me her smile. Goddamn it, I say. Didn't they give you a drum with that uniform? I say. No, they didn't, she says. She's laughing then. I ain't laughing, I ain't laughing. If I still got a heart it's breaking.

Trying to figure out this plan. We going to give Winona to her uncle and then take back Angel Neale. What happens to Winona after? They think she's going to don Sioux skirts and speak Sioux again? Not sure folks are thinking about Winona. I know they are not. Starling Carlton just loves his blessed major and will effect all in his power to succour him. Of course he will. Major the fairest man I ever met but he been filleted out with the knife of grief. Men I knew well in former days still in the company and it's so strange to be clad in blue again. Little Sarjohn he rides out ahead and bobs about on his mule like he know what he's doing. Those familiar hills now dressed in the lace and shawls of winter. Even in distress the land seems to solace you. Guess the black truth is it crosses through our hearts.

Starling Carlton leads my old company and I got my corporal work to do. There's a strange yellow-faced fella called Captain Sowell who leads Company A. Looks like his cheeks were shaved from wood and he got Dundrearies just like Trooper Watchorn years ago. Man's got a thorn bush each side of his nose you'd say. Starling Carlton ain't inclined to speak to me so I don't ask him nothing. I doubt if he trusts me but I ain't planning nothing but to keep Winona safe. Now she's ordered up beside the major who's mounted on his fine black mare. When you see a horse like that you know you been riding a sorry nag all through Nebraska and Wyoming. Her coat gleams in the silvery glamour of the snow-light. It's a long time since I rode with the major and all the old medicine of loyalty floods into my heart. Suddenly I feel sorely four or five sorrows. The loss of old comrades in times past. The dead in battles. The murder of Mrs Neale, a gentle woman. Somewhere in the back of all that are other matters. The shady ghosts of my family long gone by in Sligo. Sligo. A word I hardly even sounded in private thought in a decade of years. The filthied dress of my mother floats behind my eyes. My sister's pinafore ruined by Death. The thin cold faces. My father lengthwise like a smear of yellow butter. A stain. His tall black hat as crushed as a squeezebox. Sometimes you know you ain't a clever man. But likewise sometimes the fog of usual thoughts clears off in a sudden breeze of sense and you see things clear a moment like a clearing country. We blunder through and call it wisdom but it ain't. They say we be Christians and suchlike but we ain't. They say we are creatures raised by God above the animals but any man that has lived knows that's damned lies. We are going forth that day to call Caught-His-Horse-First a murderer in silent judgement. But it was us killed his wife and his child. The first Winona. And many more that were kin to him. Our own Winona was wrested from these plains. We took her like she were our natural daughter. But she ain't. What is she now? Plucked all two ways and there she is dressed as a drummer boy in the cavalry of the United States and easily laughing. She pleased to her soul to be answering the hurt of the major because the major's wife once showed her kindness. Winona, the queen of this o'erwhelming country. God damn it but a corporal best not weep. And John Cole lying in our bed at home and wondering what I'm doing. Ain't I treasoned him and gone back on my true word? The world ain't all just grasping and doing. It's thinking too. But I ain't possessing the brain to think it all clear. A snowfall made mostly of dark gaps and wind starts to fall on my black folly. The companies ride on with a German jackanapes in front. But no man such a jackanapes as me.

Caught-His-Horse-First don't straight off show

his face. His boys are waiting at the back of a deep glen. Trees on slopes so steep you wonder how could they manage there. Dark evergreens rushing up towards the sky as if a kinda fixed fire. A cold crowd of silver birches at the base like maidens at a wedding. The Sioux seem changed to me. Ain't got no feathers in their get-ups and their hair looks cut by barbers. They got every strange scrap of whiteman's clothes you ever saw for sale. Rags mostly. Here and there the breastplates made of thin steel wire. These Sioux haven't helped us in the war and no one favours them much now. These recent dealings ain't put a polish on nothing. But the major sitting up straight in his saddle, peering about like he might see his daughter somewhere. A strange atmosphere over us, Indian and soldier. Like a performance about to begin in Mr Noone's hall. Soldiers glancing quickly at each other and no one likes the glistening and plentiful arms the Indians bear. Daggers and pistols too. There's a kinda look to them like we being met by tramps. No-good people. Their fathers owned everything here and we was never heard of. Now a hundred thousand Irish roam this land and Chinese fleeing from their cruel emperors and Dutch and Germans and boys born east. Poured in across the trails like a herd without an end. Every face before us look like it were slapped. Slapped and slapped again. Dark faces squinting out from under cheap hats. Beggars really. Ruined men. That's what I am thinking. Then up from the copsewood yonder rides Caught-His-Horse-First. I ain't seen him for many years. He got his war bonnet on and all his clothes is good. Musta made a special effort for the day. His face looks proud and cross as Jesus in the Temple. Riding a fine and lovely stallion and no bother to keep it reined. Looks like Sarjohn speaks the Sioux. Talking for a bit. Major just sits his horse now seeming placid and still like he was inspecting troops on the parade ground. I can only see the back of his head. His uniform too is brushed and good. His hatbrim's been furled nice by his subaltern. Probably slept on his uniform last night to crease it. Even when the line of Indians shivers back and opens a little gap and the major's child is led through the major doesn't stir. It's a nest of wasps and he ain't going to kick it.

Sarjohn comes back for Winona and Starling Carlton goes on up with her and in the little strip of wintry grass between the exchange is made. Caught-His-Horse-First swings round his horse and kicks its withers with his bare heels. Like a Confederate soldier he ain't got no boots. Winona goes trotting after. The Indians flow away in a sudden unity as if the air were a pushing flood. Here's Angel Neale. Can't be more than eight or nine. The fiery woods and a little girl. She's dressed as a young Sioux squaw. The major spurs forward and leans down to her small mount. Gathers her up like a loose parcel and swings her round behind him. Any man that wants to can hear her sobs. Then we turn as a body and head back.

234

CHAPTER 20

There's old sorrow in your blood like second nature and new sorrow that maddens the halls of sense. Causes an uproar there. I'm leaving Winona. I can never see John Cole again, I'm thinking. How would I find words to tell the story? A man that only got noughts to count can't get *1* for an answer. That night our journey back's half done and the officers' tent is pitched and soon it's full of lamplight. The plains stretch black and cold about and the pickets sing their songs in low voices as if hushed by the soaring night of blotted and unblotted stars. The companies bed down and seem content as human men. A great thing's been done, the rescue of their major's heart. I can see the major scribbling on maps with his daughter at his side. There's a glass of wine on his campaign table and the light slips through it so it looks like a hovering jewel. Now and then he looks at her. I am glad to witness that. But in my head there's riots.

Two days back in the fort and the major sended his daughter the hundred miles south to the new railroad town. She got a young lieutenant and two privates for an escort. They're going to bring her all the route to Boston so she can be in the protection of her mother's people. It's rumour now that the major will resign his commission and return to his wardrobe of civvies. Guess he's wearied of the desecrated vegetables. What in the Sam Hill I'm going to do I can't tell. I send a telegraph message with the young lieutenant for dispatching to John Cole. *Held Up Stop More Soon Stop Winona Safe Stop.* That was three lies for seventy-five cents.

Starling Carlton a high-up officer so it ain't as easy to snag him now. There's a lad called Poulson is a corporal like me from Jackson. He were one of them scalawags they talk about, fought for the Union. Nice boy with a bush of red hair on top so that his cap has trouble perching. Not an elegant boy but a decent one. Captain Silas Sowell has an easy way with subalterns. He's a pious man and don't like swearing so it ain't all plain sailing talking to him. Just trying to see my path ahead. Feel my way. Major Neale got a burning face and the troopers say he often shot in the head from whisky. Guess he's looking for his medicine there. He got his daughter but he still got two graves that assault his will. Fort's much bigger these times. Wives and camp whores, broke-down Indians abound. Thousands of horses and the lads to tend them. Crows still working as army wolves and they're top-notch boys. That night I try drinking in their camp because I want to know if they know something. They're good easy men. All they do all night is make fancy jokes. Big streeling long-tailed jokes. Half in Crow and half in English. Can't follow much of it. But they don't know nothing about Winona.

A day later and I'm stumbling 'bout like this and there's something happening. Whole four regiments being raised and readied. Right from reveille every man is mustered. All the companies drawn up and the horses stamping and snorting. The major is to lead this force because the colonel's away in San Francisco. That's what Poulson says. But where we going? I say. No one knows, he says, we're to get orders later. Just one regiment left to hold the fort. Otherwise we all pour out the gates. Line after line of cavalry men. A blue snake an eighth of a mile long. We got five new Gatling guns and a whole battery of Napoleon twelve-pounders. But it's no weather for campaigning. The ground is hard and bare and even out on the plains there won't be grass. Must be a quick sortie out and then return. No one seems to know. Worse still that ratlike German Henry Sarjohn's with us. He don't look happy and he's riding with downcast eyes. Poulson says the major don't like him and I'd say even his mother found it hard. We're heading exactly the same trail was took before and I don't know to be pleased or a-feared. Looks like we're heading back to the pines and the birch trees in that arroyo where we was before. Night falls but the major pushes us on. Under cold starlight we pursue our way. I'm trying to get sense from

Poulson but he knows nothing. I got to try Starling again. I rides up to him. Hey, Starling, where we headed? He don't say a word. Just looks ahead though he can't help a tiny glance from flickering towards me. A mealy-mouthed moon half rises and dimly burns. Like a lamp going low on oil. Just after the first fingers of sunrise we come to the same V-shaped valley. A pass at the top lets us through. Beyond is a slope of grey stone and speckled snow. A creek in the middle distance tries to pick up the light of the sun. Caught-His-Horse-First's tent village lies all below. What in the name of the suffering God?

Caught-His-Horse-First must be readying for his treaty because he's flying the Yankee flag. It's stuck up on top of the biggest teepee right in the centre of the village. Big coiling and uncoiling movement from our men. Batteries set up and the Gatling guns placed swiftly. We're not two hundred yards away and if they fire a gun they can't miss for tarnation. Winona, Winona! Guessing she's down there in that damn tent. The major has issued orders and now the captains take hold of their companies and everyone getting into place. You see the Indians moving about and the early morning fires in the care of the squaws. Some of them standing up now and looking at us across the gap. Seem mighty surprised as I am myself. Must be about five hundred souls to judge by the spread of wickiups and teepees. The creek behind softly smoking with mist. Then the ground rising to the fringes of a forest and the dark green acres then and then heaped up high the black mountains and the haircuts of snow on top. There's a silence now spread across our troops and a silence across the village and across the forest and across the mountains. All creation is puzzled and don't know to say a thing. Now Poulson is at my side and he gives me a glance. Here's Major Neale riding along the line. To every section of fifty men he shouting his orders. As he speaks there's about twenty braves running up from the village. They ain't even carrying arms. Just running towards us. Caught-His-Horse-First at the front. He's took down his flag and is running with it. He's waving it like it could be a word. Now Major Neale reaches our section. You're to fall on them, men, and leave nothing alive. Not a blade of grass standing. Kill them all. These ain't words that the major knows. Now Captain Sowell rides over and takes issue with his superior. That's a terrible sight for a soldier. Battle is an ill without officers shouting too. All the eyes of the men, four thousand or so, look on with shock. Caught-His-Horse-First gets to the fringe of the army. He's shouting too, and the major's shouting at Captain Sowell. We can't hear what the captain's saying back.

The whole body of the troopers seems to shudder with intent. We see other braves now running through the village with rifles. We see the women and the children starting to leave from the back. A great smoulder and ruckus of squaws. A screeching and shouting crosses over to us. Captain Sowell can do no other thing but to rejoin his company. The Gatling guns start to fire at the distant women. We can see them falling like they belonged in a different world. The Napoleons open fire with another tone of screeching and a dozen shells erupt in the village. Now the men going to do what they got to. Someone orders mayhem they got to deliver it. Otherwise likely they die instead. Now Caught-His-Horse-First has hesitated. He waves back his braves and starts to run. He runs just as good as a young 'un. His legs powering through the sagebrush. The major lifts his Enfield, steadies, and fires. The great Caught-His-Horse-First goes down, killed by his puzzlement. Leave nothing alive, cries the major again. Kill them all. And down we all surge like that huge river flood of old.

Who will tell you the reason of that day? Not Thomas McNulty. Guess what's savage in men was in our men that morning. Men I knew from aforetime and the new men I knew just days. Rushing down on the village like an army of coyotes. Braves fetch their guns and come bursting back out of their wigwams. Women crying and calling. The soldiers hollering like demons. Firing and firing. I see Starling Carlton at the head of his company, his sabre pointing against the foe. His face red as a wound. His corpulence balanced and dangerous. Poised like a murdering dancer. And everywhere strength and power and terror. Even in the heart of every trooper. Terror of dying and being second

240

with a shot. Bullet in your soft body. Kill them all. An order we never known. I rush on with them and when I get to the teepees I drop down from my horse. I ain't got one notion what to do only push on to the middle. I am praying to the soul of Handsome John Cole that Winona might be there. If she ain't there it's perdition. As I run through the teepees I get a queer sense of lightness. Like I got speed I don't got. I reach the many-coloured wigwam of the chief and plunge in through the opening. It's bigger than it looked and the first chill light of morning swims there. Then I got a body wrapped against me. There's a dozen squaws there but the limpet on me is Winona. Merciful God, I say, stay near me. We got to get out of here. Thomas, she says, please save me. I going to do all I can. I don't even look at these other ladies. I ain't going to be no help to them. They just staring at me with the open blank faces of emergency. All around us the pocking of guns and the whining and cursing of bullets. There's bullets passing through the wigwam and out another side. Even in the two seconds I am with them two or three of the squaws is knocked. These are Winona's people and my brain is now aflame. What chokes my throat is love. I ain't saying love for them but for her. I don't care if she ain't my daughter but all I know is the fiery feeling.

Back out I push, keeping Winona sheltered. But where in God's hell do I go? Maybe make for the bluff again. Get her back up with the Gatlings.

241

Fortunately for me she's still in her army garb. That surprises me but I'll take help from God or devil all the one. Two drummer boys was with us on their ponies but I didn't see them come down. It's not like a proper charge. But maybe the uniform is something to save us. Even if the flag weren't. God knows a trooper don't like to shoot blue. We're nearly out of the village and the fight is fierce and loud. As many bodies now as living maybe. I'm not looking as such but I see every-thing around me like I had a hundred eyes. Men have swept through on their mounts slashing with their swords and firing freely. I don't see one trooper on the ground killed or wounded. Now many have slipped from their horses and are killing with pistols and sabres. Why haven't the braves fired back? Maybe they ain't got no damn bullets left. Maybe they ain't got nothing. I curse at my heart and plead this be my last battle. If I can only get Winona away. Now here's big Starling Carlton and he's standing five feet off. Captain, I say, can you help us, please help us. This is John Cole's daughter. That ain't his daughter, roars Starling. Starling, it is, and I beg you, stand one side of her and help me. Don't you understand, Thomas McNulty? Everything changed now. We're to do what was said. We're to kill them all and leave nothing alive. But this is Winona, you know Winona. That ain't nothing but a squaw. Don't you know, corporal? These the killers of Mrs Neale. These the killers of his daughter. Stand aside,

242

Thomas, and I going to quench her life. We got our orders and by damn we going to do them. His body looks huge and puffed out. He like an adder going to strike. Sweat like the Deluge in the Bible. Hey, Noah, where your ark? Old Starling Carlton going to drown the world. I do love this man. We been through a thousand slaughters. Now he's lifting his pride, a shining Smith and Wesson pistol. In his belt he drags a beautiful Spencer rifle. Looks like he got his heart's desire. Starling Carlton, ain't nothing and is all the world. Every soul God's fashioning. He lifting the handsome gun. He going to shoot. I can see it. By Jesus I pull on my sabre like a doctor draws a thorn and it moves across the brief space of three feet and one half of the blade meets with Starling's big face and cuts in and cuts in till I see his eyes bursting and he don't even have time to fire and down he is felled, my old crazy friend. And I push on past him and I don't look back only crazy like him looking round to see any other snake or killing man might take Winona.

We keep running as best we can through the wigwams and out onto the frozen grasses. I'm looking about for my horse but she must have got the hell out of there and I didn't blame her. Got to make the higher ground behind the batteries. That the only place will seem like home. I got Winona by the hand now and we two soldiers running. Truth to tell she not much smaller than me. If there's bullets coming after us it's only a

243

hive of strays. Ain't no Indians firing now. Not a one. And as we reach the line of Gatling guns we pass Caught-His-Horse-First lying dead. The murderer of Mrs Neale and Hephzibah and here now the incredible price. What grace in this or God I could not say. Not much.

Seems like it were all the devil that day. Kill them all. Leave nothing alive. Everything was killed. Nothing left to tell the tale. Four hundred and seventy. And when the men were done killing they started to cut. They cut out the cunts of the women and stretched them on their hats. They took the little ball sacks of the boys to be dried into baccy pouches. They severed heads and hacked off limbs so they was not going to no heavenly hunting ground. The troopers came back up the hill lathered in blood and gore. Spattered with tendrils of veins. Happy as demons in the commission of demon's work. Exultant and shouting to each other. Drenched in a slaughter-house of glory. Never heard such strange laughter. Big hill-high sky-wide laughter. Clapping of backs. Words so black they were blacker than dried blood. Remorse not a whit. Delight and life perfected. Slaughter most desirable. Vigour and life. Strength and heart's desire. Culmination of soldiering. Day of righteous reckoning.

And yet in the days going back across the plains there was just deep exhaustion and queer silence. The mules drawing the guns with earnest intent. The mule-skinners herding them on. Troopers who had gathered back their mounts wearily submitting. A gopher-hole tripping up a horse enough to send a trooper falling like a greenhorn. Can't even eat their grub on the middle stop. Can't even remember their private prayers. Killing hurts the heart and soils the soul. And Captain Sowell looking as angry as old Zeus and as sick as a poisoned dog. He don't talk to no one and no one talking to him.

The other silent creature be Winona. I keeping her stuck close to me. I don't trust anyone. What we walked through was the strike-out of her kindred. Scrubbed off with a metal brush like the dirt and dried blood on a soldier's jacket. Metal brush of strange and implacable hatred. Even the major. Same would be if soldiers fell on my family in Sligo and cut out our parts. When that old ancient Cromwell come to Ireland he said he would leave nothing alive. Said the Irish were vermin and devils. Clean out the country for good people to step into. Make a paradise. Now we make this American paradise I guess. Guess it be strange so many Irish boys doing this work. Ain't that the way of the world. No such item as a virtuous people. Winona the only soul not thrown on the bonefire. She seen the worst now and seen it before. It makes her silent, so silent the silence of winter is like a clattering. No words in her now. I got to keep her close. Got to get back to John Cole and keep her close. I ask her plain what she wants me to do. I ask her three times and get no answer. Try a fourth time. Tennessee, Tennessee, she says.

CHAPTER 21

Out on the plains falls a deep sea of snow covering the battle site two days to the north. Covering the Sioux dead till the spring. The few dead troopers were took back before the snows and the burial details been busy in the boneyard. The buglers blown their frosty tunes. Cold clamps the upland and the bottomland with clamps as sure as iron. Tamps down the surge of trees and stills the creeks. Manhandles the bears into their dens I guess. Now from the further country of Montana Territory come the white wolf maybe and the white fox maybe and some say even the white bear. The trail going south-east's wiped out and all the scratch and scrape of man with it. It ain't peace because storms stomp madly over it and the upper sky is a smithy for lights and bangs but it ain't our violent war.

The fort's full of rumours. I got to wait till my papers is rescinded by the major until I can go. So Winona is lodged by the major in his cold quarters now emptied of all he loves. I guess he feels he must protect her all in all. She takes off that drummer boy's garb and climbs back in her travelling dress.

Major says she can take anything of his wife that fits and he ain't got no use for nothing now. He says that without showing sorrow which makes me more sorrowful than a bulldog's face. The whole business wretched and strange. Then getting even stranger when the colonel returns from California. So happens Captain Silas Sowell is his son-in-law so that's a voice he listens to. Captain Sowell still furious with the reddened fixed face of fury. Harry Sarjohn furious too in that his good faith with the Indians is all shot to perdition. Guess they're a joint tornado. I get all this from Poulson my friend. Rumour, rumour tearing round the fort. I long to catch that stage down to the new town. It stops just outside the gates and that's a busy six horses and a rackety coach. Army keeping the road clear so that's good. Got to have some way to run supplies up from the railroad depot. Going to be a long locked-in winter looks like. Me and Winona can't be caught here. Then outside of all expectation the major is arrested. Captain Sowell saying he went berserk out there and is guilty of gross misconduct. Vengeful sorrow working havoc on the Sioux. The Sioux was just readying up for a new treaty just as the flag being flown was saying. Caught-His-Horse-First due in Washington with the other chiefs of the plains. Now all this was put into outrageous jeopardy. Yes, that's so. It were a murderous act, that's the truth. Weren't nothing to do with nothing except the major's grief and that's most likely.

The queer kick in the rumour also tucks Starling Carlton into the story. Brave captain found dead and Harry Sarjohn says he saw a trooper do it. With a sabre. He don't *kennt* that trooper but he can point out his face maybe. Now, I never seen him near us. But he's sneaky alright. He got the sabre right, God damn it. You'd think he'd be pleased I was trying to protect a Indian since that's what his other caterwauling was about. So there's going to be a muster on the parade ground. Well that's a lot of faces. But I ain't in the heart's position to risk such a thing. I got to fold in Winona, I got to. So I goes to the camp barber, a decent man I knew from aforetime, by the name of George Washington Bailey. He a black man, the best barber ever stropped a blade. I ask him to close shave me like he often done and get every mortal whisker off. I'm wearing my hair what's called Southern long, that is, as long as another man's sense of right can bear. Then I cross the drear and wind-haggard ground to rouse Winona. Stage leaving four o'clock. Got two hours. I don't even go get my travelling gear and I got to leave my saddle and my horse. Winona too. Going to be army horses now I guess. Farewell. We don't lack for the dollars to get us home that's one thing. I skip in back of the major's place. Now he quartered elsewhere in the lock-up. So I guess there's luck in everything even havoc. I keep thinking crazy thoughts like they must of dug one big hole for Starling. I'd a never in my life wish to see that bugger dead and now it's me that killed him. Might be a small thing set inside that day of killing.

The major's rooms is quiet and cold and Winona ain't lit no stove or nothing. So I tell her we going at last but first I got to find a goddamn dress and then she got to help me daub my face. Winona knows where was the major's bedroom and going in there's like breaking someone's tomb. I ain't got no hearty wish to do it but needs must. Nothing's cleaned out of Mrs Neale. Her row of dresses hangs in the fancy wardrobe. Feels just like we was robbing her real body. Down comes a dress and God forgive me but I go to search out stockings. I can forgo the damn bloomers and the like because the skirt of the dress is to the ankle but I took the bloomers anyhow. I ain't robbing no goddamn bloomers anyhow since poor Mrs Neale in truth gone by. Then I pulled my hair tight on my crown and we choose a no-nonsense hat from among a aviary of birdlike fancies. Stuff that down. All the time feeling like a thief. What the hell has life come to, stripping the dead? I got to say I notice Winona don't see it so. She liked that Mrs Neale and maybe she loved her. Guess a dress is a token of her soul. She sits me at the dressing table and goes to work. Could be Grand Rapids afore the show but it sure ain't. Smears on the make-up, does the eyes with kohl, and paints the lips, looks at me dubious and shakes powder over all. I look like a ten-cent quick job whore. It's not going to be stage lights so we got to get it right. She rubs off the kohl so then I look like my best beau punched me. It don't matter. Tones down the lipstick. Then by God we're set if ever we could be set. Stuff all that business in her carpetbag and I obliged to steal the major's razor. I don't know how long this new-fangled journey will take us but I can't become no bearded lady.

Big heavy sky of threatening snow outside. A huge glob of dark cloud leaning on the roofs. There's a detail coming in and they make their clatter on the ground. Those boys been out some days and they look pulled and wearied. Shipshape too and sort of trimmed. Strikes me this work is kinda crazy noble and I never had that thought before exactly. Not just on the nose like that. Strange boil of love for them like the trout makes in the river. Their handsome youth given o'er to toil. Troopers paid the clippings of tin. That don't change. Riding out to chaos and no sign much of that glory. First lieutenant at the head salutes me as I pass, I nearly salute back, strike me dead. Keep my hand stuffed in a muffler. Yep, stole a muffler and a coat to add to my crimes. Winona took a cloaklike coat may have been a daughter's. It don't fit well and her arms look long but the cold is vicious-minded. Then out the gates and the sentry also stiffens and salutes. He don't know me clearly but I guess he thinks all women's worth a greeting. I'm sweating worse than Starling. The stagecoach is there but it's more of a mud-wagon. A globule of passengers inside already. Driver won't have Winona getting in so she climbs up top and I struggle up with her. A dress just a menace to mountaineering. You can go in, ma'am, he says. Just not the Injun. Don't matter none, I say, I'll sit up here. I see corporals now going about everywhere. Like I drank bad whisky and seeing visions. Corporals, corporals, everywhere. Out on constable duty, I'll swear. Everyone I imagine looking for the killer of Starling Carlton. I fetch my eyes forward. Goddamn move this goddamn stage. The huge cloud surrenders and snow washes down, passing at a swirling angle. All that old world of bugles, lice and sabres disappears and the stage lurches off.

It's just a filthy old affair being thrown about for a hundred miles. You can climb down for victuals but soon it's the pitching ride again. Round and round till your stomach swole and you're hurling that set of kippers into the fond air of Wyoming. Three other victims up there with us starting to howl with sickness without making a sound. One a runner for some prospectors said to be sniffing for gold in the back hills. Good luck and yous'll soon be Indian stew. Another man a scout I recognise, he was on the recent programme of so-called removal. Through chattering teeth Winona talking to him in her own bits of lingo. I ask her what they talking about and she says they talking about the snow. You talking about the weather? I said. Yes, sir, she says.

Big train blowing steam and smoke at the depot.

It's like a creature. Something in perpetual explosion. Huge long muscle body on her and four big men punching coal into her boiler. It's a sight. It's going to be dragging four carriages east and they say they'll go good. The light pall of snow hisses on the boiler sheets. Wish I could report well of the third-class wagon but it's evil cold and damp and me and Winona got to sit in close as cats. Not an inch to move because our fellow voyagers thought to bring their whole possession with them. We even got goats and the mark of goats is stink. Man next me is a nightmare pile of coats. Can't say what size of corpse he is he is so wrapped. We've bought some pies in Laramie and a bag of that famed cornbread. Famed to twist your belly. We're told we'll see a hundred stops or so but the train moves like a giant dancer for all its bulk. Out front the snow-guard parts the snow just like a ship through blustering foam. The snow thrown up pours back across the roofs and in it comes through glassless windows to be brother to soot and sister to choking smoke. Here is new-fangled luxury I guess. We tear on through country would of took long wretched hours by horse, the train traversing like a spooked buffalo. In two three days we're going to see St Louis. That's just a blank miracle. We go so fast I believe we leave our thinking parts back the line, only our battered bodies hurtling forward. Dizzy and frozen. If we'd had the dollars handy for first class, by God we would a spent them if they was the last dollars we'd ever seen. At trembling stops we buy grub and the great engine drinks and clanks and shudders. It sure be a manly beast, that girl. Me and Winona talk the yards of time. Her top wish now is to be with John Cole. Something in John is calming right enough. For me over these long years he's sacred. I never think bad of John, just can't. I don't even truly know his nature. He a perpetual stranger and I delight in that.

Each day we find a quiet spot and wield the razor. Forgot to bring the strop so it slowly blunts. Cuts lines and nicks across my face like I was breaking into yellow fever. Winona daubs me good. Crazy thing is I'm cold and wet and sore but I'm growing happy since we moving far from Death. That's what it seems. Winona loosening too, and laughing now. She just a girl and should be laughing regular. She should be playing maybe if she ain't too old. Certainly acts the lady and knows how. We like mother and child right enough and that's how it plays. I give thanks for that. Maybe in my deepest soul I believe my own fakery. I suppose I do. I feel a woman more than I ever felt a man, though I were a fighting man most of my days. Got to be thinking them Indians in dresses shown my path. Could gird in men's britches and go to war. Just a thing that's in you and you can't gainsay. Maybe I took the fortune of my sister when all those times ago I saw her dead. Still as a scrap of seaweed. Her thin legs sticking out. Her ragged pinny. I had never seen such things nor suspected there could ever be such suffering. That was true and it will always be true. But maybe she crept into me and made a nest. It's like a great solace, like great sacks of gold given. My heart beats slowly I do believe. I guess the why is dark as doom but I am just witness to the state of things. I am easy as a woman, taut as a man. All my limbs is broke as a man, and fixed good as a woman. I lie down with the soul of woman and wake with the same. I don't foresee no time where this ain't true no more. Maybe I was born a man and growing into a woman. Maybe that boy that John Cole met was but a girl already. He weren't no girl hisself for sure. This could be mountainous evil. I ain't read the Book on that. Maybe no hand has ever wrote its truth. I never heard of such a matter unless from us prancers on the stage. In Mr Noone's hall you just was what you seemed. Acting ain't no subterfuge-ing trickery. Strange magic changing things. You thinking along some lines and so you become that new thing. I only know as we was tore along, Winona lying on my breast, I was a thorough-going ordinary woman. In my windblown head. Even if my bosom was my army socks stuffed in.

Now in St Louis we see changes since the old times. Vast wharf-houses as tall as hills. All the freedmen sprung up here like a crop of souls and near every face you see along the river be black and brown and yella. There ain't nowhere their work don't touch. They doing the hauling and the hooking and the roping. But they ain't looking so much like slaves no more. The boss men is black and the shouting roars out of black lungs. No whips like heretofore. I don't know but this looks like to be better. Still, me and Winona don't see one Indian face. We ain't lingering to find out the weevils and the bad worms in these new visions. But we flick through and there were something there don't offend though in all truth St Louis smacked into desolation by the receding war and shell-ruined houses here and there still these times even if a-building. Sense of two worlds rubbing up. Am I American? I don't know. Me and Winona take our place with the other mudsills in the fifth-class section. It's a damn pleasure to do a bit of river travel. That old Mississippi is a temperate girl most times and her skin is soft and even. Something so old is perpetual young. River never crinkles and creases or if she does it's storms. We got clement days though the woods along is clamped with ice and endless miles of white foliage festooning. Vines climb into the halted trees and frost wraps round their limbs till you think the woods be full of icy snakes. Then the great expanses of the farms and cotton fields all waiting for the errant sun and the baccy grounds sheared by fire. Those skies that God loves to show and can't but favour with a gorgeous pallid light. Though still I gaze about and fear we're followed I do find succour in these powerful waters.

Now healing from the sights of slaughter my

255

fond Winona blossoms back to talk and she like a flower now that scorns even spring. A famous flower that likely blooms in frost. A lovely child with her scented breath and up from her limbs rising a smell of life and beauty. I guess she might be fifteen years, my daughter, but who can say. I call her my daughter though I do know she ain't. Let's say my ward, my care, the product of some strange instinct deep within that does rob from injustice a shard of love. The palms of her hands like two maps of home, the lines leading homeward like old trails. Her beautiful soft hands with tapering fingers. Her touches like true words. A daughter not a daughter but who I mother best I can. Ain't that the task in this wilderness of furious death? I guess so. Got to be. My breast is surging with a crazy pride to be bringing her back homeward. We've sent a telegraph from St Louis to say that we return since till we reached the river I never dared to stir a nest. I can see John Cole take that news and stand with trembling heart in anticipation of her coming. Out on the porch gazing for us returning birds. We'll be walking in part from Memphis since some links in the stages broken. But we'll make steady progress walking on and watch the farms and feel steadier and steadier the approach of home. No matter what dangers and evils roundabout we will reach that moment of meeting again. These was my thoughts. The wide river slipping under the flat bottom. The songs of the chorusing passengers, the card-players' silences. The blacks working all the tasks of the boat like they was bringing these exempted white souls to paradise. Something stopped, something in between. Sweet river travel.

Get down to Memphis. I know my clothes just stink. Bloomers urinous and shitty. It's got to be. But we take a night's rest in a boarding house and wash ourselves and then next morning as we stirring to go was that queer feeling of greeting the lice moving back onto clean limbs. They was residing in the seams of our dresses all night and now like those emigrants along that old Oregon trail they creep across the strange Americas of our skins.

Then the long cold walk to Paris. Then the farmhouse in the distance. Then John Cole's arms around us.

CHAPTER 22

It's John Cole tells Rosalee and Tennyson I got to keep the dress on. I tole him all recounts in our private bed of what occurred and including every small matter and every great. I tole him all and recounted the sad end of Starling Carlton. John Cole says in human matters there often three things rivalling. Truths fighting one with another. That's the world, he says. Lige Magan loved that sweating man and it grieves him sore that he is dead but John Cole don't tell him I ended him. John Cole would of fought by Starling Carlton and often did and would of stood between him and harm but it were wrong in his careful estimation to want to end Winona. Darkly devilish wrong. John Cole tells Lige we don't know what's coming but it's best now if Thomas McNulty not here. Rosalee don't make no mountain out of it. Tennyson don't seem to care. Still talks to me but now like I was a woman. He very polite and lifts his hat when he see me. Morning, ma'am, is his way of talk. Morning, Mr Bouguereau. That's how things go on. That mourning dove been getting peachier and peachier but she still resident. John

Cole been sneaking her titbits from his dinners. That ain't no crime.

We're tucked in the house till spring and outside rages all the usual blather and violent tempers of storms. John Cole took Winona for a pupil and he got two books bought to help him called *The American Lady's and Gentleman's Modern Letter Writer: relative to business, duty, love, and marriage* and *An Improved Grammar of the English Language.* She going to be writing and talking like a emperor. The drifts pile up against the barn. Covers the rough graves of Tach Petrie and his boys that was dug for their long sleep. Covers the sleeping roots of things. The outlaws, the orphans, the angels and the innocents. Covers the long woods.

Then from the woods as spring ascends we hear the other wood doves call. General Lee cocks her head. Co-co-co-rico, looking for a mate before the year is older. When her wing heals I'll let her go for sure. Co-co-co-rico. Looking for each other, like the shooting stars. Like the Tennessee owls. Like every damn thing.

Come proper spring we hear some news from far Wyoming. Captain Sowell been killed by hands unknown and in the absence of an accuser Major Neale been released. We hear he's honourably discharged and gone home to Boston. To hell with the army that locks him up I guess. We don't know what happens to his charges and we don't know nothing about the looking into of the death of poor Starling. Maybe the German don't count for much. We look at this from all sides like General Lee when she gazing upon an item and we hope we may consider it good news. John Cole mighty troubled since it seem to him that Silas Sowell was sorta right. Indians ain't vermin to be burned out of the seams of the coats of the world. Witness is his old great-grandma inside of himself. Riding the caboose of John Cole. If I wasn't no sharpshooter we'd a never seen none of this trouble maybe, says Lige Magan. Never meant to shoot no girl. That long long ago, says John Cole, that long long ago. Lotta goddamned water and a lotta goddamned bridges since then. Major was calling for me to stop and I heard him, why in hell did I go on with it? says Lige. You just forget about all that, says John Cole. I thinks about it every night of my days, says Lige, I surely do. I didn't know that, I says. Yep, he says, every night of my days.

We're going to put in crops of wheat and corn this year and give the land a rest from tobacco. Gives you a shorter year too. Ain't none of that curing in barns and grading and the rest. I hitch up my skirts good as any country girl and work aside the men. Winona runs the wagon in and out of town for this and that and looks like the towns-people of Paris growing accustomed to seeing her about. Stop seeing just an Indian and start seeing Winona. John Cole reckons the young boy behind the counter in the dry-goods store's sweet on her. He says it won't be the worst thing if she gets connected to commerce. She ain't going to be marrying yet, I say, in time-honoured motherly fashion. Then lo and behold don't she gain employment clerking for the goddamn lawyer Briscoe. She got the best copperplate in the county, he says. Comes out on his gig to see us. Guess it don't look too disreputable. A white couple and an old army man. Nice black folks. That's what he sees I guess.

One evening in the summer me and John Cole was sitting out on the porch watching the shadows lengthen on things. Lige was asleep on his chair. Those crazy whippoorwills giving over and over the same little song. Winona working in the kitchen on Briscoe's accounts. Queer how you sitting there and before you see them you know someone's coming. Way over along the river track then they appear, about a dozen men riding. The new dark buffets them and yet over to the westward a huge trembling sun still burns herself out in the ashen sky. Pale colour of a bird's egg marks the upper heavens. You gotta give the world credit for beauty. The riders ride forward steady. Just coming along like they knowed the road. Soon enough we see they're army. The jackets that once we weared ourselves and the rifles stuck in their scabbarding. Looks like two officers and a bunch of boys. Well goddamn if that don't look like Corporal Poulson in the distance. That's what I say to John Cole. Lige Magan stirs in his slumbers and comes awake. He don't say nothing. We got rifles as usual lying along the porch but not that no one would see them. A colour sergeant and two corporals don't fret much to see army. On they come. Then John Cole standing just as you might on account you wanting to greet. Leans against the porch support just easy and dandy. Pulls at his hat. It's hot and his chest been sweating into his shirt. Just hoping then I'm shaved and trimmed as good as I need. Run a finger over my cheek to check. Anyhow the dark has reached our porch and sits in in bundles with us. Whippoorwills drop silent. Far off a summer thunder rolls along the hills. It's not a storm will reach us I reckon. Too far away. Got to stop my hand from greeting Poulson because in this guise I don't know him. Then that tack-tacketing of hooves and approach of horses never quiet. Don't know the other fellas unless one or two but faintly. Can't recall.

Evening, says Corporal Poulson to John and Lige. Ma'am, he says, and lifts his hat to me. What's your business, Corporal? says Lige, as friendly as a Quaker. We're on deserter business, says Poulson. Rode down from St Louis. This here Sergeant Magan, this here Mrs Cole, says John Cole, and I was Corporal Cole, I believe in your own regiment, that right? You just the men we looking for, says Poulson, just the men. It's our melancholy task to seek for Corporal Thomas McNulty, deserter. And we was told he might be here 'longside you. I knew that man and he were a good man but fact is he left before his time. And you know the penalty. So,

262

I'm thinking, this ain't about Starling Carlton. Goddamn major never signed my papers afore he were arrested. So, have ye seen him here or no? Maybe he out working or the like? God knows we don't want to combobulate ye. But we're duty bound. We got a list of nigh-on thirty men ducked out. The colonel wants it cleared. How can we fight our wars otherwise? You can't, says John Cole. I'll bring you to your man. So John Cole gives me a start saying that. Is he about to give me up? Yank up my skirts and show my balls? John Cole goes down the steps and Corporal Poulson dismounts. I thank you kindly for your help, he says. It ain't nothing, says John Cole. Should I be ready with my gun? says Poulson. No, no, says John Cole, he's quiet enough. So then he leads them through the sheds and round the back he brings them to the little boneyard. Stops at one grave with its blanket of summer-withered grass. Nods his head to Poulson. There he lies, he says. Who that? says Poulson. Corporal McNulty as you was saying. That him lying there? says Poulson. I guess it is, says John. How were he killed? We was jumped by bandits. These other beds is where three of them abide. Thomas killed all three. Protecting his home. That sure sounds like the boy I knowed, says Poulson, a decent man. That's sad, he says, and saves us a grisly job, God knows. It do, says John Cole, it do. You ain't marked the grave? says Poulson. Well, we know who lies there, I guess. I guess you do, says Poulson.

Then Winona come out and has missed the whole thing being buried in Briscoe's sums. She got a big shocked face when she see'd them. But the meekness of the troopers calms her fears. That night they bed down in the barn and by morning they are gone.

That were quick thinking, John, says Lige. I'd a drawed out the guns and tried that way.

So now Thomas McNulty was dead official-wise as far as we can see. He lived a short life of forty years and now he was gone to his rest. That was our thinking on the matter. I was strangely sad for I was pondering on his wrestling with wars and the fights of general life. I was thinking of his hard origins in Ireland and how he came to be an American and of everything put against him that he pushed aside. How he had protected Winona and loved John Cole. How he strived to be a faithful friend to all who knew him. One tiny soul among the millions. I was lying side by side with John Cole that night in the bed thinking about myself like I was dead and here's a new person altogether. John Cole musta been in the same frame of mind because he says we got to get the monumental mason in Paris to write a stone: *R.I.P. T. McNulty*. And set it up back of the barn. Just to be sure.

It was time to give General Lee her freedom. I let her go the next morning because it was summer and summer was a good time for her to try her fortune in the trees. She flew off straight from the

264

wickiup she had lived in. Went like a blurry arrow for the woods. Couldn't be a free bird fast enough. The healed wing carried her good.

Guess there must be an address called Fool's Paradise. On that exact spot in Tennessee. A few days later the letter carrier brings a letter from Paris. We see at the bottom that it's from Corporal Poulson. I read it through and bring it in to John Cole who is cleaning out the boiler in the barn for to go again next year with the tobacco. He got most of the soot on himself and he's coal-black. His hands is worser than a scuttle so he tells me read the damn letter. I am cold now in the blasting heat of the day that moils about even in the dark barn. So I reads him the letter. First worse thing is it's got my name on it. Corporal Thomas McNulty. Dear Corporal McNulty, it says. Well you must oblige me by allowing that you must think me Henry M. Poulson the biggest fool in Christendom if you think I did not see plain with my eyes that that bearded lady was yourself. Well I carried my boys away since I did see also with my eyes those rifles racked along the porch and by God if your friend Mr Magan does not look like a shooter. I saw you fight brave and well and you have a long association in the army of these states and as you may know I fought for the Union even though I was a Southern boy and I know you also set your life in the balances of liberty and evil. It was not my intention therefore to make outlaws of your friends as you would be if you

were to fire upon lawful officers. I ask you therefore and I might also say I beg you to put on your
britches like a man and come into town where we
are waiting to pluck you. By reason that you have
things to answer as I believe you will allow. I am,
sir, your most humble and obed't servant, Henry
Poulson, corporal.

He writes a good letter, says John Cole. What
the hell we going to do? Guess I'll just go in and
do what he saying, I say. What? No. You ain't, says
John Cole. This is something I got to sort out, I
say. They ain't coming after me for poor Starling.
I can ask Major Neale to come speak for me. I
was on a short commission and he was going to
strike my papers but they took him. He's cleared
now so he'll speak for me. It's just a misunder-
standing. They'll see. Hang you high more like,
says John Cole. They shoot deserters mostly, I say.
Yellowlegs shoot, bluecoats hang, says John Cole.
Either way, you ain't going. But I ain't making no
outlaw outa Winona, I say. If I stay, Poulson comes.
That stops his talk. We could go on the run, he
says, the three of us. No, sir, we could not, I say.
That be just the same thing. You a father, John
Cole. Then he's shaking his black head. The soot
drifts down like a black snow. What you saying,
you going to leave now and leave us here without
you? he says. I ain't got no choice. A man can ask
for an officer to speak for him. I bet seven silver
dollars the major will do it. Well, he says, I got to
clean out this boiler. I know, I says. So then I'm

pulling away from the darkness of the barn to step into the burning air. You'd swear God had a boiler going somewhere. The light grips my face like a octopus. I feel like I am a dead man right enough. I ain't got no faith in that gone-crazy major. Then I hear John Cole's voice behind me. You get back here as quick as you can, Thomas. We got a lot of work to do and can't do it light of hands. I know, I say, I'll be back soon. You goddamn better be, he says.

It's more in sorrow than in anger that I take off my dress and put on the clothes of man. I smooth out the dress and brush it down a while and then hang it in the old pine chest that Lige Magan's mother owned. It still got her farm dresses in it. Rough old things she wore in her time. I guess Lige looks in there and then his mother lives again a moment. Times when he was little clinging to those hems. Well I must report that the tears fall fully. I ain't indifferent. I ain't a stone. I'm sobbing like a fool and then Winona comes into the square of the door. She's standing there like a painting of a princess. I know she's going to do proudly in her world. The fierce light that was in the yard has crossed into the parlour and now tries to leak into the bedroom. It gives her slight form a soft white glow. Winona. Child of my heart. That's how it was. I was wretched ruined now. Got to go into town, I say. You want me to run you in? she says. No, that's fine. I's going to take the bay horse. I might have to take the stage to Memphis later.

You can fetch the horse in the morning. I'll tie her at the dry-goods store. Sure thing, she says. What you doing in Memphis? Going to purchase tickets for the opera John Cole likes. That's a brave plan, she says, laughing, that's a brave plan. You be good now, girl, I say. I guess I will, she says.

So I ride into town. That little bay horse goes on nicely. She got the best walk of any horse I ever owned. Just clipping along with a tack-tack-tack on the dry earth. Sweet life. I was sore in love with all my labouring in Tennessee. Liked well that life. Up with the cockcrow, bed with the dark. Going along like that could never end. And when ending it would be felt to be just. You had your term. All that stint of daily life we sometimes spit on like it was something waste. But it all there is and in it is enough. I do believe so. John Cole, John Cole, Handsome John Cole. Winona. Old good-man Lige. Tennyson and Rosalee. This lithesome bay. Home. Our riches. All I owned. Enough.

On I ride. Nice day for a hanging, as folks say.

CHAPTER 23

Poulson ain't a bad fellow. But something alters when there's a bunch of men and one of them is in chains. I guess that's true. They got a converted ambulance in Paris town and we're set to ride up to St Louis in that and then entrain in a army caboose to Kansas City. All gonna take a few days and at the start I seem to be jesting with the other boys but then them chains confer a bit of silence on me I guess. Poulson says I'm to be tried at Fort Leavenworth. I ask him if Major Neale know anything about it and he says he hisself don't know but because of my good service they'll surely look for mitigations. I dearly hope so. Just in that moment I believe I might have the luck and suddenly I got a thought that I might be heading back down to Tennessee. If you ain't ever felt a feeling like that I can't describe to you how it's just like your head was a melon full of sugar and water. I ask him can he send a letter and he says he don't see why he can't. Says they'll likely call the major anyway seeing as how he was my commanding officer when the crime took place. Alleged crime anyhows, he says. Desertion. What's the penalty for that if guilty? I says. I guess they shoot you mostly, he says. In the caboose the fellas is mostly playing cards and making jokes and they're just trying to make each other laugh and guffaw like all soldiers do and the train is making haste to Kansas City.

When we get to Fort Leavenworth I ain't feeling so *optimistic* as the fella said. The wrist chains have eaten into my flesh and the leg chains are trying to catch up with the wrist chains. I'm thinking it would a been better to make a run for it with John Cole and Winona. I was brave starting out but I ain't so brave just now. My body is tired and Poulson and the lads is just eager to check in their saddles and gear and have a carouse I guess. They deserve it. It was a long trek and they ain't done nothing wrong. Poulson says he gets thirty dollars for the capture. Fair enough. He gets me signed in too like a bit of extra gear and then I'm sitting in my new quarters like a new-bought dog and I feel like howling. But I don't. Ain't no future in howling. I'm wondering can I write to John Cole and get him to come straight up with Lige and bust me out of here. It's a giant fort and the place is milling with troopers and other sorts and what look like raw recruits and all the biblical multitude of hangers-on. I'm going up for trial in a couple weeks they tell me and till then I can eat the duck soup and be quiet. God damn it. They call me Corporal which in the circumstances has an ominous ring to it. Little man that turns the keys says I'll be alright but I guess he says that to all the glum-looking boys.

I don't know nothing that's going on since I'm tucked away like a bale of tobacco in the dry-house. So when the big day she comes I'm just mighty relieved to see Major Neale sitting in the room when I'm shunted down to be tried. They got a big long shiny table and a few officers looking pretty at ease and Major Neale is shooting the breeze with a captain when I come in. Turns out to be the 'president' of the court martial. Guess I'm someone called Corporal T. McNulty, Troop B, 2nd Cavalry. That's who they say I am anyhow. I just don't mention Thomasina in that moment. The charges is read and now I must allow the officers tuck in their legs somewhat because until then they was tending to keep them stuck out in front. The papers make a nestling sound and something in the room gets smaller. I guess it might be me. Desertion. And then they describe what they think it is I done and then they ask what the plea is and another man says Not Guilty. Then Major Neale speaks for me and he's explaining about the temporary service he hooked me up in due to his daughter being rescued through means of my kindness. Something along those lines. Then he's bumping up against his own arrest and he mentions Captain Sowell in a hard sorta voice and he's asked about Captain Sowell and there's a very queer stirring in the room. Like someone dropped ink in a glass of water. The major says he don't know

271

nothing about Captain Sowell only that he died. But he makes an effort then to haul the enormous train engine back on the track and says it was on account of all that what was happening to him that he was obliged to neglect the papers that would of discharged Corporal McNulty in the usual way. He said Corporal McNulty at great peril to his own self helped him in a time of urgent need and went a long way in a down payment of hope against his despair at that time. Then I see how much worse the major's skin has gotten. It's red as a crab's foot. Not because he's embarrassed but because he ain't well is my suspicion. So then the president of the court he asks if there's another witness could add something to this story and the major says he don't know. So then the major brings it all a bit further in the wrong direction and says with an angry voice that it was Captain Sowell accused him with another witness of cruelty in his campaign against the Sioux that took and killed his own dear wife and one of his daughters and took his other daughter Angel captive. When he says this his face is now purple so it must be not only sickness.

Captain Sexton – now I hear his name proper – is just as flamed up now as the major and he don't like the major's high tone not one bit. I come all the way out from Boston to help my corporal and speak for him and I ain't on trial here. I never said you was, says the president. God damn it, says the major, that just what it feel like. And bangs his right hand on the table. The papers and the glasses jump. Who was this other man that went witness against you? says the president and Major said some damn German called Sarjohn. Oh, says the captain, I know that man, is it Henry Sarjohn you mean? Yes, says the major. Henry Sarjohn is lieutenant of scouts at Fort Leavenworth, he says, why, I think I will call him. So Captain Sexton pulls the plug on proceedings till Sarjohn can be called. Good holy Jesus.

If the president had called Beelzebub I couldn't of been more alarmed. One man on God's earth I didn't want putting eyes on me was that Sarjohn. Why in the name of tarnation did he have to be in the damn fort? I guess he could of been a hundred miles away and still called. Tarnation. So I'm eating soup and shitting it out another few days. A man can have noble thoughts and they roosting there in his head like a row of birds but life sure don't like to contemplate them sitting there. Life's gonna shoot them birds. Then they have everyone back including the German. Henry Sarjohn is a lieutenant now by God and they say the scouts is mostly half-breeds around here with Irish fathers and Indian mothers. That's suppose to be amusing but I just don't find it so. Major Neale don't attend which I am told is his right as a retired officer and then the president asks Sarjohn his side of the story and what the hell happened to Sowell. So the little German tells us what happened which was, he don't know. They got up

273

a case against Major Neale and the major was detained and then Sowell was found killed and then the case was thrown back by the court. That's all he knowed about it. Then he looks at me as hard as a rook. He puts his head in real close. *God damn it* – I nearly spake aloud though I am forbid. For that man's breath smells of things that are dead. And then he says, and that's the man that killed Captain Carlton. Who? says the president, real surprised. Captain Starling Carlton, I seen it, says the German, and I been keeping an eye out this long time. I knew I'd know him when I seen him plain, and there he is. This weren't good for the temperature of the court and it weren't good for me. I am took back to the cells while they goes on talking I guess and then in a few days another charge is laid against me and this time it was of murder. The court believed me guilty of the charge. That's what they said.

I guess I was. I don't know how many loved Starling Carlton and even if it were only a few I was one of them. But he was lifting his hand against Winona. I don't see any other way round that no matter how often I go back in my mind and look at it. Captain Rufus Sexton says the court has decided I was guilty and so I am to be laid in chains and took out when the time was right and shot for my crime. No one speaks for mitigation because who there could speak for it?

They was fearsome days then. I am allowed to write John Cole and tell him my news and he comes up from Tennessee but as a condemned man they ain't of a mind to let him see me. I am sore sorry about that but at the same time since I carry John Cole *inside* I reckoned it must not be allowed to make no odds in the long run. I *imagined* him near me and I *imagined* I kissed his face. I imagined he said nice things to me and I imagined me saying back I thought he was the best man I ever knowed. I weren't leaving the world without saying one more time I loved John Cole even if he weren't there to hear it.

Bitterness eats the bitter. But if I was a murderer I'd a liked to kill that German. Just saying that because it's true and accurate. He was doing his duty as he saw fit to do, some might say. I'd say he is a damn meddler and I will leave it at that. Who killed Captain Silas Sowell deceased, I wonder? No one knowed and my guess was no one ever will. As John Cole said, he had a point of view and that got to be honoured. You can't go in and be slaughtering everyone like a passel of King Henrys. That ain't the world as it was made to be.

Now the sentence was gave and the summer was sitting outside my window. A huge jewel of sunlight hangs high on the wall. And I remembered often-times riding through such heat with a longing in my heart just for what the days of life ahead might bring, nothing else. I did hear them every Friday bringing down men. I would be shot as the sun came up, 'with musketry', as they decree. There'd be a day without me and then a night and then forever more. Life wants you to go down and suffer far as I can see. You gotta dance around all that. A child must come out to dance and dance around all obstacles and dance in the end the creaky quadrille of age. But. I was trying to see how it all happened and how everything came to that point and I was trying to spot the moment I was maybe pushed from the true path but I couldn't see nothing like that. What did I do truly? I saved Winona. There was comfort in that. If I could of saved her without putting a sabre into Starling's face I would of.

I wrote to John and I wrote to the poet McSweny just to say farewell but a letter come back from our old comrade Mr Noone that the poet McSweny were R.I.P. and he was sorry to hear I would be also soon – he didn't use just them words. John Cole wrote me a letter would tear the heart out of a hangman, and tucked in with it is one of them famous missives of Winona. She has put in a sprig of some wild flower. Copperplate writing. Magan's Farm, Paris. June 3rd, 1872. Dear Thomas, we are sure missing you in Tennessee. If only the army will let you come back we will kill the fatted calf says Lige Magan. He has harrowed the near fields and he sure misses your touch with those rascal horses. In the meantime there is only time to say I love you as a consequence of John Cole is champing at the bit to get to town. I miss you real bad. My heart is sore. Your fond daughter, Winona.

I weren't going on too bad till I got that.

I don't know but most likely I was forty years of age. That's early to go but plenty died in the war younger. I seen a lot of young men go. That ain't the point so much until it's you going. I know I got a number on the prison roster for men to be shot and sooner or later it go up. Well, the day creeps closer. A printed notice is nailed to the door. You wouldn't believe the sweating caused by that. My heart is weighed down by pain and longing and it just ain't no fit state for a Christian. Even the rat who flits along the wall feels sorry for you then. You ain't worth nothing to yourself. You ain't worth a Lindenmueller cent. My head floods with fear and my feet are icy. Then I'm howling. The jailer comes in. His name is Pleasant Hazelwood, I guess he's a sergeant. Ain't no real use caterwauling, he says. I'm rocking like a drunkard back and forth. Fear burns my belly like a nest of Mexican chillies. I'm shouting at him. Why ain't there no God will help me? Ain't no man neither, he says. I run against the wall like a blind rat. Like I might find a gap. Everything gone from me. I stand there with my breast heaving. No battle is worser than this. Sergeant Hazelwood stands in close and twists his hands about like two newborn pups and then grips my arm. I seen a thousand men just like you, he says, it just ain't so bad as you think. Kind old bugger and him as ugly as a moose. Kind of a angel sent to me in the guise of a fat turnkey smelling of shit and onions. But it ain't helping. Not truly. The devil's franked my ticket and God ain't in it. How can I make my peace with Him if He ain't there? I plunge down again into violent misery like a rock thrown into a torrent.

One evening shortly after very late I get a visitor. I know it ain't John Cole but Sergeant Hazelwood gives me notice. Says a gent is here to see me. I guess I don't know too many gents unless they're officers. Sure enough it's Major Neale.

Well he ain't a major now, is he? Come in in his beautiful suit that some tailor in Boston has laboured over. He's looking much better. The few months has done him good. Tells me Angel is going real well at her schooling and he wants her to go on to the university to please her mother. Alright, I says. He has a big bunch of papers with him. He's gone back to all the fellas was in the battle and asked each and every one what they knew or saw. Finally he says he gets to Corporal Poulson. He kinda has the same account as the German Sarjohn but there's a difference. He says Corporal McNulty were trying to stop a Indian girl being killed. That old Starling Carlton's blood was up and nothing would do him but to shoot her with his pistol. A-course, yes, I'm thinking, since he were trying to follow your damn orders, the loyal old bastard – but a-course I don't say that aloud. Poulson says he sees it all and keeps his mouth shut till the major asks him. That's the army way. Whatever you say say nothing, just in case. So Major Neale goes over to Washington and takes up the case there. And then he goes down to the head of the army of the Missouri. Well, he says, slowing down now in his account, they can't stop your sentence. Laws don't allow it. When he says this my heart drops to my boots. But, he says, they can commute it to hard labour for one hundred days and then you will be freed. The major says if I don't mind breaking stones a while then that's what I can do. I says, Major, sir, I thank you, I really do. Don't be thanking me, he says, I thank you. You saved my daughter the only one remaining to me and you fought like a dog in the war and your service under me was always exemplary. I says I am sorry his wife is gone and he says he is too. He lays his right hand on my shoulder. I ain't washed in a month but he don't flinch. And he says he will always remember me and if he can ever be of service to me again in the future I know where he is. Well, I don't know where he is but I don't say nothing because that just what people say. Another thing I don't say aloud is, Are you the boy that killed Silas Sowell? I say I sure will be glad to get back to Tennessee where my people abide and he says he's certain they will be glad to see me.

So I am one hundred days making big stones into small stones. In the time of the hunger in Sligo a lot of men did that work, trying to earn the pennies to feed their families. It were called Relief Works. Well, I am feeling mighty relieved. I am happy to strike down at those stones and my fellow prisoners are mighty puzzled at my happiness. But how could I been otherwise? I am going back to Tennessee. The day come when all my work is done and they kit me out in a set of clothes and they set me on the road outside the prison. The clothes is tattered but give me my modesty, just. Set free like a mourning dove. In my exultation I forget I ain't got a bean of money but it don't concern me and I know I can rely on the kindness of folk along the way. The ones that don't try to rob me will feed me. That how it is in America. I never felt such joy of heart as in those days traipsing southward. I never felt such pure charge and fire of joy. I am like a man not just let loose from death but from his own discomfited self. I don't desire nothing but to reach our farm and witness the living forms of John Cole and Winona step out to meet me. The whole way sparkles with the beauty of woods and fields. I had wrote I was coming and soon I would be there. That's how it was. It were only a short stretch of walking down through those pleasing states of Missouri and Tennessee.